TH

"Like a master chef, Judith Fertig takes the tale of a gifted baker starting all over in her old Midwestern hometown and layers it together with an intriguing mystery buried deep in the community's Depression-era past."
—Beatriz Williams, *New York Times* bestselling author of *Along the Infinite Sea*

"In a small town where secrets run deep and over generations, Fertig shows friendship, family, and food can bring people together and heal old wounds."
—Jill Shalvis, *New York Times* bestselling author of *Still the One*

"A heartwarming story of community, love, and food so delectable you want it to leap off the page into your mouth."
—Linda Rodriguez, award-winning poet and author of *Every Hidden Fear*

"A dash of complex romance stirs up a cast of characters linked through time by a precious bauble in a delicious setting."
—Jeanne Ambrose, award-winning writer, cookbook author, and editor of *Taste of Home* magazine

"Wonderful, entertaining . . . A warm, intriguing novel laced with mouthwatering descriptions of cakes!" —*The Huffington Post*

"This book is a treat for the senses. And it was heartwarming to see that as Neely helped other people, she was also helping herself."
—*First for Women*

continued . . .

"Not only do I want to meet (and be friends!) with Neely after reading her story; I want to taste every one of her deliciously therapeutic treats. How I wish I knew what flavor she would choose for me!"

—Denise Mickelsen, cooking, baking, and gardening acquisitions editor at Craftsy

"A lovely book that blends the past and present with delicious cake . . . Grab this book with a sweet treat and cozy up for a delightful read."   —Rainy Day Ramblings

"Fun and sweet and entirely enjoyable . . . A great beach read for this summer. Just make sure you bring some cupcakes along in your cooler."   —Cherie Reads

"[Fertig] is a talented writer who can titillate one's senses and at the same time create a mystery that unfolds gradually but with enough zip to keep the reader fascinated . . . A great read that should be on every reader's list of summer fiction to enjoy at the beach, mountains, in one's yard in a comfy chair, or just about anywhere, any time! Delightful and highly recommended!"   —The Best Reviews

BERKLEY TITLES BY JUDITH FERTIG

The Cake Therapist
The Memory of Lemon

the *Memory* of *Lemon*

JUDITH FERTIG

BERKLEY BOOKS, NEW YORK

BERKLEY

An imprint of Penguin Random House LLC
375 Hudson Street, New York, New York 10014

THE MEMORY OF LEMON

This book is an original publication of the Berkley Publishing Group.

Copyright © 2016 by Judith Fertig.
Penguin supports copyright. Copyright fuels creativity, encourages diverse voices, promotes free speech, and creates a vibrant culture. Thank you for buying an authorized edition of this book and for complying with copyright laws by not reproducing, scanning, or distributing any part of it in any form without permission. You are supporting writers and allowing Penguin to continue to publish books for every reader.

BERKLEY® and the "B" design are registered trademarks of Penguin Random House LLC.
For more information, visit penguin.com.

Berkley trade paperback ISBN: 9780425277959

Library of Congress Cataloging-in-Publication Data

Names: Fertig, Judith M., author.
Title: The memory of lemon / Judith Fertig.
Description: Berkley trade paperback edition. | New York : Berkley Books, 2016.
Identifiers: LCCN 2016009052 (print) | LCCN 2016009113 (ebook) | ISBN 9780425277959 (paperback) | ISBN 9780698182745 (epub)
Subjects: LCSH: Bakers—Fiction. | Women cooks—Fiction. | Weddings—Fiction. | Family secrets—Fiction. | Self-realization in women—Fiction. | BISAC: FICTION / Contemporary Women. | FICTION / Romance / Contemporary.
Classification: LCC PS3606.E78 M46 2016 (print) | LCC PS3606.E78 (ebook) | DDC 813/.6—dc23
LC record available at http://lccn.loc.gov/2016009052

PUBLISHING HISTORY
Berkley trade paperback edition / June 2016

PRINTED IN THE UNITED STATES OF AMERICA

10 9 8 7 6 5 4 3 2 1

Cover art: *Flower Infinity Spiral* by Elovich/Shutterstock.
Cover design by Rita Frangie.
Interior text design by Laura K. Corless.

This is a work of fiction. Names, characters, places, and incidents either are the product of the author's imagination or are used fictitiously, and any resemblance to actual persons, living or dead, business establishments, events, or locales is entirely coincidental.

Penguin
Random
House

1

LATE MARCH
MILLCREEK VALLEY, OHIO

Neely

Lydia, the twenty-something bride-to-be, sat stony faced on the settee in my front parlor.

This was not the way I wanted to start the week. Since I'd opened my bakery in Millcreek Valley's bridal district in January, I had learned a lot about wooing, in the business sense. When I did wedding cake tastings, I took potential clients away from the cheerful light and beveled glass cases of Rainbow Cake and drew them quietly, seductively into the more intimate setting of my home right next door.

Here, I hoped they would be charmed by the French gray walls, the glint of heavy hotel silver serving pieces, the fire in the late Victorian hearth, and the little cakes, buttercream frostings, and mousses I had made for them.

But this bride was unmoved.

We had tried tiny cakes in chocolate, browned butter yellow, poppy seed, white with a faint hint of almond. We'd sampled blood orange, fleur de sel caramel, pomegranate, dark chocolate, white chocolate, pistachio, raspberry, and countless other frostings and fillings. I'd even offered a lemony cupcake with its surprise-inside blueberry filling—our signature flavor combination for March—but to no avail.

Lydia would take a tiny, polite bite and put each miniature cupcake aside on her plate. The more we tasted, the more the reject pile grew, and the more rigid her posture became.

Lydia's mother had put a substantial deposit down and reserved the date for her daughter's June wedding—she was lucky that I had just had a bride cancel for that exact day. Booking a wedding cake, a wedding anything, only a few months out was iffy. But money talks loudly enough. The only problem was trying to find a time when Lydia's "wedding team" could interview her about the millions of details that went hand in hand with a society wedding.

Roshonda Taylor, wedding planner to the stars, was gorgeous as usual in her salmon sheath dress that showed off skin the color of her favorite caramel macchiato. Gavin Nichols, gifted interior designer and space planner, sipped his coffee, careful not to spill it on his pristine starched shirt, navy blazer, and khaki pants. If someone had told us back in our blue-collar high school days that as thirty-somethings we would be planning a high-style wedding together, we maybe would have moved our prom from the rickety Fraternal Order of Eagles hall to somewhere more expensive and glamorous. But probably not. We learned early: You have to work with what you've got.

And what we had here was a crisis. Somehow we had to navigate the choppy waters between what the mother wanted and what the bride envisioned.

The bride had been putting us off for weeks. And now this.

As a new business owner, I could not afford to have unhappy high-profile clients. Word of mouth was everything to wealthy mothers and brides. *Who did your flowers? Where did you get those antique lockets for the bridesmaids? Don't use so-and-so.* You never wanted to have your business name fill in the blank for *so-and-so*.

I refilled Lydia's teacup with a chamomile blend and poured more French press coffee for her mother and the other wedding team professionals, who must feel like I looked. My reflection in the silver teapot cast back my auburn hair tied up in a fraying topknot, wide green eyes expanded to extra wide from anxiety, and a now-familiar Claire O'Neil Davis expression—a duck seeming to stay afloat effortlessly while paddling furiously underwater.

I just couldn't get a read on the bride, other than the obvious. She didn't like my cakes.

This was a first.

I was a pastry chef with tons of haute cuisine experience, and I had enjoyed my fair share of success in New York before bringing my skills and myself back home to Millcreek Valley. Just a few short months later my signature desserts were gracing society functions, private dinners, corporate events, and glamorous galas. My wedding cakes were sought after.

So I wasn't entirely convinced I was the problem here.

I knew that my little sample cakes and the fillings and frostings were delicious, even if Lydia couldn't recognize it.

But I also knew that my abilities in the kitchen were only part of the secret to my success. It was my other gift, the way I could use my intuition to "read" a client through flavor, that helped me win over the crankiest and most difficult of brides. The ones like Lydia. But something was preventing me from working my usual miracles today.

Every time I tried to turn on my internal flavor Wi-Fi, I got no signal.

This was also a first.

My slightly magical palate was the way I made sense of the world. It revealed an inner state, an emotional core. Sometimes flavor answered the question I didn't know I had. Just like Gran and my dad, I knew flavor was both a way to read people and a way to understand myself.

Should I have left my New York life behind to start again here in Millcreek Valley? A few weeks back, the comfort of sweet cinnamon had reassured me: *Yes*, it whispered. *One step at a time.*

Yet it always seemed easier to pick up on someone else's flavorful inner state than on my own.

When I sat with clients and opened my mind to them, a taste usually came through. It might be sweet, sour, salty, or bitter. After a moment, it would blossom into a full flavor. The sweet ripeness of apricot, the sourness of a Key lime, the earthy saltiness of Mexican chocolate, the aromatic bitterness of nutmeg.

In a flash, a feeling would follow the flavor. Joy. Skepticism. Lust for life. Quiet acceptance.

And from that feeling would come a memory, a scene called back to present day. A moment whose real meaning and importance I might never fully know.

And I didn't really need to know everything. I used my gift to

The Memory of Lemon

see my clients' stories so I could design desserts—in this case, a wedding cake—to fit each customer like a couture gown, not an off-the-rack dress in desperate need of alterations.

If I got the cake and filling and frosting flavors right, they would resonate with my clients, reaching them in those down-deep places where they would begin to feel that everything really would be all right.

If I got the flavors right.

I couldn't get them right if I didn't get an initial impression. What was the deal with Lydia? Why couldn't I read her?

Usually, by this part of a wedding cake tasting, I'd be casting images of wedding cakes on the smooth plaster walls with my laptop, casually dropping a few celebrity client names from my New York days, and my current clients would be choosing a design.

But we weren't there yet. And I was beginning to fear that we wouldn't get there. I looked over at Lydia again, who sat stiff and silent.

"Sweetheart, what do you think of the lemon with the lavender? For a hot summer night, that might be very refreshing," Mrs. Stidham asked. Her expensively cut and streaked hair and the whiff of $350 perfume from Jean Patou were at odds with her too-tight, too-short leather skirt and the animal print top. Her French manicured nails were immaculate, if impractically long.

The mother had remarried, I assumed, as Lydia's last name was Ballou.

Lydia moved her plate, piled high with discards, from her lap to the tea table. She crossed her arms in front of her chest. Where her mother was groomed and flashy, Lydia looked like a sixties folk singer. She wore no makeup and her long, curly, mouse brown hair was parted in the middle. She had on a shapeless lace dress, which hung on her thin frame, and a short-sleeved beige cardigan. Her beautiful, dark blue eyes could probably look soulful when she wasn't being obstinate.

"Mother," she finally said, "I told you I didn't want cake. I want wedding pie."

Well, I can't help you there, I wanted to say. My bakery was called Rainbow Cake for a reason.

Roshonda jumped in.

"I think what Lydia is trying to say is that although Neely's—I mean Claire's—cakes are delicious, maybe we've strayed too far from the Appalachian theme we talked about," Roshonda said, giving me the eye.

Appalachian. Hmm. Why was I just hearing about this now? When I thought *Appalachian,* the first thing that came to mind was definitely not cake. Roshonda's meaningful look, with a slight tilt of her head toward Mrs. Stidham, told me that this first go-round was what the mother wanted. Traditional wedding cake.

Obviously, Lydia had other ideas.

A bit reluctantly, trying to leave my bruised ego behind, I was warming to the Appalachian idea.

Bourbon and branch water. Dulcimer music. Wildflowers in jelly jars. Biscuits and country ham. That did have a certain charm.

"I know you've talked this over with Roshonda and Gavin, but why don't you tell me about the kind of wedding you want," I said to Lydia with a smile. "What is your inspiration?"

Lydia sat up straighter, unfolded her arms, and put her hands in her lap. "Some of my happiest memories growing up were the

The Memory of Lemon

summer escapes I spent with my grandmother in the hills of northern Kentucky, along the Ohio River," she said.

Her mother reached over and, with a dramatic gesture, took her daughter's hand. Lydia rolled her eyes, kept her arm stiff, and didn't lean in to her mother. *Awkward.*

"To be fair, Mom tried really hard. She worked two jobs to support us," Lydia said, looking sideways at her mother and then back at me. "We lived in a tiny apartment above a bar. The neighborhood wasn't safe, so I couldn't go outside if she wasn't at home. Every night, I'd try to go to sleep in spite of the drunks yowling on the sidewalk and the cigarette smoke and beer smell that drifted up through the floorboards.

"At my grandma's in Augusta, it was like paradise. It was quiet and peaceful. Nobody bothered me. I would spend hours in the woods, by the creek, in her garden, in her skiff on the river. And that's what I want to re-create for my wedding: that simple paradise," Lydia said.

Her mother released Lydia's hand, then fished around in her handbag for a handkerchief.

I gave Lydia those few moments of silence that always prompted more of the story.

"I remember the wonderful feeling I had as soon as we drove out of our crappy neighborhood," Lydia recalled.

"You would start singing all those silly songs that you made up," Mrs. Stidham said, twisting the handkerchief in her hands. "If you saw a blackbird, it was a song about a blackbird. If you saw a barge on the river . . ."

"'Barge in Charge,'" said Lydia, suddenly smiling. "One of my greatest hits."

"I still can't get that song out of my head," her mother said. Lydia turned toward me. "And when we finally arrived at the ferry, I started to feel free again," she continued.

Out of the corner of my eye, I saw Lydia's mother stiffen. Weddings dredged up all kinds of things. No mother wanted to be reminded that her daughter felt unsafe and unhappy as a child. Mrs. Stidham bit her bottom lip.

"As the ferry went across the river," Lydia continued, "getting closer to the old buildings along the waterfront, I felt the wind in my hair and the pull of the river under my feet. It was like stepping back in time and going home, if that makes any sense."

"Vangie, Lydia's grandmother, made any place feel like home," said Mrs. Stidham. "And she made Lydia feel safe and special, as she did for my brother and me. But as I got older, I saw another side of Augusta. I couldn't go back to that kind of life. Small-minded people knowing your business, judging you. Like most small towns. But I understand it was probably the best part of Lydia's childhood," she said, tearing up. Mrs. Stidham smoothed out the handkerchief to dab her eyes. "Maybe, sweetheart," she said, turning toward her daughter, "we could still get that sense of simple paradise if we brought in a lot of trees in big pots to the ballroom at the River Club, like Kate Middleton's family did for her wedding at Westminster Abbey."

"Mom, I thought we had already agreed that the River Club was out."

One unconvincing tear managed to escape Mrs. Stidham's false eyelashes—probably real mink or yak hair or something like that—and roll down her cheek.

A fake lime flavor, like you tasted in cheap candies, settled

The Memory of Lemon

in my mouth. Unlike the sharp, somewhat aromatic flavor of real lime zest and juice, the fake stuff tasted like chemicals. It was the flavor I recognized as manipulation. *Hmm.*

I took a sip of coffee to banish it.

I studied Mrs. Stidham. I had the feeling that crying in an attractive way usually worked for her.

Lydia seemed unmoved, as I was.

I always Googled my clients before their wedding cake tastings so I was as prepared as possible. I'd found out that Gene Stidham was a self-made man, a guy who had invented a popular playing card game in the 1970s—Duo—that launched his company. He could have sold the rights very profitably to Mattel or Parker Brothers, but instead he had slowly added board games and then video games to his business portfolio. When the popularity of video games started to plateau, his company got into mobile gaming. Duo Gaming had made him a megamillionaire. To his credit, he had become a notable local philanthropist who had a soft spot for children's charities.

It didn't take much searching to find photographs of Gene and Cadence Stidham in evening dress, attending one big event after another. She was attractive in a nouveau riche sort of way and taller than him. He had thinning hair, glasses with clear frames, and a pleasant demeanor. Not a guy you would pick out of a crowd and say, *He looks successful.*

But I could still imagine how they had gotten together. Maybe, once upon a time, a down-on-her-luck single mother with a waiflike daughter had pulled at his heartstrings. I wanted to know more, but I couldn't bear the fake lime flavor another moment. I'd try at another meeting.

At this rate, we'd have to have quite a few more meetings because we weren't getting anywhere. I took another sip of coffee. When I looked up, Lydia was staring at me. Everyone else was, too.

Quickly, I had to pick up the thread of our conversation. *Simple paradise. Augusta. Wedding pie.*

"And is there a special reason you'd like pie instead of cake for your wedding?" I asked Lydia.

"Grandma Vangie taught me how to make pie. She made the best pies."

I nodded. "Well, I don't have pie today, but see what you think of this." I passed her a sugar cookie, which she—thankfully—took and began to nibble.

I had to think fast.

"Let's start with the little things and then we can work up to wedding pie," I suggested. "We can do these sugar cookies in virtually any shape and flavor you want for a bridesmaids' luncheon and wedding guest favors or simply as part of the wedding dessert buffet. I have these wonderful edible transfer wafer papers that you can apply to a sugar cookie so it looks like a vintage postcard or a perfume bottle or a china pattern."

Lydia scowled.

"But I don't see those designs for you," I quickly added. "I see botanical prints of Kentucky wildflowers or woodland plants like ferns on these cookies. We put the cookies in handwoven baskets so the guests can gather them like herbs from your grandmother's garden."

"Yes!" Lydia said, suddenly animated.

The Memory of Lemon

"And maybe the flavoring for the cookie could be a Kentucky flavor, maybe something that could have come from your grandmother's garden or the woods near her house. We can figure that out later."

Lydia beamed and turned to her mother, who looked crestfallen.

Uh-oh.

"You have to understand, Claire, that this wedding is for Lydia and Christopher, first, but it's also a big social occasion for my husband," said Mrs. Stidham.

"I would imagine that Mr. Stidham has a lot of friends and business associates he'd like to invite," I said.

"My husband has been very good to Lydia and me, and I don't want to disappoint him," Mrs. Stidham said, twisting her handkerchief again in her lap, as the fake lime flavor started to reassert itself.

I swallowed hard, trying to banish it.

"Gene wants the best of everything for Lydia, as I do. Designer gown. Luxurious reception. The finest champagne. It's expected from one in his position . . ." She trailed off, looking away. Her chin jutted out. She wanted her way.

I noticed that as she became upset, a hint of her Kentucky drawl returned. *Interesting.*

"Almost all of my big weddings feature signature sugar cookies," I reassured her. "It's just a question of what you do with them."

"I do appreciate everything you and Gene are trying to do for me," Lydia said forcefully, turning to face her mother. "But it's my wedding. I don't want glamour and glitz. I want something real. I want my wedding to be meaningful. You and Gene give enough big parties as it is. Can't this be what Christopher and I want?"

We were back to the classic standoff: Bride versus Mother.

When Lydia got up to use the restroom, Mrs. Stidham whispered to us, "Isn't it funny? I love Augusta. I truly do."

The fake lime flavor came in on a wave.

"But having Lydia's wedding there would be hard for me. I've spent most of my life trying to get away from the log cabin I was raised in, and then living paycheck to paycheck as a single mother." Thankfully, the awful taste was ebbing again.

"Thanks to Gene," Mrs. Stidham continued, "those days are long gone. I want to make up for everything I couldn't give Lydia earlier in her life. She could have a destination wedding in Paris, in Tahiti, no expense spared," she said, dabbing her eyes again. "But my daughter wants a hillbilly wedding."

2

LATE MARCH
INDEPENDENCE, MISSOURI

Jack O'Neil

The spring blizzard had blasted down from Canada, covering everything in sparkly white. That may have been bad news for commuters and daffodils, but it was good news for Jack O'Neil.

Jack's buddy Marvin was doing the rounds of the parking lots on old Route 40—fast-food drive-ins, no-tell motels, and porn palaces—with the snowplow hitched to his pickup, making a little extra money. Marvin had taken the dog with him. He said he'd bring back a pizza and some soda.

Jack had stayed behind for his tour of duty at the beat-up desk in the motel office.

The No Vacancy sign was crooked in the City Vue's window, but he wasn't expecting any travelers in this weather. I-70, which ran parallel to Route 40 a little ways to the north, was closed. Plus, the City Vue did a brisk if downtrodden business in temporary assistance, housing the needy sent there by Social Services.

Most of the City Vue tenants were on welfare and rented by the week, so there was little need for hospitality. But you never knew what might happen. The numbers he needed were right by the old push-button phone: the Independence, Missouri, police department; the ambulance service; and the fire department. If you called 911, you got all three and a lot of flak afterward. It was better to be particular and ask for only what you needed in the low-rent district.

Jack had worked some construction the past year so he could afford a warmer place to stay in deep winter. Ever since he got frostbite on one of his toes—it looked like freezer burn and hurt like hell—he didn't sleep rough when it got too cold.

Yet it wasn't like he had the TV on and a weather report he could check. Hell, he didn't even have a cell phone. In Independence, and neighboring Kansas City, the temperature could plummet fifty degrees in twelve hours. Despite the layers of sock, plastic bag, sock, plastic bag, then boot, he almost lost that toe and could have lost others during a cold snap last year. No way was he going to be a cripple.

So when Marvin, another regular at the nearby VA hospital, had offered him this temporary gig, Jack took it.

By April, it should be okay to go back to his old place.

Here at the City Vue, where it was warm and dry, he could keep things safe. Like the letter from his daughter that the guy from Project Uplift, the nonprofit group that fed the homeless, had brought by. Jack kept the letter in his shirt pocket, which he patted from time to time to make sure it was still there.

He sat back in the swivel chair that didn't swivel anymore and looked around the room. A rack of Technicolor postcards of the Kansas City skyline was furry with dust. Fake paneling peeled off the walls. The dropped-down ceiling tiles were yellowed with nicotine, even though Marvin had stopped smoking years before.

Jack opened the desk drawer and drew out a sheet from a stack of stationery so old, there was no zip code. The paper smelled musty.

But it was free.

One of the perks of the job here, along with a room for him and the dog.

In the back of the drawer, he found a ballpoint pen almost as old as the postcards. Amazingly, the darn pen still wrote.

He opened with *Dear Claire*, then put the pen down, unsure what to say next. He had left when she was fifteen. He hadn't spoken to her since, barely able to send a postcard from wherever he landed over the years.

There was so much, he didn't know where to start. *Better keep it short this time*, he told himself. When he finished, Jack put the letter in a City Vue envelope and wrote out the address he knew by heart in Millcreek Valley, Ohio.

He leaned back in the chair, just to rest his eyes, and fell into that old dream again.

He's dangling by strings like a marionette, his arms and legs in a silky fabric, jerking at some invisible puppet master's whim. Abruptly, the strings go limp and Jack collapses in a heap.

He wakes up in the dark, in pain, a smell of wood smoke in the air. And piss. A girl with blue hands reaches down to him. She's trying to tell him something, but he can't understand her. Her round face glows red.

When Jack woke up, a blue light was seeping through the opening in the sagging draperies. Jack looked down at the floor and shook his head.

More than forty years of this same goddamn dream. Wasn't it time for it to make some sense?

Or for Jack to quit searching for clues? Or to stop dreaming it?

In the old days, this would have made him turn to the bottle.

But he was learning to feel his feelings. And now he was goddamn hungry.

Where were those lemon cookies that the people from Project Uplift had brought in the previous day? Lemon always reminded Jack of home, of his mother's famous lemon pie. His daughter, Claire, also loved it. Jack wondered if all families had a favorite flavor.

He had avoided anything lemon for years. He hadn't wanted to remember the people he left behind: his daughter, Claire; his mother, Dorothy; his sister, Helen; even his wife, Cindy. Maybe she had divorced him by now. He wouldn't blame her.

He hadn't wanted to remember his hometown, Millcreek Valley, or the house in which he'd grown up. And he especially hadn't wanted to recall his time in Vietnam.

But if he wanted to get better, the docs at the VA hospital kept saying, he had to let it all come back. He had to feel the

feelings. Talk it out with other vets. Write a different ending in his mind.
Maybe then he could go home again.
Meanwhile, there were no more cookies.
Where the hell was Marvin?

3

APRIL

Lime and Coconut

Neely

The second meeting with Mrs. Stidham and Lydia had gone about as well as the first. We still weren't getting anywhere. And the wedding was in June, two months away.

As they rose to leave, taking with them a little box of cookies and our robin's egg blue wedding packet, they still seemed uneasy. I would have made pies and tarts for them to taste, but Mrs. Stidham had stonewalled us, perhaps hoping to wear her socially errant daughter down.

It was clear that neither the soothing charm of my parlor nor my winning recipes had worked their usual magic—again. The bride and her mother loved each other, deep down, but there was also mistrust and selfishness. And that played out in the very different ideas they had about the wedding. They each wanted their own way. And we still had no solutions.

I couldn't help fix the problem if I didn't have information. The fake lime flavor that Mrs. Stidham emanated was part of a story she was trying to hide, but it wasn't the "tell." And I wasn't getting anything from Lydia yet.

As I walked them out my front door and onto the wide covered porch for the second time in as many weeks, I pointed out my concrete goose with its chef's hat and baker's apron, the tongue-in-cheek yard art that Millcreek Valleyites dressed up for every occasion. I purposefully placed it right by the front door to help soften any wedding-jangled nerves before I conducted wedding cake tastings.

"I don't get it," Lydia said, pointing to the goose. "What's with the goose?" Her mother looked equally puzzled.

"It's sort of a Millcreek Valley mascot," I said. "Millcreek Valley used to be known as Gansdorf, or Goosetown, when the first German settlers moved here in the 1840s." Blank looks.

But still I blathered on.

"The hardware store on Millcreek Valley Road has a whole flock of concrete geese, if you want to take one home to dress up," I added. "Maybe if you style her up perfectly, yours will finally lay that golden egg we're all hoping for."

"This one stays out here on your porch, though, right?" Mrs. Stidham asked, catching her bottom lip in her teeth again. "What I mean is, you don't bring the, uh, geese to weddings or anything like that, do you?" Obviously, Mrs. Stidham was happy enough with her own rather sizable nest egg, courtesy of Dragon's Warcraft, Duo Gaming's wildly popular mobile game. She didn't need a fake bird to make things happen for her. Even so, I thought there might still be a chance for a connection here—that with a well-placed quip, I might be able to make her see the humor in this moment.

"Oh, no, I would never bring this old girl to a professional event. She's way too heavy," I deadpanned. I hoped my delivery was dry enough to elicit a giggle or even a smirk. But nothing.

"Hmm," they both said, as they practically ran down the steps and to their car.

I closed the front door and sank against it.

"They didn't get the goose thing, I take it," said Roshonda.

I shook my head.

"How are we going to make this wedding happen?" I moaned.

"Here, I'll pour a coffee for you," said Roshonda. "Gavin?"

He put his hand over his cup.

"Give yourself some, too," I said to Roshonda as she poured.

"No, thanks. I feel like I'm going to jump out of my skin as it is."

The three of us sat for a while in silence.

"We'll find a way to make everybody happy," Gavin suddenly said. "We have to." He shot his starched cuffs out of his sport coat, a nervous habit he'd had since junior high band concerts.

Nervously, I nibbled a sugar cookie, but it stuck in my throat. I sipped coffee and felt the lump move ever so slowly downward.

"Well, at least money is not an issue," said Roshonda. "That's one good thing."

"We have to get the mother past the idea of Kentucky as poor hillbilly cabin and toward Appalachian artisan, rustic chic, old-fashioned garden, small-batch bourbon," added Gavin.

Roshonda shook her head. "We should just go there," she said.

"Go where?" I asked.

"Augusta," she said. "On the ferry, over the river, into Kentucky. We have to find Lydia's grandmother's place and see it all for ourselves. Maybe it would work for the wedding and reception, maybe not. If it's really some smelly old cabin, Mrs. Stidham is never gonna go for it, no matter how much Lydia pouts. We need a place with *potential*."

We all knew what that meant. In wedding-speak, it was a term that combined availability, affordability, and style-ability.

"So, we don't invite Mrs. Stidham and Lydia to go with us?" I asked.

"Hell, no," Roshonda said. "They can't agree on what day it is. The three of us go there. We check it out. We eliminate it or we work up a plan that will showcase it as a five-star wedding venue that will please our hillbilly bride."

"I can't go Saturday. I've got the Mill Creek Yacht Club Regatta," Gavin said.

Roshonda and I rolled our eyes at each other. The "yacht club" was a grassroots group of environmentalists and supporters of clean water who paddled down the Mill Creek in canoes and kayaks to assess the state of the waterway. They held their regatta of ragtag boats in spring, when the weather was cool, as the Mill Creek was still far from pristine and during the height of summer smelled like the bad old days of industrialism.

"Hey, I even talked Big Ben into going this year," Gavin said.

"I can just see the two of you in a canoe," said Roshonda. "You'll look like Arnold Schwarzenegger and Danny DeVito in *Twins*."

I laughed. Ben Tranter was a former college football player with

The Memory of Lemon

the musculature to match—the polar opposite of rail-thin Gavin. Ben and I had known each other since grade school. We dated briefly in college, but our romance derailed (all my doing). Then we parted ways. He now owned a private security firm that catered to the many one-percenters in our region. When I moved back to our hometown from New York City late last year, Ben and I began circling each other again, this time with grown-up thoughtfulness. The feelings were all there, at least from my perspective: I knew I didn't have far to go before falling deeply in love with this man. But it was complicated. Not least because I was still technically married to my narcissistic, soon-to-be ex-husband, Luke.

"How about Sunday?" Roshonda asked.

We all were free, so I added *Field trip to Augusta* to my planner.

"Can I ask Ben to go with us?" I asked.

"Don't see why not," said Roshonda, giving me a sly smile. "Could be fun."

Our meeting broke up, and I went back to the bakery.

Every time I walked in the door of Rainbow Cake, I experienced the same feeling of well-being that you enjoy when you sink into a hot bath on a cold day.

The robin's egg blue walls, the little cakes on tiny stands that popped up and down the chocolate-colored marble counter, and the vintage glass display cases made my heart glad. Gavin had done a fabulous job making my vision come true.

The far wall displayed our colors and flavors for April: lime and coconut. The chartreuse backdrop made the little pastel Easter egg cakes, a white bunny cake, yellow sugar cookie chicks, and coconut cupcakes with lime filling stand out. It also made me yearn for spring.

"We were wondering when you were going to grace us with your presence." Maggie Lierman, whose short blond hair and milkmaid complexion belied her toughness as Rainbow Cake's manager, handed me my apron. "Rough morning?"

"I just want world peace," I said as I put the apron on, and then I gave Maggie the short version of culture clash, wedding-style.

We caught up on special orders and surveyed our shrinking inventory of unsalted butter (and then called our supplier, who was on speed dial) before another wave of customers ambled in to be waited on.

Usually Mondays were slow, but not today.

"See you tomorrow, Neely," Norb called as he went out the back way. Norb Weisbrod was my tried-and-true baker who came in at three o'clock every morning to get the day's cakes, cookies, and pastries done before our first customers arrived. Rainbow Cake was my bakery, but when Norb was in back mixing and baking, it was *his* space. Woe to anyone who interfered with his concentration or his routine. The difference between home and retail baking was *consistency*. Norb had that in spades, so I was happy to let him be.

But now that he had gone for the day, I needed to finish up a special order for lime and coconut cake. I had already made the pale green lime curd, its sharp citrus tang perfectly balancing the smooth blend of butter, sugar, and eggs. Its aroma and flavor banished the fake lime that I associated with Mrs. Stidham and now dreaded every time we met for Lydia's wedding.

Norb had baked three tender layers of our yellow cake, made with the softest cake flour. I had to put the layers together with a billowy frosting that looked and tasted best the day it was made.

And, of course, I needed to grate fresh, sweet coconut, familiar yet exotic.

For the frosting, I put the sugar and egg whites in the top part of my trusty double boiler over a saucepan of simmering water. As the ingredients warmed and dissolved into a clear mixture, I used my hand mixer to whip them into a glossy white cloud. Magic!

I smoothed the aromatic lime curd over the top of the bottom cake layer, then placed another cake layer on top, spread it with more lime curd, and repeated the process with the third layer. I used my spatula to whirl the frosting over the sides and top of the cake, making stiff peaks wherever I could. Then I showered it with tiny curls of fresh coconut. The tantalizing scent transported me to a white, sandy beach lapped by a turquoise sea under a tropical sun. Lime and coconut were the getaway flavors my bakery customers needed in April, tax time.

All too quickly, the bell on the front door jangled again and snapped me out of my island paradise. I looked up at the clock. Yes, the mailman was as on time as ever. I put my spatula back in the frosting bowl and walked to the front of the bakery. He handed me a stack. "I might as well give you these, too, if you don't mind," he said and piled my personal mail on top. He winced as he put his hand on the small of his back. "Saves me a trip."

With Maggie behind the counter, I went back to the inner sanctum of Rainbow Cake. Its milk chocolate walls, marble work surfaces that stayed cool for pastry and chocolate work, and orderliness calmed me. I sorted through the mail, dropping the junk in the recycling bin and piling the rest on the counter.

Coupons, ads: Pitch. Invoice, invoice, wholesale bakery catalog: Keep.

I tore open a letter from Luke's attorney. Blah, blah, blah. Something about our prenuptial agreement. The tone was vaguely threatening, reminding me that according to the terms of that long-ago document I had naively signed, Luke held all the cards. I was at his mercy. He could take back the worldly goods he had so generously bestowed upon me—Gran's house and the bakery, both of which I had bought with money he had given me. In other words, if I were smart, I'd forget about this silly divorce business and go back to being Mrs. Luke Davis, the little woman. At least in public. Fat chance.

I tossed the letter on the marble countertop, which was way too good for any contact with Luke. Basically, he was stalling, bringing up some nonissue that he hoped would prevent me from filing for divorce in a timely fashion. The NFL football season was over. Now it was golf, with every gridiron great sponsoring a golf tournament for charity at a five-star resort with plenty of sun, beer, and babes. And, of course, Luke, the NFL quarterback always tagged by sports journalists as *this close* to making it in a Super Bowl, couldn't miss any of them. What else was new?

The other letter. Hmm. I didn't know anyone at the City Vue Motel in Independence, Missouri.

The stationery looked old and smelled like cigarette smoke, but the spiky handwriting was familiar.

My heart in my throat, I stood up and began to pace. The workroom now seemed to close in on me, so I strode out to the baking area. Norb was gone, so the area by the ovens was quiet.

The Memory of Lemon

I sat on his stool by the rolling metal rack of sheet pans and began to read:

Dear Claire,

A guy at Project Uplift stopped by and gave me your letter. I have read it so many times, it's about to fall apart.
It sounds like you're doing well with your bakery. You can do anything you set your mind to, honey.
Please forgive me for the harm I never meant. I've been messed up for as long as I can remember, but I'm getting help now.
For some reason, I've been thinking about my mom's—your gran's—lemon pie and dreaming of home. And you know what that means, don't you, sweetie?
I never intended to be gone this long. But one thing just led to another and here I am. I have nobody to blame but me.
In my mind, you're still a beautiful fifteen-year-old with your whole life before you. You deserve the best.

Love you, for what that's worth—
Dad

P.S. Please write back.

It was too much to take in.
My dad.
In January, I had gotten a postcard from him with a return address of Project Uplift, a nonprofit group that fed the homeless

in Kansas City. He had abandoned my mom and me when I was in high school. I had mixed feelings about him, to say the least, but still, I didn't like imagining him destitute, without a roof over his head. I had kept the postcard, but hadn't responded right away, not sure what to do.

And then the sour flavor of anger that had tormented me for weeks also brought a surprise gift—a glimpse into my dad's high school days, when his drinking problem had started. I had seen him sneaking sips of whiskey in a neighbor's garage to calm his worries about going to Vietnam.

At the same time that I had this vision, I had been ending things with Luke, my charming, handsome, successful husband with the chronic wandering eye. I realized that I had stayed with Luke for much longer than I intended. But not for the most obvious reason. I hadn't been hanging on to Luke because I desperately needed a male in my life after my father abandoned his family. I had taken Luke back time after time because I had been unconsciously trying to keep my dad's pattern from being mine as well. Love 'em, leave 'em, then fall off the face of the earth.

After I finally gathered the courage to leave Luke and start over, I had a breakthrough idea.

Why not write to my dad?

Now my homeless, missing-in-action father had written me a letter that actually said something. And was from an actual address. Not just a plain white "thinking of you" postcard from a town he was just passing through.

We were having a long-distance connection, the very old-fashioned way.

I typed the address into Google on my iPhone and found

the City Vue on old Route 40. I touched the red locator balloon with my fingertips, as close as I'd gotten to my dad in years, then hugged the phone to my chest.

Dad.

How many red locator balloons would it take to track his journey from Ohio, over the years, to where he was now? Jack O'Neil, the wanderer.

I held the letter with shaking hands and read it again. This time, a surge of anger surprised me with its intensity.

He had been thinking about *pie?* What about us? His daughter, his mother, his sister, his wife whom he'd left all those years ago. The people who had to pick up the pieces when he fell apart.

But one thing just led to another, my dad had written.

He was right about that.

After he left, Mom and I lost our house and had to move in with Gran. Mom and Gran's relationship soured.

Aunt Helen never married. Mom refused to move on.

And I won't even get started on me.

Jack O'Neil had been a human wrecking ball, and we were all still picking up the pieces. He had thought only of himself, not the people he said he loved. How could we ever trust him again?

What did he want from us now? Forgiveness? A new start?

I folded the letter and shoved it back in the envelope.

4

FEBRUARY 1818
IRELAND

The Wanderer

Eliza Shawcross sat in the morning room, a fine woolen shawl around her bony shoulders to keep out the chill. Even with the coal fire burning in the grate, she could barely feel her feet in their hand-stitched leather shoes. Her feet always seemed to be cold.

Her ash brown hair was parted in the middle with side curls peeping out from under her lace cap, the mark of a married woman. Now in her thirties, Eliza knew she had lost whatever bloom she once had. Although her hair had dulled over the years, her gray eyes remained sharp and clear. Her mouth scraped across her face in a thin, bitter line as she gripped the quill pen, blowing on her fingers to warm them. The Ballykinsale household account book lay open on the desk. Her own black-penned lines showed the same elegant hand as her late father's. But her attention was elsewhere.

From the long window, she saw the boy raking the front garden, picking up the dead leaves and limbs from the boxwood and holly beds, the aftermath of the previous day's gale. That afternoon, he should start on the back—the pleasure garden and the kitchen garden—where the rigid protection of cold stone walls had saved the plants from the worst of the storm.

Sean O'Neil was a handsome boy, actually a young man now, Eliza had to admit. Chestnut hair, green eyes. A good, sturdy build to him. Intelligent. He could read and write; she had seen to that. And a hard worker, like his parents, and just as Irish, through and through.

His mother, Cathleen, had been a comfort to Eliza, keeping vigil each time a child washed from her body before its time, swept away on that cursed, bloody tide. Bringing her that special tea she brewed with a strip of dried orange peel.

"For a new day, missus," Cathleen would say each time.

Eliza removed Cathleen's funeral holy card, printed with the image of Jesus pointing to his red heart encircled by a crown of thorns, from where it was hidden under the desk blotter. The priest at the Anglican church in Queenstown would regard this as a vulgar and lurid display of overwrought feeling. "Papist," he would sneer if he saw it. He would also be shocked to learn that Eliza had paid for these cards as well as the funeral.

Cathleen and her husband were two years gone, killed by a runaway team of horses hauling barrels of salted butter to the Queenstown harbor. The butter had been seen to first, the kegs passed hand to hand down to the dock and onto the ship, while the O'Neils bled to death in the street. Eliza could only imagine how long they lay there before that shabby priest with the whiskey breath came to administer their last rites. Mr. Shawcross had their bodies taken in a cart for burial in St. Brigid's cemetery.

So it was in Ireland these days. Catholic. Protestant.

Looking at the holy card, Eliza again felt the pain for what she was about to do.

She had never been a beauty, and Eliza knew that Charles Shawcross had married her as much for her father's estate as for the small personal charms she could claim. On the rare occasions when he came to her at night—in yet another attempt to produce a child—she gritted her teeth, even as she opened her body. It was always the same. He patted her much as he would a skittish horse he was about to mount. Then he turned her on her side in the dark and lay behind her. Without a word, he pulled up her linen shift, his hot breath on the back of her neck. He never spoke her name. Perhaps he pretended she was someone else.

She was a brood mare who couldn't foal. Yet Eliza still did her woman's duty. The promise of a child made this bearable. When it was over, he gave her a kiss on her cheek, then went back to his room. She slept alone.

Eliza got up from the desk and stood in front of the fire, holding on to the mantel as if for strength.

Her husband had started looking at the boy with more interest than was seemly. Sean had assumed his father's duties as head gardener of Ballykinsale shortly after Mr. O'Neil was gone, and he had performed admirably, impeccably, from the first. Anyone could see that.

"He needs my guidance," Mr. Shawcross had said once again as he helped himself to kippers and boiled eggs at breakfast that morning. There was always an explanation for his seeking out the boy, offering a word of advice, a manly pat on the shoulder that had begun to linger like a caress. The boy didn't see what was coming. Maybe her husband didn't, either.

"I'm riding to Queenstown today, my dear," he had told her, sipping his tea from a thin china cup. "There's a man with a promising dapple gray that I've had my eye on."

"Shall I tell Cook to keep supper warm for you, then?"

"No, no, I'll dine in town, and be back after you're abed."

And so the time had come. Eliza rang for the maid. "Please ask Padraig to have the pony cart ready in an hour. I'll be taking Sean with me on an errand to Queenstown. Then please go to the attic and bring down my large leather case to Mr. Shawcross's room."

It was a risk to involve the maid, but the valise was too bulky for Eliza to manage on her own.

With a feverish energy, Eliza unlocked the linen press in the upstairs hall and removed a small bag of gold coins from the back of a drawer. In her husband's dressing room, she gathered two linen shirts and a paisley cravat. A silk waistcoat from their courting days. A fine broadcloth coat in bottle green that her husband had not worn in years and would not miss. A pair of breeches now too small for him. Silken hose and fine leather dress shoes. A warm woolen muffler she had knitted him for Christmas and he had yet to wear. She placed it all in the valise.

Slipping into the gardener's cottage, she quickly gathered what few clothes Sean possessed. He was already wearing his good boots and a thick sweater. She took Cathleen's coral brooch and Thomas's pipe so Sean would have something to remember his parents by.

Padraig brought the pony cart around the circular front drive, where Eliza waited in her bonnet and cape. Sean helped her into the cart, and she handed the reins over to him. He didn't notice the large valise behind the seat, but "hee-yupped" the pony to canter down the drive.

At the dock in Queenstown, Sean took the valise from the back of the pony cart and handed it to Eliza.

"No, this is for you," she said. "And this." She handed him the bag of coins. "Keep it safe."

The boy looked shocked and scared.

"Mr. Shawcross wanted to surprise you," Eliza said, "and it looks like he did. After what happened to your parents, we want you to start fresh in America. You'll have clothes, money, and this." She gave him a letter of introduction, which she had written in the style of her husband. Who would know so far away?

"Keep it safe, by your heart," she said, steeling herself as she folded the letter and put it in the small leather case that had been her mother's.

"Missus," Sean said in a whisper, his eyes brimming with tears.

When the *Eleanora* sailed out of Queenstown for New York, hours later on the afternoon tide, the snow was coming down in thin petals, like the blossoms of the Ballykinsale whitebeam savaged by the gale.

Eliza leaned on Padraig, trampling the white blooms into the snow as she hobbled from the stable yard to the kitchen, wracked with silent grief. The startled cook settled her before the fire and poured her a mug of hot, sweet tea flavored with a strip of lemon peel and laced with brandy.

Slowly Eliza came back to herself. She took another sip. It would do. But it couldn't begin to thaw the cold place that had settled in her heart.

EARLY SPRING 1820
AUGUSTA, KENTUCKY

When the viburnum—the wayfaring tree—bloomed a creamy white, it would be time to prune the roses, but he wouldn't be there to do it.

Sean O'Neil threw the last of the boxwood clippings into the bonfire. He had once again restored order to the garden, a sun-warmed refuge from the dark wildwood on either side of the river and as far as the eye could see in the hills beyond.

He could clear his head in a garden, where the sunlight could make its way in and the plants could breathe.

He straightened up, brushing the debris from the linen shirt he wore like a smock. When he arrived in New York, his clothes had been the clothes of a gentleman, but his old work boots told a different story. Soon, he had sold the fine bottle green coat to a tailor and had bought instead a dead man's buckskin trousers at a market stall. They better fit his new life.

The Memory of Lemon

Traveling on a flatboat from New York to Philadelphia, he had kept his letter of introduction safe in all weather, and there had been all weather, such like he had never known in Ireland. Melting heat, sodden heat, dry heat. Bone-jarring cold, rain that fell sideways, waterspouts on the river.

But the letter from Charles Shawcross had opened doors at the Bartram family's botanic garden across the Schuylkill River from Philadelphia. He would have liked to stay there and study the native plants that the Quaker John Bartram had brought back from his travels. In the Bartram garden, Sean had seen the beautiful magnolias, mountain laurels, azaleas, and rhododendrons flower in spring and the sugar maples, black gums, viburnum, and sumac blaze with color in autumn, a world of difference from the plants he had learned to cultivate at home.

He could have learned so much.

But there was always that bit of unpleasant business about being Irish, and Sean had had to move on.

And now he had to move on, yet again, from Ezekiel Peabody's garden in this little village on the banks of the Ohio River, although this was not about Sean's accent or his clothes or the presumption that he was as low as a Negro.

The herb woman had come that morning to dig the last of Mr. Peabody's comfrey root, the plant Sean knew by the Gaelic name *lus cnámh*. The root was black, but its inner flesh was almost stark white. She once used it to make liniment to ease the old man's aches and pains. But no more. Mr. Peabody had been dead a fortnight.

Peabody's son and his wife now occupied the home—and the

garden. They had brought their slaves, a housemaid called Sullah and her husband, Pompey. Pompey was a quiet, hardworking man, but he was no gardener. He couldn't tell comfrey, with its bell-shaped lavender flowers, from sage, or *sáiste*. Sean hated to think what the garden would look like in a year's time.

But it was not his problem.

The new Peabodys did not want a gardener.

The young Mr. Peabody had been kind enough to suggest a man he knew in Queen City who might have need of one, a physician who owned a fine house, one Daniel Drake, who also happened to be Irish. Sean hoped Queen City was bigger than Augusta and friendly to people of his kind.

At least Queen City wasn't wilderness.

This big raw country was not to his liking. It was wild like the worst of gales, and he never knew what next would blow into his life. It kept him on edge.

When the flatboat left in late afternoon for the forty-mile, all-night trip to Queen City, Sean helped the herb woman tie up her mule on deck between the bales of tobacco and hemp. She untied her baskets of potions and tinctures and her gunnysacks of roots and herbs and set them on the deck. She regularly made the trip to Queen City to sell her medicines and see her daughter, Sarah, recently married.

Together, Sean in his buckskin and the herb woman in her straw bonnet and heavy wool shawl stood on the flat deck, feeling the river run its westerly course beneath their feet.

Sean marveled at the flocks of brilliant green parroquets that glittered in the buttonwood trees, those tall, pale trees with the peeling bark that he knew as *craobh sice*. Their pale yellow flowers dropped silently into the muddy green water.

When they floated by cattails that grew in marshy areas where little creeks fed into the river, he counted scores of blackbirds with red and yellow markings on their wings.

As night fell, the lanterns in the forecastle shone their dim light on the dark river water. Sean had heard tales of giant fish and turtles that could snap off a man's leg. The flatboat kept close to the steep banks. If they hit a sandbar, the men would use the long poles to move them away to deeper water. If they hit a snag and capsized, it was a shorter swim to shore.

Sean sat on the plank deck, his back against his valise, packed with everything he owned in the world.

Abigail Newcomb, the herb woman, sat next to him, smoking her clay pipe. He was grateful for her calm, steady presence. He stole a glance at her, her face shadowed by the bonnet. There was something that reminded him of his missus, who had been so kind to him in Ireland. Mrs. Shawcross and the herb woman might be around the same age, he thought.

Someone played a banjo for a while and sang a few mournful songs, but then got tired and put the instrument away.

Sean and the other passengers were left with the sounds—and the terrors—of the night. The scream of a big cat from somewhere up in the hills made Sean's skin prickle.

"That's a ghost cat, a panther, some call it," the herb woman murmured. "They hunt at dark. I had one get up on the roof of my cabin when my Sarah was in her cradle, like to scared me to death."

There was a rustling in the underbrush: a slither and then a splash into the water.

Sean stood to look out over the dark water. He wished he had a rifle.

The herb woman reached up and touched his hand with something smooth and cold. As he turned toward her in the shadowy light, he saw the small stoneware jug she offered.

"Courage in a bottle," she said.

He took a swig and wiped his mouth with the back of his hand. Whiskey with a little spice and something sour. He felt the fiery liquid go down his gullet and then he tasted something familiar.

Suddenly, he felt hollowed out and yet weighed down, as he hadn't let himself feel in a long time. He was back in the kitchen at Ballykinsale, sitting in front of the fire, stunned to learn that both his mam and his pa were dead. Cook had given him hot, sweet tea with something else in it, just like this—fiery and sour.

He felt the presence of the missus, with her kind gray eyes and her hand on his shoulder, and knew he would never see her again, either.

He took another swig and then stumbled as some big creature passed under the flatboat. He felt a steadying hand at his side.

"Sit here with me," the herb woman said, pulling him back into the present.

He sank down heavily beside her, almost spilling the precious elixir that had brought his old life back so vividly. Would he ever feel at home again?

How much farther did he have to go to find that place?

The Memory of Lemon

OCTOBER 1820
QUEEN CITY, OHIO

Under a clear October sky, the woods bordering this river town and the hills on the Kentucky side had burst into color. Maple trees flamed orange, the dogwoods deepened into a reddish purple, and the redbuds glowed a golden yellow. Only the sycamores, with their ghostly peeling bark, did not put on an autumn display. Their leaves simply dried up and fell.

John James would not notice the trees, as his wife, Lucy, knew. He was looking for birds. With any luck, a blue heron, a bald eagle, or a passenger pigeon. He had taken the boys, Gifford and Woodhouse, with him. And when they returned at dusk, they would all be together again. Lucy treasured this time when they all lived under the same roof because she knew it would end soon. It always did.

Lucy, small and dark haired with a ramrod posture, saw them in her mind's eye making their way along the marshy areas of the Mill Creek. Back in Pennsylvania, when she and John James were courting, she would have gone with him, returning later to paint a watercolor in her sketchbook or play an arpeggio on her pianoforte, the descending notes like falling leaves.

But now there was no sketchbook and no time to paint. There was no pianoforte. There was only this bare little house and the arts of a gentlewoman's life that she now taught to private school students. For pay, not pleasure.

The only piece of furniture she did not miss from their old

life was the painted pine cradle that had rocked their two baby girls, buried only a year or so apart in little graves down the river in western Kentucky.

Lucy looked out the window onto the dusty street. It did not help to ruminate on life's misfortunes, she thought, but she had no one to talk to but herself.

She loved her husband. She *loved* him. He was handsome, affectionate, intelligent, and good to her and the boys. But it was difficult, sometimes, to live with him, just as it was once difficult to understand his French-accented English with Quaker "thee" and "thou" added for good measure. That was how he had learned English when he recovered slowly from yellow fever years before, and that was how he spoke it still. Lucy had always found it charming, but most people didn't know what to make of him, even here in this frontier town, where one would meet every kind of vagabond in buckskin clothes and coonskin cap.

John James Audubon was a born dreamer. Lucy had to be the practical one.

His $125 monthly salary at the new Western Museum, promised by Daniel Drake, had not materialized, nor was it likely to. The financial panic that had doomed them in Kentucky now surged like a tidal wave upriver to Ohio. Daniel Drake was about to lose his fine house, his garden, and his carriage. After a few weeks of exacting taxidermy and painting realistic backdrops for wildlife exhibits planned for the new museum, John James had wisely packed up and brought his work home.

With no other means of support, he turned again to portraiture, charging five dollars for each work, as he had in Louisville. He limned General and Mrs. William Lytle in three-quarter

The Memory of Lemon

profile and was paid before they, too, became victims of the crash. When portraiture was scant, he gave drawing and painting lessons at Miss Deed's Seminary for Young Ladies. But this could not go on.

If Lucy's stepmother walked through the front door of the tiny house, she would know Lucy for a fool, and it could only be a matter of time before the Audubons moved back east to be a millstone around the family's neck at the Bakewells' farm, Fatland Ford.

In the front parlor, the room with the best light, a tableau sat temporarily forgotten on the rough wooden table. The dead Carolina parroquets, with their glittery green plumage, vivid yellow neck and breast, and brilliant orange on either side of the beak, were strung like puppets with wire to the dowel rods attached to a wooden base that her husband used to simulate their natural, living postures. Clumps of straw-colored cocklebur, the soil still damp at the weedy roots, made the scene ever more lifelike. The little burs that the parroquets loved to eat stuck to everything in the room and were the bane of farmers and sheep and horses—and women who tried to keep a clean house. But Lucy knew better than to attempt tidying up. Her husband could change his mind about the day's outing, come back inspired, and work by candlelight long into the night, drawing and painting.

The charcoal sketch of the parroquets, on paper they couldn't afford, lay crumpled in a corner of the room. It was only good for sketching, not nearly fine enough for John James to wet his brush for watercolor or waste confident smudges of oil pastel crayon. *I am slowly desponding,* he kept telling her.

She was glad he had taken his gun with him that day. She

hoped he would find refuge in the woods. And perhaps he would bring back a wild turkey or plump little quail that she could wrap with fatback and roast on the coals.

Restless, she put on her bonnet and gathered her market basket. She had learned to cook on their hearth without the help of a servant, but baking bread was still a mystery. There was no point in wasting good flour and the yeast from the brewery when she could just buy a large loaf for a comparable price.

In the open-air market a few blocks away, Lucy paid the baker and put the loaf in her basket.

"Missus."

Lucy walked away, but the voice got louder. "Missus."

Lucy turned toward the next stall and the older woman in a calico dress and linen apron, with a straw bonnet tied under her chin. She was sitting on a three-legged stool behind a table filled with bunches of herbs, bottles of potions, and liniments.

"Yes?"

"I have something for you."

Lucy frowned. Was this some kind of trick?

"I do not think I've had the pleasure of your acquaintance, ma'am."

"Abigail Newcomb, at your service." She did a sort of curtsy, as a workingwoman was still expected to do to a woman of a class above. Abigail also extended her work-worn hand, a gardener's hand, to Lucy.

Lucy sensed a feminine strength that passed from the older woman's hand to her young one, and she held on a second or two longer than she intended.

The Memory of Lemon

"I come up from Augusta on the flatboat every fortnight or so," said Abigail, matter-of-factly. "Visit my daughter, Sarah, and grandbaby, Little Abigail, and do a little business here." She gestured at the table. "I've seen you and your boys. And your husband so keen on the birds. I've been wanting to give you this."

The herb woman handed Lucy a thick bundle of short, slender sticks tied together with a strip of homespun, just big enough to fit into a tankard.

"Spicebush," the woman explained. "You brew a tea with a few sticks. Let them steep in boiled water. Tastes like allspice, if you know it. Helps you remember the ones who are gone, but you don't feel the melancholy."

Lucy looked at her sharply. How did she know?

"I bring Sean, here, the dried spicebush leaves. Sean misses his old life in Ireland, and he says that the sour tea tastes like what the cook used to make for him." The herb woman pointed to a young man dressed improbably in a fine linen shirt and buckskin trousers, loading a cart with thick coils of hemp rope.

"He used to have fancier clothes when he arrived in New York, Sean told me," recounted Abigail. "The clothes of a gentleman. But the bottle green coat didn't hold up well tramping through the woods."

"The fine muslin dress from my courting days fared much the same," Lucy said.

"He has a letter of introduction, does Sean O'Neil," Abigail continued. "He's a gardener by trade, but not much call for that here, where the big woods are still so close. A good worker, should you ever need someone to tote and fetch. Most days, you can find 'im here, somewhere in the market. I hope he settles," she said, and they both gazed in his direction.

Lucy thanked the herb woman and put the bundle of sticks in her market basket. She was saying good-bye when a man hurried past carrying two withy cages, woven from willow branches. One cage held redbirds. The other, glittering green parroquets.

"I can't abide a free thing caged," the herb woman said with a sigh.

Lucy's own heart sank at the sight. And then she knew.

She would have to let him go. She would help him pack his gun and tackle, his violin and flute, his much-loved copy of La Fontaine's *Fables*. Sheets of art paper, two feet wide and three feet long, rolled into a long tin case. His watercolors, brushes, chalks, and pencils. His wire for mounting specimens. His portfolios. The ledger with the marbled blue endpapers he had just bought at W. Pounsford, the bookbinder, three doors north of the Presbyterian church. Paper for letter writing.

John James Audubon would travel down the Ohio, then the Mississippi on a cargo flatboat, drawing birds from here to New Orleans. In seven months, he promised, he would have his collection of American birds.

And they would be together again.

But not here.

"Mrs. Newcomb." Lucy turned and touched her arm. "You have been very kind to me. In return, my husband could render your likeness before he goes downriver. He's very good with sketching and then coloring with chalk pastels. What they call a portrait, but on paper."

Lucy knew it was an odd offer, and Abigail Newcomb looked

appropriately puzzled. Only the rich had pictures of themselves hanging on a wall.

"If not of you, maybe your daughter and her baby?"

Abigail's eyes lit up. "Then I can see them whenever I want. Like they were with me."

5

Neely

I peered out of Rainbow Cake's front window on Saturday morning. The empty sidewalks reflected the bleak day. Where were the brides, their mothers, their friends? Anyone?

Maybe the cold drizzle and overcast skies had kept everyone snug in their beds.

In the empty bakery, I penned the last lines to a short letter to my dad. Although I was of two minds about renewing our relationship, I'd decided to risk it. Who knew how long he'd stay in Missouri before he moved on again? I had to take the chance while I could.

I wrote in longhand on printer paper:

> *My problem might seem a little silly—the bride who wants a hillbilly wedding and her snobby mother who is hiding*

something. But what really bothers me is that I'm not getting any kind of a flavor feedback from them. Maybe I just need to be patient.

Did that ever happen to you when it was something important?

Write back when you get the chance, and hope everything is going better for you, Dad.

Claire

I had wanted to sign off *Love, Claire,* but I just couldn't. I folded the letter and put it in the envelope. Maybe Dad would have some advice. Maybe not. Maybe he'd move on and never even get this letter. Dear old Dad.

I wondered if I should include anything else. A photo? A business card? A brochure from the bakery? Yes, the brochure. Just information, not anything too personal. If I enclosed a photo, he might send one back of him. And I wasn't ready for that.

I placed the letter on top of the bills I was paying. A lot of bakery supply vendors still believed in paper invoices, doing their best to keep the post office in business.

This morning, when I checked my business checking account online, before the bakery opened, I noticed the balance was teetering on the brink of going to red. Our retail orders were down this week, although our wedding orders were up.

Now I just had to make sure the weddings were successful. No easy feat, especially ones like the pie wedding. I refused to think about that until our trip to Augusta the following day. The joys of the self-employed. Always something.

The Memory of Lemon

Justin, our barista, was wiping down the counter around the La Marzocco coffee machine for the umpteenth time, so I put him to work. It was a measure of how busy we weren't that he had the time to make an intricate spiderweb pattern in the milky foam of my latte. I took a sip, then looked at the pattern again. I grimaced. What I now saw was a shaky dollar sign.

That—and the caffeine—filled me with nervous energy. If I had to pay Luke back for the monies I'd used to get this business started, could I really make it? Could I even get a bank loan? Could I survive with all that debt to carry? When I compared sales figures for February and March, it had looked like March formed a canyon compared to February's peak. April was a plateau so far. What I needed was a mountain range. And a bunch of hungry shoppers.

I looked around the almost-empty bakery for something to do. The glass cases displayed spring-themed sugar cookies. Surely the wise souls of the Queen City area could brave a few raindrops for a really great sugar cookie. We also had breakfast cupcakes—though Maggie insisted on calling them muffins—of every flavor, as well as to-die-for cinnamon rolls. *C'mon, people.*

At the far end of the bakery, our canvas curtain heralded April's lime and coconut theme. Little bags of coconut meringue polka dots with lime buttercream filling were there for the taking. I was proud of our little cakes shaped like a cracked-open coconut—white coconut cake interior with a dark chocolate "shell," complete with a lime cookie straw inserted in the center for imaginary sipping. Lime bars with a coconut crust and lime curd filling sat on a snowy white cake stand. If they all didn't go that day, I'd be packing them up to deliver to the nuns and caregivers at Mount Saint Mary's.

All that work . . .

Jett Patterson, a local high school student, would soon arrive to begin sculpting delicate sugar cake decorations for the Martin/Obermayer wedding the next weekend. Jett's artistic talent was as weighty and emphatic as the heavy black makeup she applied to her lips and eyelids.

Maggie kept the books and waited on customers. Norb did most of the baking. Suddenly, I felt useless. While a smattering of people sipped their beverages and ate their pastries, I started to pace, latte in hand.

Maggie gestured me to come back behind the counter.

"Why don't you catch the first part of the regatta? It would give you something to do."

"Am I that obvious?"

She gave me a look.

"Why don't *you* take some time off? I'm sure you've got things to do on a Saturday."

"The other grandparents are keeping Emily this weekend. I don't have any money to shop. The weather is crappy. And the thought of a whole day spent with my mother watching reruns of old sitcoms, well . . ."

"All right, all right. I'll have my phone with me if we suddenly get busy."

I ran next door to change into my running shoes, added a sweater, arranged my hair into a topknot, and pulled on the hood of my bright yellow rain slicker. I looked like a unicorn on traffic duty. I pulled off the hood and redid my hair into a low ponytail.

It wasn't that far to where the regatta was gathering at Vorhees

Landing, but I decided to drive in case I had to get back to the bakery fast.

The canoes and kayaks were angled on the sloping east bank of the creek, ready for push-off. Under a makeshift tent, volunteers passed out water bottles and name tags. Dave Pearce, his angelic blond curls tamed by an old baseball hat, was the organizer. Even in grade school, he was always bringing fossils and crayfish he had found in the creek for show-and-tell. He now headed the tri-state environmental board overseeing the water quality of the rivers and creeks that flowed from southern Indiana and Ohio, into the Ohio River, and across into northern Kentucky.

The next person I recognized was Lydia. She was holding hands with a tall, earnest-looking guy wearing wire-rimmed glasses and a puffy jacket. The groom? I made it a point never to assume, so I ventured carefully as I approached them. "Good to see you again, Lydia. Have you done this regatta before? It's my first time to see it."

"Mrs. Davis—"

"Oh, please call me Neely."

"Neely, this is my fiancé, Christopher." I shook his hand.

"I'm working on the desserts for your wedding," I explained.

"I'm not much into sweets," Christopher admitted, "but whatever Lydia wants is fine with me."

"You mean whatever my mother wants," Lydia said, darkly.

"We'll find a way to make everyone happy," I said. "So how did you get involved in the regatta?" I asked, desperate to change the subject.

"Lydia and I take our canoe and do river cleanup days almost every weekend in the spring and fall. When Lydia is committed to something, she gives it her all," he said, squeezing her hand.

Lydia's demeanor, which I had first taken to be steely and stubborn, now took on a different slant. She was an activist. She must feel a deep connection to our little part of the world, and she was trying to make it better. I admired that about her.

"Five minutes, ladies and gentlemen," commanded a familiar voice from a bullhorn.

I said my good-byes to Lydia and Christopher and walked over to Ben and Gavin, who were sipping coffee. "So you two really are doing this."

"Neels." Gavin gave me a one-handed hug.

"Come here, you," Ben said as I reached up to put my arms around his neck. He held me a little longer than was strictly friendly, but Gavin didn't mind, and I certainly didn't.

"I'm so glad to see you," I whispered in Ben's ear and gave his arm a squeeze.

"And I'll see you again tonight," he whispered back. "Dinner. Pick you up at seven." His warm gaze made me feel lighter, more buoyant, as if slow bakery traffic on a rainy Saturday was no big deal. There were more important things in life. I wanted to bottle this feeling. But, happy or not, I hadn't yet filed for divorce from my high-profile husband, which meant that my budding romance with Ben needed to remain under wraps for now—especially at events like this one where we were surrounded by several dozen nosy Facebook and Instagram friends.

Like it or not, I could see the wisdom in my attorney's advice. Rich men—like Luke—were used to getting their way. When they didn't want a divorce, they could make life *really* unpleasant for

The Memory of Lemon

the women who wanted to leave them. Like me. Especially *unfaithful* wives who made their public-image-conscious husbands look weak or inadequate in the bedroom.

I wasn't about to make that mistake. Besides, I hadn't been unfaithful. Yet.

"Hey, I saw her first." Gavin pretended to strong-arm Ben and grabbed for me. He wore designer jeans and his baseball hat backward like the preppy, hip-hop-listening environmentalist he was—today.

Ben laughed and released me. "I think we need a team look." He turned his baseball cap backward, too.

"If this was an actual regatta, I might agree, Tranter," said the voice from the bullhorn—Dave had now joined us. I turned to face him, long and lean and nerdy as ever. "But it doesn't matter who comes in first," he continued. "Our big 'win' today would be noting an improvement in the biodiversity of this unique ecosystem."

"You had me at 'biodiversity,'" Gavin teased, "but then you had to go all 'ecosystem,' too. Is fun not allowed, Pearce?"

"People have been having fun on the Mill Creek for generations and look where it's gotten us," said Dave.

Ben gave Dave a couple of big pats on the shoulder. "Dave, we got it. Gavin brought his binoculars. He's our lookout man. Got your clipboard, Nichols?"

"Clipboards are so football. We're using the Mill Creek Regatta app." Gavin pulled out his phone and pushed a few buttons. "All you do is tap here for blue heron or turkey vulture or red-winged blackbird. Or navigate over here to report illegal dumping or suspicious effluent."

"In fact," said Dave with a wide smile, "we're going to be paddling on treated effluent."

We stared blankly at him.

"Effluent starts off as raw sewage, then goes through a water treatment plant," explained Dave.

"Sewage, transformed. Just adds to the experience," said Gavin, who, nevertheless, turned a shade paler.

"Well, it looks like you two are in good shape. Too bad I'm not," said Dave. "My tracker—my girlfriend, Shelley—missed her flight from Chicago this morning." He turned to me. "How about it, Neely? Want to be my tracker?"

I looked at Ben and he smirked back at me. Inside joke. In high school, Ben had listened to me complain about getting stuck with Dave Pearce as a lab partner semester after semester because our last names threw us together alphabetically. Dave was nice enough, but prone to annoying lectures and tangents. Well-meaning, but officious. Now here I was, with the chance to be Dave's science buddy all over again, this time on a lab that floated in effluent. The irony was thick—a fact not lost on Ben, who was chuckling indiscreetly behind his coffee cup. I had to smile, too. Ben might love to tease me, but it was always a pure-hearted sort of ribbing. I felt lucky to have finally found a man who could give me a run for my money *and* always have my back.

My phone buzzed with a text message from Maggie. "So sorry, Dave." *Not.* "I've got a new appointment," I said, happy that the day's business was picking up. "Dave, if anybody can do two things at once, it's you."

"See you later, Neely," Ben said meaningfully.

The Memory of Lemon

"Remember when this was the Maisonette, very old-school French?" Ben asked, as he opened the brilliant red-orange door of Boca that evening.

I did remember, but I didn't want to spoil this occasion with a sad trip down memory lane. I was at the Maisonette with Luke and several other people the first time I realized he had been cheating. I brushed that thought aside and gave Ben my warmest smile.

"Boca's food is supposed to be great."

Inside, the pewter bar with a men's club vibe was buzzing. Ben had wanted to go to a famous and expensive steakhouse that major sports figures liked to frequent, but I had steered him here. I had envisioned a sports-free evening for this next milestone in our relationship. Maybe Boca was a mistake, though. It was busier than I expected.

The maître d' guided us up the contemporary glass-walled staircase to a private dining alcove under a pendant lamp with a drum shade. Two sculptural leather wingback chairs in vivid orange cozied up to a round table. The brick walls were done in that old European peeling paint finish. Old World meets New. This was more like it—far from the madding bar crowd below.

When we sat down and I saw how Ben looked at me, I felt suddenly shy. And nervous. This was what I wanted, wasn't it? Still, I felt like I was jumping in at the deep end.

Nervously, I steered the conversation to the shallows.

"Dave Pearce hasn't changed at all," I said.

"You two would have scored an A-plus on your wildlife check-off. Same as biology tests in high school, only he didn't look at your answers first," said Ben.

When the Prosecco came to the table, we clinked glasses.

My hand was shaking a little bit as I took a sip. I so hoped we didn't see anyone who knew me or who knew Luke. In my world, being separated meant I could date other people, especially since I was leaving a husband who had no room to talk. But in the high-stakes, big-money divorce world, this was risky.

"Our first real date in how long?" Ben asked.

"Light-years," I said. "I think the last time was when you took me for pizza and a movie our sophomore year in college." The last date had actually been the frat party in which Luke had recognized "that girl from the bakery" and I was a goner. I wanted to forget that, too.

"Well, you look just as beautiful as you did then, Neely," he said.

"Liar." I smiled. But I did look good. I wore a form-fitting black lace dress and my good diamond earrings. My hair was up in a loose knot, with that messy, just-got-out-of-bed look that was so hard to achieve. I had spritzed on Chanel No. 5. And I made sure I had on sexy lingerie. I wasn't sure where the night would go, but I wanted to be ready.

Ben, in his navy blazer and crisp striped shirt, looked like he had gotten what little sun there was that day during the regatta. Ben was his own man. He didn't care how other people judged him. I found that confidence very sexy.

The signature potato puffs that came to the table were airy like a soufflé. Paired with the bubbly, the combination made me feel almost effervescent.

The Memory of Lemon

It was like stars twinkling. Or a camera flashing.

When I tried a second potato puff, I gently gilded it with the buttery sauce pooled on the side of the plate. Instead of the sinful bite that I expected, however, it turned extremely salty on my tongue. I wanted to spit it out, but instead I gagged it down, followed by a big gulp of water. Ben ate his nonchalantly, as if nothing was wrong. Maybe the chef had oversalted my sauce. Or maybe not.

I had learned to pay attention when I tasted the salty flavor of fear.

Another tiny flash.

When I looked up, I saw a well-dressed, well-groomed man approaching our table, just putting his little camera away in his pocket.

"You two look cozy," he said. "I hope I'm not interrupting anything."

The salty flavor intensified, and my body started into full anxiety mode as fear kept repeating itself.

Here I was in a sexy dress, an iced-down silver bucket of Prosecco at the table, wedding ring missing in action. How was I going to explain this?

Why should I have to explain this?

I was separated from my husband. I was having dinner with an old friend. I wasn't committing a crime, just trying to fly under the radar a little bit.

Ben rose from the table and shook the man's hand. "Neely, you remember Charlie Wheeler. We used to give him crap about being a punter, but he has done all right for himself. Big-city lawyer." Ben patted him on the shoulders as if Charlie still had football pads on.

"What brings you back here, Charlie?" I croaked. I hoped he couldn't see my heart thudding in my throat or the shaky way I held my champagne flute. Charlie was Luke's attorney, but that was no big deal, right? Luke, of all people, knew we had called it quits, knew that Ben and I had known each other since grade school. Why was I overreacting?

"Just business. And I could ask you the same. Looks like you two are off to a great start." He gave me a cool, appraising look.

"We are. Lots to celebrate," I said, lightly, I hoped. "Ben said he'd take me to dinner because the bakery turned a profit," I lied. "So, here we are, way ahead of projections."

"Well, cheers to you," said Charlie, raising one eyebrow.

He wasn't a fool. But I decided to call his bluff.

"Why don't you join us?" I asked.

Ben shot me a puzzled look as I tried to telepathically tell him I was sorry that I could be ruining our date night yet again.

I hoped Charlie would decline, say he was meeting clients or wanted an early night.

But he didn't. "Don't mind if I do. And dinner will be on me. This is the most excitement I've had since I got back to Queen City," Charlie said. "Which tells you a lot about this trip." He grinned.

As our attentive waiter was bringing over another chair for our table, Charlie held him back for a minute.

"You two get close there and let me get another photo. A memento of the trip and old friends," Charlie said, taking his camera out of his pocket again. I didn't want him taking another photo, but I didn't want to look guilty, either. I forced myself to smile. He took the photos and sat down.

The Memory of Lemon

When Ben sat down, I squeezed his hand under the table, and then he seemed to accept the charade.

"You got my letter last week, Neely?" Charlie asked.

"I did."

"It's not personal, you know, just business. Have to take care of my client. But let's not talk about that now."

Let's not, I thought. But that didn't mean the prenuptial agreement wouldn't be on my mind for the rest of dinner.

"So, tell me about this regatta," Charlie said, before our entrees arrived. "I've been to the Henley Regatta in England, all ascots and straw boater hats and lots of champagne."

"Well, this was more like sweatshirts and ball caps and empty Budweiser cans," Ben said with a laugh.

"It's about the environment around the Mill Creek," I said. "Water quality and wildlife. Muskrats and blue herons and carp."

The waiter put my plank-roasted fish in front of me. The sauce smelled divine, but I knew everything would taste salty to me.

"I hope that's not Mill Creek carp," Charlie joked.

I grimaced.

But Charlie plowed on. "Bet you two didn't know that old John James Audubon himself once ventured up the Mill Creek from the Ohio River, the opposite of the way Ben went today," Charlie said.

"I didn't know that Audubon was ever in Queen City," Ben said.

"Just a short while," said Charlie. "One of my clients collects hand-colored Audubon prints, and they're stunning. Worth a fortune. Especially the birds that are now extinct. Passenger pigeons. Carolina parroquets."

Charlie and Ben leaned back a bit from the table as the waiter put a sizzling steak in front of each of them.

As we took our first bites, I tried to imagine what Queen City must have looked like in Audubon's day, when all of this was new and green. When passenger pigeons and Carolina parroquets were unaware that their days were numbered.

"The Queen City Library has an original folio of Audubon's birds and they turn it to a new page every day," Charlie said, washing down his steak with a glass of red wine, the pricey Brunello he had selected. And that Luke was probably paying for.

I wished I could turn a new page and end this evening.

After an interminable meal and the start of a tension headache, I tried to explain myself to Ben on the way home.

"I'm sorry. I didn't mean to ruin our date. I should have suggested someplace off the beaten path. Can we try again next week?"

"I'm booked with work every Saturday night through June," said Ben, morosely. "Our timing sucks."

"I'm sorry. I didn't want it to be like this."

We drove in silence.

"What's the big deal, Neely? Just tell me."

Just the thought of this new threat shot a bolt of ice-cold dread through me. I explained to Ben about my prenup with Luke. How the "unfaithful" clause applied only to me. If I were proved to be unfaithful, and Luke chose to enforce this clause, not only would I walk away from the marriage with very little, but Luke would be entitled to a portion of any properties and monies accumulated during our marriage—namely, my house and business.

The letter from Charlie Wheeler had stated Luke's intent to

The Memory of Lemon

enforce that clause. I had dismissed it as chain rattling, but now I knew they were going after me.

Ben wanted to know why I had ever agreed to such a thing, but I didn't have a satisfying answer. In those early days with Luke, I couldn't even begin to imagine what the end of our relationship might look like. Instead, I only thought of happily-ever-afters. So I had signed the agreement, unread, no questions asked. Back then, I assumed I wouldn't want or need a slice of my husband's astronomically large salary if we split. But now I was less certain. Luke had wronged and humiliated me so many times—surely I was owed *something* for that. And there was Gran to consider, too.

"If it were just about me, I could happily divorce Luke and not ask for a cent. I would have just admitted to Charlie Wheeler that we were dating. But I've got Gran to think about. Her care at Mount Saint Mary's is expensive. In another few years, the money she received when I bought her house will be gone. And then what? Mom and Aunt Helen can't take that on. The bakery is doing well right now, but not that well."

I twisted my hands in my lap. Tears filled my eyes, but I was too stubborn to give in to crying.

I waited until I was calmer to continue. "If Luke drags his feet on a legal separation, I can still file for divorce when I have established residency in Ohio, which will be on May 15. Then I don't have to worry as much when I go out with you."

"But Luke was a bastard. He's got no room to talk. This isn't 1860."

"It's the way things work if you're trying to divorce a wealthy man and want a settlement, even a modest one. Big double standard."

"Is that why Charlie was taking all those photos? Not just for old times' sake?"

"I don't know," I said miserably.

"Maybe Luke doesn't want to let you go," said Ben quietly.

"It's too late for that. I've already gone," I said, reaching across to touch Ben's arm.

"But he can make it really difficult for you."

"I don't think Luke would do that. He's got too much pride."

"Then why is he looking for proof that his wife has been unfaithful?"

We looked at each other and then sat in silence.

Ben drove carefully to my house, but didn't look over at me, didn't reach for my hand. He leaned over to open my car door, but didn't get out.

"We can't see each other, then, Neely," he said, looking straight ahead. "It's too risky for you. Luke has enough money that he could have you followed twenty-four/seven. Maybe he's having you followed right this minute. Someone could be taking photos of us sitting here. The last thing I want is to hurt you."

"But I will see you. Tomorrow. We're all going to Augusta, remember?" I said. "We can't let Luke control our lives."

"I have to think about that. Good night, Neely," Ben said.

I walked into my house alone. He waited, as I knew he would, until I was safely inside before he pulled away.

How differently this evening has ended from what I intended, I thought as I pulled my nightshirt over my head. My sexy lingerie lay at the top of the hamper, not trailing a way to the bed. Now was the perfect time for a pity party.

Why couldn't I be with the man who truly, unselfishly, loved me? I had given Luke everything I had and he still wanted more—a one-sided marriage that allowed him to stray and forced me to stay.

And then I got mad.

Luke didn't own me. I had left him and I wasn't going back. I would figure this out. I was not going to lose Ben.

But how was I going to fight back?

6

Neely

After my Saturday night date debacle, I was dreading our trip to Augusta. Why had I asked Ben to go with us? It had seemed like a good idea at the time. Maybe he would simply beg off. I wouldn't blame him. The clash between Mrs. Stidham and her daughter, Lydia, had taken an abrupt backseat to my personal dilemma. Roshonda, Gavin, and I might find a compromise to the mother/daughter stalemate through our visit to the family's Kentucky home place today, but I couldn't see a way yet to make things better with Ben.

The early morning drizzle did nothing to change that. I hoped Ben would still come with us. I would soon see.

I was relieved to see Gavin drive up with Ben in the front

seat. I left the bakery with a to-go carton of coffees and two boxes of my famous cinnamon rolls for the drive. I did a quick visual scan of the parking lot and Benson Street, both empty, before I got in the backseat with Ro.

I passed the coffees around, gave everyone a napkin, and opened the boxes.

Is there anything better than the scent of a still-warm cinnamon roll? Yes: the taste of one. Maybe that would give two star-crossed, would-be lovers a little comfort.

"I can't eat and drive," moaned Gavin.

"You mean you're worried you'll get crumbs on your jeans," Ben said, between bites. "Crumbs and a crease don't mix."

"Let me drive, then. Crumbs would only improve my outfit," Ro said, gesturing to her slightly rumpled appearance, which her quilted jacket didn't help. "Crumbs would add a little texture. Isn't that what interior designers say?"

"Hmph," muttered Gavin, fastidiously licking frosting from his fingers. "Let me finish this, and then we'll get going." He looked slightly horrified as Ben flicked a cinnamon roll crumb onto the upholstery.

Looking closer, I saw that Roshonda had little flakes of the previous day's mascara under her eyes.

"Late night, huh?"

"Nobody's business what kind of night I had," she said and then smiled at me in a cat-that-ate-the-cream kind of way.

"Well, I'm glad someone had a good time," Ben grumbled.

My heart sank.

Roshonda's look to me said, *What???*

The Memory of Lemon

I sighed and made the cutoff gesture to her. I didn't want to get into all of that now. It would cast a pall on the whole day.

Roshonda rolled her eyes and went back to nibbling all the frosting off her roll.

"Let's get in the zone for this," Gavin said, drinking the last of his coffee and patting his lips with a napkin. "Bluegrass music. A little Emmylou Harris to start our Kentucky trip?" He chose a disc from the console and slipped it into the CD player.

We drove out of the parking lot with "Blue Kentucky Girl" in Emmylou's distinctive meandering voice, a little tattered at the edges.

Gavin and Roshonda started singing. Ben and I just listened.

Bluegrass music tells it like it is. Lives full of high spots and low points. Lost loves. Moments of amazing grace. We just had to get through it all.

We took the tangle of highways to Route 52, the Ohio River Scenic Byway, which followed the river through little towns like New Richmond and Point Pleasant. To our right was the Ohio River, wide and slate gray as the sun just started to peep out from the low clouds. The sloping banks on either side were shedding the drabness of winter for new spring greenery.

Shortly after we passed Ulysses Grant's birthplace at Point Pleasant, we saw the sign and turned down the gravel road to the ferry landing.

We got out of the car to wait, watching the six-car ferry chug its way back from the Kentucky side. The air was warming, and we could see fog drift up from the cold water.

"This reminds me of that old movie *Brigadoon*," said Gavin.

"Gene Kelly is on vacation in Scotland and comes across this enchanted village shrouded in mist. Brigadoon comes alive for only one day every hundred years. The mist parts, and, of course, he falls in love with this beautiful girl who can really dance..."

"Who wouldn't?" asked Roshonda, who, memorably, had tried to teach us the Roger Rabbit and the Tootsie Roll back in the day.

"Cyd Charisse! She was the beautiful girl who could dance." Somehow I knew that.

"And they're separated by forces bigger than they are..." Gavin continued.

"Like a hundred years between dates," chimed Roshonda.

Gavin and Roshonda laughed.

Ben and I were silent.

Again, Roshonda gave me a look.

Gavin drove the car onto the ferry, and then we all walked onto the deck. Soon, the ferry plied its way back across the river.

Like Lydia said, I could feel the river beneath my feet.

As we got closer, the Augusta skyline came into view. I was glad I had done my homework, so I could recognize what I was seeing firsthand. No wonder this late-eighteenth-century river town had been the setting of several movies. A row of houses fronted the river: an old brick Georgian from the late eighteenth century with a fanlight brought from colonial Virginia, a few white Greek Revivals, a carpenter Gothic, a Victorian painted lady, and at the end of Riverside Drive, the stucco facade of the old Methodist church, built in 1819.

"Genteel. Charming. Sort of a visual history timeline. It

would make a great Christmas card," said Gavin, framing the view with his hands.

"Or a wedding invitation," Roshonda snapped the view with her camera. As we got closer to shore, she said, "She was right. It is like stepping back in time."

"This could work," Gavin said suddenly, inspired. "We could make something beautiful here."

"Sure could," Roshonda agreed. "People always say they want a destination wedding, and then they pick someplace where half their friends can't afford to go. Here you get the best of both worlds. It feels like you're somewhere else, but you're fairly close to Queen City."

"I'll bet the ferry company would keep going past its ten o'clock last call if the price were right," Ben said.

"Note to self," Roshonda said, typing it into her phone.

Ben had actually spoken. Maybe the day was going to improve.

"Or guests could just stay in Augusta. We'll have to check out the accommodation situation here," I said. "I wouldn't like to drink at the reception and then face an hour and a half drive back to Queen City."

I touched Ben's arm, but he didn't respond. He wouldn't look at me. I turned away, my eyes stinging with tears. How was trying to do things the right way somehow wrong?

I guess I was still following the rules. But that's what pastry chefs do. There is a proportion range for everything—ratios for the amount of dry ingredients to wet, how much batter can go into a pan, the time it takes to beat an egg white until foamy and one that is at its full billowy peak.

I wanted to be with Ben, but I wanted a cushion for Gran, too.

She would need it soon enough, and I had earned it twice over during the years I'd set aside my own dreams for my cheating husband's. I pulled a tissue from my purse and acted like the breeze had blown something in my eye.

We all got back in the car right before the ferry docked. I had to settle down, focus on the job at hand and not my personal life.

Gavin drove up the ramp in front of that gorgeous Georgian brick and we were on Riverside Drive, heading east. He took it slow so we could admire the historic homes as we passed.

In front of the old Methodist church, now a residence, we turned right onto Bracken Street and then left onto a gravel road that wound through the trees and up a hill, away from town.

According to Lydia's hand-drawn map, the log cabin we were seeking was off the beaten path, tucked back in the hillside near Bracken Creek.

With the windows down, I could hear a little waterfall somewhere. New leaves were just budding on the trees, but the ivy and other creepers high in the tree canopy provided a dappled light. A clean, sharp smell came in on the fresh breeze, and just as quickly, I could taste it. Really taste it. Citrus and spice mixed together.

I had a momentary flash.

An older woman and a younger man, sitting next to each other in the lantern light, traveling down the river on some kind of flat barge by night. The two of them again in a market stall, in some rough-hewn town, with a tiny, dark-haired woman carrying a market basket.

Just as quickly, they were all gone.

This didn't make any sense to me just yet, but I felt we were in the right place.

"If Lydia wants her wedding here, we'll have to shuttle the guests to the cabin," Roshonda said, typing a note into her phone again. "We can't have women in stilettos or teetering great-grandpas traipsing up this road."

We made a sharp turn up and to the right, following the road, and came out onto a clearing, a plateau on the hilltop, fringed with trees. And there were two cabins, with aged, silvery logs and clay chinking that still looked pretty good. A dogtrot, sort of a covered breezeway, linked the two cabins. A split-rail fence enclosed the garden, laid out in a foursquare pattern. To the side was a big barn, and that got Roshonda excited.

"A barn wedding! I've always wanted to do one," she exclaimed, jumping out of the car.

"It's a tobacco barn," said Gavin.

"How can you tell?" I asked.

"See how they've left the wood dark and not painted it red or white? That's to increase the heat from the sun. The roof is high-pitched, and when we look inside we'll see tiers of beams where farmers hang bundles of tobacco leaves to dry. There will be a big door on each gabled end that opens to help the hot air circulate."

"You never cease to amaze me, Nichols," Ben said. "You could kick ass on a game show."

"Hey, if this barn looks decent inside, we've all won the lottery with an event space," said Gavin.

We walked through the split-rail gate to the grassy area leading to the barn.

We needed Ben to push open the weathered barn door. It was difficult to see the interior at first, until Ben opened the barn door at the other end. The light flooded in and we gazed at a simple, spare space of soaring proportions. It was rustic and yet somehow elegant at the same time.

"I can see those strings of Italian lights inside, along the beams," Gavin said. "Or crystal chandeliers. Such a contrast. Yes!" He pulled a little gadget out of his pocket and aimed the tiny red beam from the front barn door across to the back door. "Sixty feet," he said. "Probably three times that for the width of this barn. You could have a big party in here, all right."

As he and Roshonda conferred about dance floors and bar stations and porta-potties, and Ben checked out how the barn was constructed, I left to wander in the garden.

Here would be my inspiration for desserts. I took out my notebook and sketched the rough design of the garden. Maybe this design on a flavored sugar cookie? At this point, I didn't know what I would use and what I wouldn't, so it was best to write it all down. Heirloom roses were starting to bud, probably rugosas or damask roses, ancient varieties that bloom once a year and are highly scented. Maybe rose in something?

Herbs were also coming up. I recognized mints, dittany, borage, horehound, and others used a long time ago for tinctures and liniments. I bent over to touch the lemon balm. I couldn't resist rubbing the aromatic leaf between my fingers and then tasting it.

Fresh lemon. The young man on the barge came to mind. Who was he? He made me think of my dad. And then I wondered when I might get another letter from my father. If I ever would again. I still didn't trust that I could rely on him for anything.

And then I stopped.

I wasn't going down that rabbit hole today. I wanted to enjoy the garden and do the work that I loved.

In another section of the herb garden, I recognized plantings of scented geraniums. I could use these old-fashioned herbs as well. My favorite, Rober's Lemon Rose, was an intoxicating blend of citrus and floral with an elegant, sort of filigreed leaf. Maybe a flavored sugar sprinkle, like a sweet gremolata, on soft sugar cookies? Maybe the leaf as an edible garden garnish on a flavored custard tart? I jotted notes to myself.

I crushed each variety of leaf between my fingers, enjoying the scent. Apple geranium. Velvety chocolate mint. Nutmeg geranium with its tiny leaves that smelled—and then tasted—so evocatively of spice.

Immediately, I saw the old-fashioned woman in her straw bonnet give a small bundle of sticks to the tiny, dark-haired woman. A remedy of some sort? Something to brew a tea?

This was a long-ago story I didn't need to know today. Again, I swept it from my mind and focused my attention on the garden.

Another quadrant had trellises for climbing plants. English pea tendrils were inching up the wires. Reddish stalks of rhubarb leafed out in abundance. I recognized scallions and the famous Kentucky limestone lettuce that was so crisp and delicious. Someone tended this garden in the family's absence. I wondered who.

I cataloged as much as possible before wandering over to the two little cabins joined by the dogtrot. Both doors were locked, but I peered in the windows. There wasn't much to see. The rooms were sparsely furnished.

Again I tasted spice, and I thought I heard a fiddle playing. I looked back toward the barn and saw that all three of my friends were still engrossed in it. I sat down on the steps of the dogtrot, held my notebook and pen, and stilled my mind.

Thoughts of Ben and Luke and Charlie Wheeler tried to invade my peaceful moment, but I brushed them away.

I crossed the threshold into my happy place, where I transformed colors and flavors and stories into desserts. I imagined Lydia's wedding in the tobacco barn. Wedding pie. Tarts and cookies with the flavors of her grandmother's garden.

As I let my imagination soar, I had a feeling that the stories that came from lemon and spice would lead to more than just creating the perfect wedding desserts. Much more.

I breathed in and breathed out, centering myself. I had to be patient. The flashbacks would come when they were ready. When I was ready.

I closed my eyes, imagined the citrus and spice on my tongue.

Lemon, which usually signified clarity and sharpness, now also whispered, "Wanderer."

Spice lingered, as it always did, the flavor that evoked times past. Comforting. Healing. And then it, too, was gone.

My body thrummed with the energy I knew to be vivid intuition.

Wanderers. Healers. They had something important to tell me. Not long since, I had used my gift to reunite long-lost sisters.

Maybe this time I could bring a wanderer home and heal a family.

Lydia's family?

Or mine?

I began to sketch.

7

AUTUMN 1825
AUGUSTA, KENTUCKY

The Healer

Abigail Newcomb sat in the rush-seated chair on the dogtrot, the covered area that connected her two one-room cabins. With a needle and stout thread, she strung pods of leather britches beans through their centers to hang and dry for winter.

Her hands were busy, but her mind wandered. She looked down the rise and out over the water below, as placid and river green as if it knew every mystery of life.

The river had its moods, just like people. Frothy on a bright, windy day. Murky during spring floods. Dark and somber in winter. Blue, green, brown, black, gray. The river was like a friend that spoke to her.

Abigail rose, hanging the latest length of beans from a peg in the rafters of the small cabin on the left side of the dogtrot, which she used as a workroom.

She always loved the woodsy smell of the tiny work cabin, a commingling of drying herbs, flowers, and roots. For Abigail, it was the scent of comfort: bunches of dittany for the tea that soothed headaches and colds, leafy sage for sore throats and hoarseness, feverfew for easing pain, spicebush for melancholy. On hickory-hooped screens supported by narrow wooden benches, recently dug comfrey roots were drying; they were good for dysentery and female debility or in a salve for aching joints. On another screen were the orange-red rose hips she had snipped from her rosa rugosas. She would make a cheerful cordial with the inner seeds of the hips, sour in flavor, which helped put the bloom back into little cheeks after a winter of salted and dried foods.

This little cabin was also where her husband used to plane a board, turn a spindle, or notch dovetails so the bottom and sides of a drawer would fit together. The really heavy work of sawing boards from a hewn log he did outside, as she did her gardening and gathering.

She took a splint broom and swept dried leaves and seeds from the floor. She redded up the baskets and tools, so everything was tidy. She set out the plate of soup beans and a generous hunk of corn bread, covered with a homespun cloth. She had brought the food over from the identical cabin on the other side of the dogtrot, the space she used for cooking and sleeping. She placed a bucket of spring water, a hollow gourd full of soft lye soap, and a length of soft flannel nearby. The old quilt lay folded on a bench.

There was nothing more to do. She shut the door and sat down again in the dogtrot, halfway between her working world and her abiding world. She listened to the sounds of night falling.

As the light faded and the far bank of the Ohio turned from green to purple, her ears pricked up.

She loved the rustling and the whoosh of air as her dark-bodied guinea fowl flew up to roost in the trees bordering the garden. Awake, they chirped when they searched the ground for insects to eat. But they would caw loudly, and then make squeaky cries, if anything disturbed their sleep.

When darkness fell, Abigail retreated to the other tiny cabin. When she shut and barred the door for the night, the glow of the fire illuminated the walls, and the night sounds quieted. She was snug and safe here, protected by each wall of nine hewn logs of oak and elm and poplar that her man had felled, dragged here with the mules, and notched into place. She had done the chinking with stones and the white clay she had dug up from the creek.

He knew his wood, did Isaac Newcomb. Hickory, strong yet streaked dark and light; not pleasing to the eye for furniture, but strong enough for a tool handle. It also produced a fragrant smoke to flavor a kettle of soup beans or smoke a ham. Isaac favored cherry, with its smooth fine grain and a reddish color, for a chest of drawers or a side table. Oak was too hard to work by hand, but it made a stout cabin log. Isaac liked tulipwood for a hanging cupboard, as it wasn't too heavy to suspend by a peg on the wall. Abigail didn't have the knickknacks and folderol to display that city women favored. But the rendering of her daughter and grandchild by Mr. Audubon took pride of place, tacked up on the wall right by her chair.

When she and Isaac had been in this cabin just a year, he took his winter-made cupboards downriver to Queen City and came back with her fiddle.

Just the feel of it made her glad. Sitting in the old blue rocker by the fire, she nestled the fiddle between her chin and shoulder, feeling the smooth contours of this happy marriage of two woods. Spruce, with its vertical, wavy grain, on the top front, and the golden brown, striped tiger maple on the body.

Together, they gave the best sound. Some said a mournful sound. But it was all the company she needed of an evening. She could summon him back with song. She could summon anyone, it would seem, drifting between two worlds.

Abigail had heard that the dead did not always know they were dead, and it was unfinished business that kept them tethered to their old life. Isaac had been a good man. What was his unfinished business that he could not leave this place?

As she raised the bow, it seemed almost to shimmer in her right hand. The motion traveled down her arm, building up to a sinuous wave that skimmed over the strings and made the first beseeching note. The melody swelled, crested, then broke, as clear as water from the cave spring.

> *Black is the color of my true love's hair*
> *His face so soft and wondrous fair*
> *The purest eyes*
> *And the bravest hands*
> *I love the ground whereon he stands*
> *I love the ground whereon he stands.*

She half closed her eyes and saw Isaac again, a wraith floating in the darkest corner of the cabin. She sighed. It did no good to call out to him or try to touch. He would only disappear.

She played the rest of the song and then old favorites like "Shady Grove" and "Barbry Allen."

When her arm got tired, she put the fiddle down and sang in her thin and reedy voice. As the embers died, pictures flickered through her mind of their courting days in Philadelphia, when they had walked down the paths of Bartram's Garden to the river's edge, pledging their love as the moon rose and the water glimmered with milky light. When they sang, the river echoed their voices.

The guinea fowl called out from their perch in the trees.

She heard the workroom cabin door swing open on its rusty hinge, then softly shut. Another traveler had found the way to her home and she was glad to be able to offer this stranger a place to rest, if only for a night. Abigail put her fiddle away in its case and placed it back on the carved shelf that Isaac had made.

And when she was ready to climb the ladder to her pallet bed in the loft, she sang good night to her beloved.

Oh, I love my love
And well he knows
Yes, I love the ground whereon he goes
And still I hope
That the time will come
When he and I will be as one
When he and I will be as one.

For the first time since Isaac had passed years before, she had a powerful knowing that made her body tremble. The sensation shivered from the top of her head, down her spine, to the soles of her feet. She would be with her husband again.

Soon.

Judith Fertig

LATE FEBRUARY 1826
AUGUSTA, KENTUCKY

"I can't go back there," the young girl said. Her dark, thin face had a sheen that belied her shivering in the early morning chill.

She had startled Abigail, who hadn't expected to see anyone still in the workroom cabin. The travelers were usually gone by daybreak.

Abigail slowly walked toward the girl. She leaned over and pulled the quilt up over her rounded belly, taking in the clean head scarf, the too-big shoes neatly arranged beside the pallet bed, and her worried eyes.

"Let me get a fire going and I'll make us some tea. Get you some breakfast. Been travelin' long?"

The girl nodded yes and then grimaced.

Abigail put the back of her hand to the girl's forehead. No fever.

She rose and walked through the cabin door, across the dogtrot, to the twin cabin on the other side. She stooped at the fireplace and swept a few coals into her heavy iron frying pan, then brought them across.

Back in her workroom cabin, Abigail swept out the previous day's ashes and laid the fire, adding kindling and seasoned oak logs that a thankful first-time father had split for her. In a few seconds, she saw the satisfying plume of smoke rise with the first flame. The fire began to crackle and put out heat.

There was still water in the copper teakettle, so she added a bunch of dried dittany. She set the kettle to boil next to the fire.

"Did you eat what I left last night?" Abigail asked.

"Yes, ma'am. Thank you."

"I've birthed many babies around here. Do you want me to see how your baby's doing?"

The girl nodded.

"Well, if we're going to be on such intimate terms, maybe we need to introduce ourselves. I'm Abigail Newcomb."

"My name's Safronia Birdsall. My people call me Fronnie, but he calls me his little bird," she said with a tremor of distaste that she couldn't quite hide. "That be Mr. Birdsall, over by Ol' Washington."

"I know of him," said Abigail, trying to keep a neutral expression. The Birdsalls owned a big brick house in Old Washington, about twenty miles to the south and east, and a tobacco farm worked by their slaves. She had ridden over on the cart with Isaac when he delivered a cherry chest of drawers for their sons' bedroom. The trip took so long, they had had to spend the night. Mrs. Birdsall gave them a cramped, cold attic room; they took their supper with the house slaves. "You've been walkin' a good day or two."

Abigail splayed her hands over the girl's belly while she looked at her face. Skinny, not much over thirteen, fourteen years old. Scared, but plucky—or desperate. Abigail pressed firmly in a circular motion, checking on the progress of the baby, humming a tuneless song as she did. The girl's hips were thankfully wide enough, but that didn't always ensure an easy delivery in one so young.

"Was that you playin' the fiddle last night?" Fronnie asked.

Abigail nodded.

"At the last house, they said that'd be the sign to go on in."

Abigail felt the baby kick down low. She smiled at Fronnie. The girl tried to smile back, but turned her head to the side as a tear trickled down her cheek.

"What's the matter, Fronnie?"

"I cain't tell no one."

"You can tell me." Abigail stroked the girl's arm through the blanket.

The girl closed her eyes tight as another contraction took hold. A minute or so later, Fronnie turned to look at Abigail.

"Miz Birdsall, she hate me. And Mr. Birdsall, he just turn his back."

Abigail did not have to wonder why that was. She knew all too well.

Fronnie sat up slightly, propped on her elbows. "I don't want them sellin' my chile. I seen them do that to the other girls. Sol' off a chile like it was a calf."

Abigail sighed, then smiled at Fronnie. "Nobody's goin' to hurt this baby, now that it's ready to come into the world."

Fronnie relaxed a little bit.

"My sister Celie ran off, up in the Ohio country, to Leb'nun," she said. "Celie's free now. I reckon I can git me and the baby there. Once we get over the river, we're free, too."

"Well, not today," said Abigail, patting the girl's arm. "Won't Mr. Birdsall be sending riders out looking for you?"

"Nah. He's at the tabaccah auction in Maysville. That's why I took off when I did."

When the tea was ready, Abigail poured her a cup. "I put some black cohosh and cramp bark in it, too. Helps speed things up," she told Fronnie.

Fronnie sat up and sipped the tea.

Another pain gripped the girl. She clutched her belly and breathed hard.

By late afternoon, as the shadows drew in, Abigail built up the fire so that Fronnie and her baby girl would stay warm. She brought her rocker and a yarn blanket over from the abiding cabin so she could sit and watch over them.

"When did you say that Mr. Birdsall was comin' back?" Abigail asked Fronnie, as the young mother suckled her baby by the fire the next afternoon.

"Well, he come back on Sunday after breakfast. Miz Birdsall, she be at church all day."

We will have to leave tonight, then.

She hated the thought of taking this girl with a new-mint child out into the cold, but it had to be done. It wasn't safe to stay here longer.

While Fronnie and the baby rested, Abigail lit the lantern and hung it from the tree branch so that the Lovejoys would know she was coming across. She gathered six little squares of blue and white ticking that she had intended to use in a coverlet, but would now be the baby's diapers. She grabbed her wool shawl and her late husband's buckskin coat and wool muffler.

At moonrise, Abigail helped Fronnie and the baby, both wrapped up in her shawl, down to the skiff at the riverbank. The river was down, maybe about two feet. But that was normal this time of year, when ice jams further upriver held back the normal current.

Abigail got them settled on the seat, Fronnie's eyes wide and bright with fear. Abigail pushed the small boat off, then jumped over the thin sheet of ice at the shallow end and into the boat. She grabbed the oars and guided them around floating chunks of ice and into open water.

Abigail turned to see her lantern beam the way home through the trees. Lucky for them, the river hadn't frozen over this year. The past week's thaw had melted most of the ice and the air was milder than it had been in a while.

Halfway across the river, she was warm again from rowing. She didn't see any riders along the Kentucky shore. The Lovejoys would shelter Fronnie and the baby, then move them along to another house. Maybe Fronnie really would find her sister again. Abigail hoped it would all turn out well. She probably would never know for sure.

On the Ohio side, Abigail used just the one oar to paddle the skiff into a cove partially shielded by tall grasses and cattails. She helped Fronnie and the baby out and motioned them up the bank. Fronnie knew to follow the guiding light of the Lovejoys' lantern and hide in the woodshed.

As Abigail waited for them to disappear into the night, the cold started seeping up through the bottom of the boat, into Isaac's big boots and through the heavy woolen socks, up her legs and into her hips. Her buckskin coat felt as hard and cold as iron. She needed to get the boat across the river and warm up by her fireside.

When she was almost halfway across, Abigail heard a crack like a rifle shot and then a boom, like a cannon.

She ducked into the boat, put the oars down, and ran her hands over her chest. She must have been shot. Maybe Mr. Birdsall had come back early, had caught her ferrying his slave across the river.

But no, she was fine. She sat up and turned around in her seat. She couldn't spy anyone moving on the Kentucky shore, but that didn't mean they weren't there.

And then she noticed the current was starting to run faster, west toward Queen City.

Abigail had a hard time rowing a straight line across. She didn't want to drift too far downriver, past Augusta and settlement, and be out alone on a cold, dark river.

Abigail used one oar to push a log out of the way. It hadn't hit the boat hard enough to stove in the side, but it was close.

And then it came to her: In the freezing and thawing they'd had that month, an ice jam must have cracked wide open farther upriver, causing the boom. The debris it had held in its frozen grasp had dislodged and was racing toward Augusta. The current would only get stronger. And if history repeated itself, she would see a roaring wave of muddy water that could swamp the boat. Sweat rolled down Abigail's face as she rowed harder. She had to get to shore.

Abigail kept the Lovejoys' lantern in sight as she rowed backward to her own. It took everything she had to block out the rushing water and the fear that crept up her spine.

She never saw the dark shape in the water, the downed tree. One minute she was racing against time. The next, she felt like she was on fire in the freezing, murky water. She tried to get a handhold on the overturned skiff, but her hands didn't seem to work. She kicked furiously, hoping to shed the boots that were weighing her down, but they wouldn't come off. She tried to heave herself up and over the hulk of the skiff, but she didn't have the strength. She slid down again into the water and went under. She kicked herself back up to the surface, gasping for air.

Stay calm, she told herself. *You're not that far from shore.*

Her hands had frozen to cold claws, but still she tried to get a purchase on the upturned skiff and turn herself toward the lantern light. But she knew the skiff was drifting with the current.

She couldn't stay in the dark water for much longer. She had to do something to reach the Kentucky bank, so she kicked out, her feet like lead weights. Her arms flailed as she tried to swim. When another log floated by, she hooked one arm over it to hang on and catch her breath. The light receded as she moved farther away into the black night.

And then it didn't matter.

She was getting drowsy. She didn't burn anymore. She didn't feel the cold. Her vision narrowed to a pinhole of light. The lantern. Home.

And then she felt Isaac's strong arms carry her there.

8

Neely

Simple paradise. Stepping back in time. Grandmother's garden. Going home.

I could almost recite Lydia's wedding mantra. Too bad her mother was not yet convinced.

Lydia's wedding team was meeting again, this time at Gavin's office.

Maybe he could paint the picture that would convince mother and daughter to go forward with the plans that Gavin, Roshonda, and I had hatched on the drive home from Augusta a few days back.

I was also going forward with flavor. From the moment we turned up the lane to go to the Kentucky cabin, the twin flavors of citrus and spice sparked long-ago stories. I wasn't sure, however, what they had to do with Lydia and her mother or how these momentary flashes would help get us over this impasse.

I knew that sunny citrus helped put things in focus, sharpened the memory, just like a squeeze of lemon juice could sharpen and clarify the taste of sweet fruit. I was also well aware that too much citrus could indicate a corrosive anger. My first wedding at Rainbow Cake had taught me that. But this was a gentle, subdued citrus, like the taste of a Meyer lemon.

Spice usually indicated grief, a loss that lingered for a long time, just like the pungent flavor of the spice itself, whether it was nutmeg or allspice or star anise. The more pronounced the flavor, the more recent the loss and the stronger the emotion. So there was some kind of loss or remembrance involved here. Yet there was also a comfort in the remembering, knowing that people had gone before you. That they waited for you on the other side.

Maybe I was pushing myself too hard. Maybe if I just relaxed a little bit, the flavor Wi-Fi would do the rest.

As I drove to Gavin's office, I noticed a black SUV that seemed to follow me across the bridge to Lockton, through the industrial area that had devolved into a blighted business district. Past the brownfields left by torn-down factories, with pollutants that hadn't been cleaned up yet.

The SUV followed me along the overpass, with I-75 thundering below, where the former Miami-Erie Canal had once flowed. It was still tailing me as I reached Gavin's carriage house office in Fairview. When I pulled up to park, the black SUV went on its way.

Another bad driver in a hurry.

The Memory of Lemon

Gavin had kept his living quarters below, his office above. His carriage house opened in the back to a private garden of lush hydrangea and scented roses enclosed with a tall hornbeam hedge. He had somehow made it classic in design yet romantic in feel. A contemporary bronze sculpture doubled as a fountain, the sound of running water doing its best to calm and center me.

When I walked up the stairs and into his office, a fresh breeze was wafting through the large windows. The loftlike space had a mid-century modern vibe complete with a black leather Eames chair and ottoman, which looked vintage fifties. A few Charley Harper contemporary bird prints hung over the credenza that served as office storage. A Sputnik-shaped chandelier lit the long, clean-lined trestle table near the bank of windows facing the garden.

"Oh, good, Neely's here," said Gavin. "And she brought the most important part of our meeting—her cinnamon rolls. She's got me hooked on these things." I gave him the bakery box and he put the rolls on a rustic wood platter. I would have made tartlets in Grandmother's garden flavors to get them in the mood, but after the first cake-tasting fiasco, I thought it better to wait until they were both on board.

Roshonda, chic in a blush pink sheath dress and a statement necklace of large crystal beads, gave us each a starched vintage napkin. "I have a box of these left over from a Victorian wedding we just did in Carriage Hill," she said.

We were laying on the charm today, in whatever way we could. If this didn't work, I wasn't sure what we would do next.

"I'm excited to hear what you thought about Augusta," said Lydia, in a purple maxidress, her hair in loose, pre-Raphaelite curls. Her fresh face wore a look of hopeful anticipation mixed with wariness.

"Yes, I'd like to know what you think," said Mrs. Stidham, who sat across from Lydia at Gavin's large trestle table. Her flawless makeup and bright turquoise silk suit suggested she had a fancy lunch appointment after this. She drummed her French-manicured nails on the table.

"Let us show you." Gavin flipped the cover off the artist's easel at the end of the trestle table to unveil his idea board.

"Our theme is a Kentucky frolic from the 1820s, one that the famous artist John James Audubon wrote about," Gavin began.

Both mother and daughter narrowed their eyes. This wasn't a grandmother's garden. This also wasn't a glitzy hotel wedding.

Gavin had unveiled their family's tobacco barn set up for a reception. Tables with burlap tablecloths. Crystal chandeliers hanging from the ceiling.

Roshonda and I looked at each other. We loved it, but would Lydia and her mother?

"Why Audubon?" Mrs. Stidham finally asked.

"He actually lived and worked in northern Kentucky and upriver in Queen City for a while, back in the early 1800s," Gavin told her. "I kinda got hooked on Audubon after bird-watching at the Mill Creek Regatta last weekend," he said, turning to Lydia and then me. "Did you happen to check out the Mill Creek Regatta app?" he asked us. "There was a link to 'Audubon in Queen City.'"

"I must have missed it. I downloaded that app last weekend," Lydia said. She tapped her phone, searching the app.

"Audubon was all about discovering and capturing the American wilderness, bird by bird. He was a naturalist *and* an artist," Gavin continued.

"I found it!" Lydia beamed, turning her phone to show us the artist's portrait in smartphone miniature.

Mrs. Stidham frowned.

"Audubon's original hand-colored bird prints bring in big money at art auctions," I added, for Mrs. Stidham's benefit. "I just had dinner with an attorney whose corporate client collects them." I had to admit, it felt good to use Charlie Wheeler a little bit.

"Maybe as a philanthropic gesture, in honor of your daughter's wedding, you and your husband could also purchase and donate a print from this American icon to a Queen City institution," suggested Roshonda. "Or offer it as an auction item to support a favorite charity. Either way, such a unique gift inspired by your daughter's wedding would be sure to enhance your community profile."

Mrs. Stidham's eyes widened with interest.

Lydia shrugged her shoulders, as if to say, *Whatever it takes.*

But at least they had found a tiny patch of common ground, even if they arrived there from opposite ends.

"After the regatta, I read his autobiography and some of his journals," Gavin continued. "He wrote about a Kentucky wedding frolic—what they used to call a party. It was all about bourbon and barbecue. Your family's heirloom crystal, which you had brought with you to this frontier outpost, set on burlap-covered tables. It showed you wanted the best life you could have, one that honored the past but looked forward to the future as you were making your own way. One that celebrated the frontier spirit and the self-made individual. And all in this Kentucky paradise."

Both mother and daughter smiled, but didn't look at each other.

Ooh, Gavin's good. A nod to Lydia's desire for a hillbilly wedding and Mrs. Stidham's pride in her husband's entrepreneurship in one go.

"Music and dancing and the local gentry in their best frocks whooping it up in a big, fabulous tobacco barn on the Ohio River. Great food. Lots of Kentucky bourbon. Live music. I think we have something really special here," Gavin said. His enthusiasm was infectious. I could feel the mood lift in the room.

I looked from Gavin to Roshonda, then to the bride-to-be and her mother. Our idea might just work.

"Audubon's bird paintings are so vivid," Gavin continued. "They'd look great, sort of large format, hanging on the barn walls. Local flavor but upscale at the same time."

One by one, he unfurled rolled-up Audubon prints of parrot-green Carolina parroquets and then Bonaparte's Gulls, showing them first to Mrs. Stidham, then to Lydia. "We would blow these up at least three times the size, but still keep the incredible detail," Gavin told them.

We were almost there.

"Just imagine your friends and family standing on the ferry as it crosses the river," Gavin said. "They'll sense the power of the river rolling beneath them. They'll smell the fresh air. They'll see the historic homes getting closer and closer. They'll start to feel they're going back in time. That they've left their other world behind, all their cares, all their worries. They're really starting to look forward to this wedding. They know it won't be like anything they've ever experienced before.

"We bring them from the ferry and the car park up through the woods to the clearing. They see the cabin. They sit in the beautiful, scented garden for a late afternoon wedding. They toast the newlyweds. And then they dine and dance a moonlit night away in the transformed tobacco barn. Magical. It will be a wedding they'll always remember."

Lydia sank back into her chair in what looked like relief and pleasure.

One down, one to go.

"And the photos! I wouldn't be surprised if *Garden and Gun* picked this up," he added, looking at Mrs. Stidham.

"I love *Garden and Gun*." She gasped. "Do you really think so?"

"If you move the wedding to Kentucky, since they're all about the South. I know one of the editors," said Roshonda. "But you have to get the best photographer. I'll have to do a little arm-twisting, but I know the perfect person. Doesn't usually do weddings, but I think she'll do yours."

"So are you both on board with this?" Gavin asked.

"Yes," they both said, a little too tentatively for us.

We weren't out of the woods quite yet.

"You'll have to have a couture gown if we want to get in the magazine," said Mrs. Stidham to her daughter. "Monique Lhuillier, Vera Wang, somebody like that. We'll have to pay a lot extra for a rush order, but Gene won't have a problem with that."

"I'm going vintage," Lydia replied, sitting up again, ramrod straight. "I already have my dress. It's one that Grandma kept."

"A dress from Vangie?" Mrs. Stidham sighed, but a text message diverted her attention. "Have to take care of this, sorry," she said to us. "A problem with the caterer today." She got up from the table and made a call, hissing into the phone from the back of the room.

"So we meet next week? Fill in the details? Map out our plan?" Roshonda said.

"Works for me," said Lydia.

Mrs. Stidham looked up and covered her phone. "Shoot me a date and time. I'll make it a priority."

When the bride-to-be and her mother had left, Gavin, Roshonda, and I waited until we could hear them driving away in different directions before we high-fived each other, barely containing ourselves.

"We've got no time to waste," said Roshonda. "They liked the idea today, but if we don't flesh this out more, we could still lose them."

She went into delegate mode. "Gavin, watercolor renderings. They need to see everything. Neely, sample tartlets. We have to wow them. I'll get the photographer with a portfolio and the caterer set up for a tasting."

We high-fived again and went our separate ways, our wedding homework assignments moved to the top of our to-do lists.

I thought I spotted the same black SUV following me again. Coincidence? I didn't care. And frankly I wasn't doing anything wrong. Let Luke's investigators note my every move if they were indeed keeping tabs on me.

On the way back to the bakery, I picked up a quinoa and greens salad for my lunch.

I was trying to eat better, a challenge when I was surrounded by tempting carbohydrates at work.

When the mailman came, I was sitting in the workroom, spearing the last forkful of dried cranberry and baby kale.

"I hope you brought something good today," I teased as he handed me both stacks of mail, for the bakery and my home next door.

"Hey, I don't send it. I just deliver it," he said. "You know that saying—don't kill the messenger."

"Maybe you need an incentive. Every time I get a big fat check in the mail, you get a cookie. Something like that?"

"Are you trying to impede the progress of the U.S. Postal Service?" he asked. "If I stopped and had cookies every day, I'd be slower on my rounds."

At that moment, I got a flash of flavor—something tangy, something sturdy that had gone soft. A flavor that sometimes went *underappreciated*. So that was how he was feeling.

A husky boy with a homemade buzz haircut stands in the elementary school parking lot, holding the Stop paddle, a reflective vest in Day-Glo yellow making him visible in any weather. He takes his job seriously. No kid under his watch is going to be hit by an inattentive parent driving on school grounds.

"Hey, nerd." A tall handsome boy with an expensive backpack walks past him, leading a pack of wannabes across the parking lot to the sidewalk. The tall boy turns and walks backward, shouting, "One hundred on your spelling test," he taunts, "too cool for school," and the wannabes guffaw.

"Hold on just a second. I'd like your opinion on something." I ran to the back of the bakery and brought out a tiny piece of upside-down strawberry-rhubarb cake that I was trying out for May. I handed it to him on a napkin.

"Rhubarb?" he asked and downed it all in one big bite. "Mm-mm," he said, wiping his mouth with the napkin. "Maybe I'll rethink your offer." He whistled as he hoisted his heavy leather postal bag as if it were suddenly lighter.

I looked through the bakery and my personal mail. The Carriage Hill Country Club still hadn't sent its check for the Member-Guest Golf Dinner desserts that had been so fiddly to make. Little cakes resembling putting greens. Why was it that the projects that took the longest to do were always the ones that were the slowest to be paid?

Bills. Junk mail. Letter.

The stationery from the old City Vue Motel still smelled faintly of cigarette smoke, but the return address had been crossed out and a new one written in, with that spiky handwriting I recognized with that familiar stab to my heart.

Dear Claire,

I've moved from the City Vue Motel, as you can see from this address. I'm living in an old trailer in a scrapyard near the Blue River in Kansas City. I'm sort of the guardian of the junk. My new part-time job. But, hell, I'm grateful.

Got a dog. Looks like a black Lab. I call him Ranger.

The folks at Project Uplift still seem to find me wherever I

The Memory of Lemon

go. Three times a week, they bring hot food and clean socks, bottled water, little individual soaps, things to keep me civilized. They mail my letters to you.

Today, they brought some really good chicken chili and scratch-and-dent dog food for Ranger.

One of the guys was playing "500 Miles," an old Peter, Paul, and Mary song that was popular when I was in Vietnam. It's all about trying to go home, my theme song right now.

Ranger just came back to the trailer from a dip in the river. When he shook himself dry, the water droplets caught the sunlight like little prisms. It's not every dog can make its own rainbows.

I remember we went to Oster's Bakery when you were a little girl and you told me that the bakery smell made rainbows. You could always do a lot more with our special gift than I ever could.

I dreamed that dream again last night, the one that starts with me falling out of the sky and then looking up at the girl with blue hands. It's the nightmare that makes me not want to fall asleep. The one that made me drink myself into a stupor for too many nights.

Been going to group therapy at the VA hospital when I can get a ride. Post-traumatic stress. That was news to me.

And I think all the years of drinking dulled my ability to taste. You and your gran know what that means. Maybe that's part of the reason why I've been lost, to myself and to the people I love.

But it's starting to come back a little bit. I hope, anyway. I won't burden you with a lot of this. I just want you to know that I'm trying.

*Love,
Dad*

Well, true to form, my dad had moved on again. I searched the new address on Google Maps. I pictured an old trailer and a black dog by the Blue River. I touched the red indicator button to make it feel more real to me.

I didn't want to get my hopes up that he would turn his life around. I had gone down that wishful-thinking path too many times already. But these were promising developments. He had stopped drinking. He was going to therapy. He was explaining himself and staying in touch.

But I was still far from ready for him to come home.

My life was hardly serene.

I had not heard from Ben since we had all gone to Augusta. I was planning for a make-it-or-break-it society wedding. And my football player husband was trying to tackle me as I was running for a divorce touchdown.

My dad had been absent from my life for almost twenty years. Was it too much to ask for him to stay away until things settled down?

My stomach rumbled. So much for the quinoa and greens salad filling me up. I wanted a spice cookie.

I took one from the display case and filled my mug with more coffee.

Mmm. Spice. It made me think of the double cabin in Augusta, of how peaceful it must feel sitting on the dogtrot porch and feeling the fresh breeze come up from the wide Ohio River, the flowing boundary that both separated and joined two worlds. Ohio and Kentucky. North and South. Mrs. Stidham and Lydia.

9

MARCH 1826
AUGUSTA, KENTUCKY

The Wanderer

Hunters found Abigail Newcomb's body, washed up way beyond the shoreline. They took Sean O'Neil to the cove to show him the exact spot.

It must have been a terrible thing to find, he thought. The gray, sodden, moldering body amid the tender green leaves of a twiggy spicebush just wakening to spring.

One of the hunters recognized the herb woman from the signet ring still on her withered hand. And someone else had sent a message upriver to Queen City.

Sean could not let Sarah and Little Abigail, barely six years old, travel from Queen City on their own. They were as close to family as he had in this big country, as a wayfarer who yearned for a home.

Abigail Newcomb had been like a mother to him. Sarah's dark hair and gray eyes reminded him of the missus, Eliza Shawcross, back in Ireland, whose kind yet stern face was still etched in his memory. It was too soon after Sarah's husband's death and now her mother's to ask for more.

They buried Abigail on the edge of the garden she had planted on the top of the hill, next to her husband.

Sean carried Little Abigail and put a protective arm around Sarah as they trudged back to the cabin. And then he set about providing for them as best he could, chopping more firewood, getting a roaring blaze going in the abiding cabin, and swinging the copper kettle over the coals to boil water for tea.

"What was it that Mother recommended for melancholy?" Sarah asked Sean.

"Spicebush," he said, remembering Abigail's gift to Lucy Audubon. Lucy and her boys had gone downriver to her people in Kentucky not long after John James Audubon had taken off on his bird adventure. Had he no more care for his loved ones than to leave them in this raw country? Sean wondered.

"But isn't that where they found Mother, in a stand of spicebush downriver? I'll never touch spicebush again," Sarah muttered.

Sean threw a chunk of dried sassafras root into the kettle instead.

When Charles Ballou came to call, the tea was ready. The newcomer from Virginia wanted to buy the property and start farming. With close-cropped blond hair, a ruddy complexion, and pale blue eyes, he didn't look like someone who had spent much time in the hot sun, thought Sean.

Sean poured Ballou a mug of tea as he sat across from Sarah, by the fire. Sean took a step back into the gloom of the cabin. It galled him that he did not have a voice in this matter. Sean gritted his teeth and sent up a silent prayer to Abigail Newcomb, telling her he would watch out for her daughter and granddaughter as best he could, no matter what Sarah decided.

"I'll terrace these hills and plant tobacco, build a big barn on the back side of the garden," Ballou told Sarah. He smiled, he charmed, he told little stories.

Sean narrowed his eyes. "Those are big plans," Sean couldn't keep himself from saying. "Have you the capital for it all?"

"Not yet. The bank has yet to know what Charles Ballou is capable of. And I'm of a mind to be doing this family a favor. Newly widowed, I understand, and I'm sorry for that, ma'am. But I could farm this for you, make improvements, keep it going."

Sarah's look was unreadable.

"But not pay her anything," Sean said, his voice deep like the growl of a guard dog. "And you think that a help?"

"You misunderstand, sir," Ballou said, rising from his chair. Sean took a step forward and the two stood toe to toe, glaring at each other.

"Gentlemen," Sarah said quietly. "Please sit." Sean stood guard until Ballou sat down. Then Sean pulled up a three-legged stool and sat, as well, leaning forward with his elbows on his knees.

"Have some tea." Sarah filled a mug for Sean and the conversation resumed.

Eventually, Sarah saw the benefit in letting Ballou work the land, build the barn, and pay her a percentage of the profit. Ballou saw the advantage in not getting in over his head, with Sarah retaining ownership of the cabin and the land.

They would draw up the papers at the solicitor's office the next day.

Sean was proud of Sarah, who'd handled this matter in her mother's calm, quiet way. But he could also see the spark of interest in Ballou's eyes for this widow with property, but scarce a glance at Little Abigail, the child she held most dear.

He was one to watch, Sean thought.

That night, Sarah fried up slices of ham that a neighbor had brought, baked biscuits, and opened a jar of her mother's wild blackberry jam.

As the evening drew in, Sarah picked up her mother's fiddle. Little Abigail sat on Sean's lap in the rocking chair near the fire, drowsy but still trying hard to stay awake.

Sarah drew the bow over the strings a few times, waiting for the music that wanted to reveal itself. When she tried the first few notes of "Black Is the Color," her mother's recent favorite, the strings screeched. Little Abigail sat up straight, startled.

Sarah loosened her shoulders, her neck, her fiddling arm, and tried again.

This time she felt the familiar tremble travel up her spine, down her arm, into her hand, and move the bow ever so gently over the strings. A melancholy note. And then another. And finally a mournful song.

> *What is this specter I can see?*
> *With icy hands taking hold of me.*
> *I am Death and none can tell*
> *I open the door to heaven and hell.*
> *Oh, Death, oh, Death, please pass by me*
> *Until my love again I see.*

Sarah fiddled and sang all the verses, letting her mind wander. But when she saw Little Abigail crying in Sean's lap with her arms wrapped around his neck, she put the instrument down.

"Maybe a lullaby?" Sean gently suggested.

Sarah took up the fiddle again. The rhythm of this lullaby reminded her of the slow sway of a mother's hips, a baby in her arms. Little Abigail relaxed and snuggled into the crook of Sean's arm.

Go to sleep, my little baby
Go to sleep, my little baby
Papa's gone away but Mama's here to stay
Gonna be right here with you, baby.
Weep no more, my little baby
Weep no more, my little baby
Can't be blue when you're wearin' silver shoes
Gonna sleep all night, little baby.

You're my sweet little baby
You're my sweet little baby
Sugar in the pie and a big blue sky
Go to sleep, my precious little baby.

"I can't play no more," Sarah whispered and seemed to collapse into the chair.

She put the instrument away in its case. The narrow, lined piece of paper glued to the inside of the lid brought fresh tears. *Abigail Newcomb* was written on the first line in her mother's tiny script. One day, when Sarah felt stronger, she would pen her own name on the next line. It was, she thought, as if the violin's maker fully expected that such a fine instrument would be handed down through the generations.

"Now that your grandmother is gone, I guess you can't be Little Abigail anymore," Sarah said to her daughter, sadly. "You can only be Little Abigail if there is a big Abigail."

"I want to be Little Abigail," the child wailed. "I don't want to change my name."

"All right, all right, child," Sarah said, reaching over to caress her daughter's tear-streaked face, so like her own. She sighed, suddenly bone weary.

Sean reached over, still holding the child close, and took Sarah's hand. "There's enough change as it is. Let Little Abigail keep her name for now." He stood up and carried Little Abigail to the pallet bed in the loft.

"Do you want me to stay?" he asked Sarah when he came back down, gesturing to the chair he had recently vacated.

"I'm no fit company for anyone," Sarah said, staring into the fire. "Go get you some sleep. I'm after another piece of sassafras root."

When she walked across the dogtrot and opened the door to the workroom cabin, the moonlight shone on a pair of eyes glimmering in the dark. Sarah jumped back, banging into the door, but didn't cry out or run away. Abigail had taught her to be brave, even in the darkest night.

"I heard the music," the stranger whispered.

"Let me bring you some ham and biscuits," whispered Sarah. "And then we'll go."

She would feed this old man and light the lantern to alert the Lovejoys across the river, just as her mother had taught her when

Sarah still lived there. It was a good thing she had felt a sleepless night coming on. Maybe a row across the river and back would tire her out and let her sleep. She would not wake Sean. Unlike Sarah, he had never learned to swim and was afraid of the water.

Change was coming. Charles Ballou would farm the land, but he would not live here. And who knew where his sympathies lay? Did he believe a slave was a person who deserved to be free or chattel that someone had a right to own?

Sarah couldn't help but feel that she was disappointing her mother. Abigail Newcomb had tried to help everyone she met, slave or free, man or woman, puny or strong. Now, there would be no one to strike up a tune on the fiddle in the evening, to signal that it was safe to come in from the woods. There would be no more food and fresh water.

The double cabin would sit empty until Sarah and Little Abigail came again. She couldn't bear the thought of selling it or renting it out. It was home. Maybe one day she or Little Abigail would return.

After that night, the dark wayfarers would have to find the way to freedom on their own.

OCTOBER 1862
AUGUSTA, KENTUCKY

Little Abigail put the violin back in its case. She had tried, but failed, to elicit anything but a mournful screech from the strings that evening. Some nights were like that. Or maybe she was losing her touch.

On the inside lid of the fiddle case, she ran her work-worn thumb down the list of women, mother to daughter, who had played and loved this instrument: Abigail Newcomb, Sarah O'Neil, and Little Abigail. Strong women. Women who knew how to persevere in difficult times.

Times like now.

Although Kentucky hadn't declared for the Confederacy and wanted to remain neutral in the conflict between the North and South, the Confederacy had declared for Kentucky.

Her grandmother would have been proud of the Augusta Home Guard who had just held off Colonel Basil Duke and his Confederate troops a week before. The rebels had come up from Falmouth, Kentucky, their aim to take the town of Augusta and its strategic spot on the river. Once they had Augusta, they could venture into Union territory.

And they almost did.

After a long, dry spell, the river was so low a sandbar had appeared. Duke's men on horseback had charged into the water, running the federal patrol boats off. But the home guard had set up shop in town, shooting down at the rebels until Colonel Duke signaled a retreat.

Maybe that skirmish had kept her O'Neil family safe on the Ohio side, Little Abigail thought. But there was no way to tell them. With the war on, she couldn't send a letter. She couldn't cross the river herself. She couldn't even conjure her mother and father; her brother, Dennis; or her favorite niece, Sadie, with a song in the dim firelight tonight.

Yet she had been right to come here.

The distance had definitely put a strain on their relation-

The Memory of Lemon

ships. Sarah and Sean were now too old to travel; young Sadie tended to them. Dennis needed looking after as well. He had taken to drink after his little boy died of cholera.

If she were back in Lockton, Little Abigail knew she could set it all right again.

Yet the turmoil of war had kept all but the most intrepid travelers at home. Little Abigail admitted that she was many things—stubborn, strong-minded, even "mulish," her husband, Jacob, once told her. But *intrepid*, no.

Upstairs on a pallet bed, her daughter, Lizzie, slept, a slip of a girl at thirteen who would soon bloom like the prettiest rose in the garden. The last time Lizzie had seen her cousins she still carried her little hand-sewn poppet everywhere, the doll that Little Abigail had made for her.

She and Lizzie would be all right, even if Jacob never came back from the war. It seemed like he had drifted out of their lives like wood smoke. Here one day, gone the next.

But he had left them bags of cornmeal hidden in the work cabin. After the first frost, they'd gather what menfolk they could. They'd kill the pig and smoke the hams and the bacon with the hickory wood Jacob had set aside. Their guinea fowl still nested in the trees. And there was the garden. And the woods. And the river.

The Ballou men had gone to fight for the Confederacy, so the tobacco fields lay fallow. There was no tobacco curing in the high rafters of the barn. It was difficult and dangerous to travel, even from here to the tobacco auctions in Maysville, so it didn't really matter.

But she and Lizzie wouldn't starve, unless more soldiers came and took what little they had.

She had the work cabin full of herbs hanging to dry, and she had pomades and potions and liniments to give to the poor and sell to those who could afford them. The spicy aroma of the workroom and a cup of sassafras or spicebush tea always put her right. Maybe a cup of that tea would have loosened her arm this evening, made the bow glide over the fiddle strings, and brought her loved ones back to her in spirit. But it was too late now.

Little Abigail wrapped her shawl around her shoulders, rose from the rocking chair near the fire, and went out to look at the river.

In the moonlight, it glimmered like a pale silk ribbon.

Oh, the river took you in, Little Abigail thought. *It told you things you wanted to believe. It held you here.*

Yes, once, the river had been the way forward. The way to safety. The flowing, living thing that could also take her back to her people, anytime she wanted to go.

Now, it was a line she could not cross.

JULY 1878
QUEEN CITY, OHIO

Lizzie had no desire to go back there, ever again. She really didn't know those people like her mother, Little Abigail, had.

Her two-week visit had seemed like an eternity.

Lizzie had gone downriver to Queen City on a steamboat and then up the canal on a smaller boat to Lockton. Her older cousin, Sadie, who lived in the O'Neil farmhouse, had been welcoming. But Lizzie felt hemmed in, like she couldn't breathe. The giant

The Memory of Lemon

brick hulk of the mattress factory blocked the light and turned the lane in front of the farm into a wind tunnel. The noise from the paper mill and the lock operating day and night and the steam-powered canal boats kept her from sleeping. The stench from the fetid canal made her eyes water.

Sitting in the little canal boat once again, headed for the Plum Street dock in Queen City, Lizzie smoothed her fitted jacket and the long, narrow skirt in sensible navy serge. Her white collar, she noted proudly, was immaculate. Her navy straw bonnet, trimmed with a blue-and-white-striped ribbon, hid her ash brown hair, parted in the middle and gathered into a low knot. She wore white gloves to hide her freckled and work-roughened hands, definitely not the hands of a lady.

Sadie's hands had looked much the same. But she was married and didn't have to concern herself with her looks. Sadie had two children still at home and an elderly father who drank too much. Old Uncle Dennis had been Little Abigail's brother, the one who lost a little boy to cholera.

Every time Lizzie heard the cork come out of the bottle, she cringed. Sadie just shrugged, as in, *That's the way things are.*

And the questions!

Why hadn't Lizzie married? How old was she now—almost thirty? What did she do all day in that cabin? My goodness!

And they had trotted in every available bachelor: the butcher, the baker, and the mattress maker.

Lizzie knew they meant well.

But she had no desire to marry. What she had seen of men—her silent, compliant father, Jacob, and the hard-drinking Ballou men who worked the tobacco fields—had left her underwhelmed. Since her father and Little Abigail had died, Lizzie owned the double cabin and the garden, the tobacco barn and fields. A husband would only mean more work and less of her own authority, although her mother had certainly managed to keep the upper hand.

If Lizzie yearned for company, it was of the feminine variety. She had formed a strong bond with Miss Albert, the schoolteacher, who lived in town during the school year, but spent her summers and weekends with Lizzie.

Miss Albert was teaching one of the Ballou boys to read, since his parents were lax about making their children go to school.

If you don't have family, who will get your property when you pass? Cousin Sadie had asked, perhaps with a hint about her own children.

Lizzie and Miss Albert had become fond of the youngest Ballou boy. He was the first one Lizzie thought of when Sadie had asked her that question. The boy was kind and thoughtful, loved music—or at least tolerated her fiddle playing—and caught on fast. He had brought his little cousin to listen. Maybe she would learn how to play the fiddle.

If Lizzie ever had a son, she hoped he would be like Harry Ballou. Maybe when it was time, she'd make out her will in his favor. But she had plenty of years ahead of her.

When the canal boat docked at Plum Street, Lizzie grabbed her satchel and walked down the gangplank to the busy thoroughfare. Sadie had been kind enough to pack a lunch and Lizzie thought she'd make her way to the levee until it was time for the steamboat to depart.

On a bench as far away as she could get from the noise and commotion, the wagons hauling freight to and from the boats,

Lizzie took out the flask of lemonade and took a sip. Her O'Neil relatives seemed to drink that by the gallon. Lizzie preferred her spicebush tea, warm or cold. But the lemonade tasted good on this hot, hazy day.

From her vantage point, the gray river looked like a mother cat resting on her side, with the boats like mewling kittens getting what nourishment they could.

The river was like that.

And Lizzie couldn't wait to get back home.

10

MAY

Strawberry and Rhubarb

Neely

"Have you heard from Ben?" Maggie asked as soon as I walked into the bakery.

"No."

She gave my arm a friendly pat, then went back to filling an order.

What was there to say? Despite the early morning sunshine, I felt cold and dreary. And alone.

Norb was baking butter cookies. Their sweet, mellow aroma began to buoy my low spirits. Maybe coffee would help as well.

I approached my good buddy, the La Marzocco espresso machine, with a little trepidation. What would the message in the latte foam suggest this morning?

Maybe if I varied my routine slightly, I'd get a more promising reply from the supernatural breakfast beverage realm. I made a

Cuban coffee that had an extra shot of espresso and a tiny sprinkle of sugar for a brew that was not quite bitter, not quite sweet. I steamed some milk until it was frothy, and then guided the white foam onto the dark surface. I was going for a simple "we are all one" circle, but ended up creating a comet with an angry tail.

Sigh.

After that strained ride home from Augusta—a trip that was big on traditional and bluegrass music, but short on conversation—I wasn't the only one who had noticed that Ben was barely speaking to me.

"You two need to kiss and make up," Ro had hissed at me in the backseat, at odds with the Everly Brothers' melodic harmony. "I can't have my best friends on the outs. And I thought getting you two back together was a good idea! Don't prove me wrong."

I had explained the stalemate to Ro, and that made her even angrier. "Can't your lawyer do something about that?" she asked. "You need an attack dog attorney, not a teacup poodle. Are you going to let Charlie Wheeler grab your lawyer by the throat and shake him to death while you stand by and watch?"

No.

I went to see Jonathan Billings, Esquire, yet again, in the Fairview offices of Voorhees, Allen, and Billings. So far my teacup poodle's advice had been to be patient. Professional athletes were all swagger and no substance in litigation, he assured me. High-asset divorces always took a long time. "Let him get used to the idea," Jonathan suggested. "Go slowly." It would all work out. Blah. Blah. Blah.

At least that had taken up some of the countless hours that week waiting to hear from Ben.

The Memory of Lemon

After our disastrous Saturday night date and the rather curt good-bye at the end of our Augusta trip the next day, Ben hadn't responded to my text or voice mail messages. Okay, I thought, maybe he needed some time to process this new complication in our potential relationship. Maybe it was because he worried that Luke had somehow bugged my phone. Maybe it was because I was too much trouble and Ben was finally sick of it. But I needed to know. I hoped I'd hear from him soon, just as I had hoped every day that week.

Once again, I texted him a simple "?".

The Cuban coffee was starting to warm and soften that cold, hard place in the pit of my stomach, the physical symptom that something was definitely wrong. I was caught in a relationship triangle, with points that led to Luke, Ben, and Gran. I felt every sharp, bitter point.

I was starting to understand why I was drawn to the balm of sweet things. I had always thought of myself as a can-do, upbeat person who'd overcome a childhood trauma. That was the persona I thought I showed to the world, the story I told myself. But when I took a quick inventory of my daily thoughts, which I alone created, I found a lot of fearful what-ifs. I didn't want to be a brittle type A masquerading as a breezy B. One quick and temporary fix, a little sugar, seemed to smooth out those bitter jabs I kept giving myself.

I took another sip of coffee and tried to think dispassionately. When I filed for divorce in two weeks, I'd face Luke again, he of the prenup that I had been too much in love to worry about. And his attorney, Charlie Wheeler. He of the "it's not personal, it's business" mantra that never rang true. I had been incredibly naive to imagine that Luke would grant me a divorce, just like that.

"I can be different," he had told me months before. "I can change." Once again, he had tried to work his old, sexy magic. But my heart had finally caught up with my body, which had physically moved away from him, and my head, which knew Luke had to be the person he was, not the person I wanted him to be. That spring night when Luke had come back to try to persuade me, I had finally tasted the truth. The comfort of sweet cinnamon had held my metaphorical hand as I left my old life behind and started over.

But just because our marriage was over for me didn't mean it was over for Luke. He probably wouldn't let me go without a fight. That was how he was hardwired. He would stand there in the pocket, like the quarterback he was, and coolly figure out a way to outsmart his opponent.

Me.

He would try and try, throw a Hail Mary pass if he had to, until the game was over.

This wasn't disaster thinking on my part. It was being rational.

And while Luke was busy playing the game, I might end up losing Ben. *Whoops. Bad thought.* I took another sip of sweetened coffee.

And then there was Gran, slowly slipping away in the memory care wing at Mount Saint Mary's. Pneumonia, a choking spell, or any number of things could take her before my divorce was final and all this tumult I had created could end up being for nothing. *Jeez. Out, damned thoughts.*

I sipped more coffee. Sugar obviously wasn't working today.

The Memory of Lemon

No matter which way I turned, I seemed stuck in a maze of my own thoughts.

It was time for the second, surefire way I had to alleviate stress—going to my dessert-lover's happy place. There was no point in ruminating and wringing my hands. I had two hours before we'd open our doors, so I finished the little upside-down Bundt cakes topped with mosaic jewels of rhubarb and strawberry. I loved rhubarb, that hardy, underappreciated garden survivor that leafed out just as the worst of winter melted away. Not everyone was a fan, especially of the bitter, mushy, overcooked version. Yet sometimes a little bitterness could bring out the best in other flavors. Bitter rhubarb made sunny-day strawberry face the realities of life—and taste all the better for it. As I brushed the cakes with a deep pink glaze made from sweet strawberry and bottled rhubarb bitters, I hoped I would change rhubarb doubters. Certainly, the little Bundt cakes looked as irresistible as anything I had ever seen in a French patisserie. The glaze would set to a dull sheen while I worked on the new display for May.

I looked forward to this changing of the bakery guard. Our customers seemed to respond as well; our foot traffic and corresponding sales rose at the beginning of each month. For May, I hung the rosy pink canvas curtain as a backdrop for our strawberry and rhubarb theme. Out came the spring green platters, cupcake wrappers, plates, and napkins as a color contrast to our goodies.

I still had to work on strawberry-rhubarb hand pies—small turnovers of puff pastry—and tartlets. For Lydia's wedding, I needed signature tartlet shapes that would equal my creativity with cakes. With the puff pastry and pâte brisée doughs chilling in our walk-in refrigerator, I had a date with a rolling pin later on this morning. I wanted to wow Lydia and her mother at our meeting that afternoon.

I knew Lydia probably had her grandmother's lard crust in mind, but pâte brisée held up better. Nothing worse than a pie or tart with a soggy bottom.

By the time Rainbow Cake opened, the little jeweled Bundt cakes sent out their sweet beacon from narrow rectangular platters, pink-frosted cupcakes sprouted tiny stalks of rhubarb made from marzipan, and bags of pale pink meringue polka dots, sandwiched together with strawberry rhubarb jam, were ready to go. Irresistible.

And just in time. The first customer in the door was the Professor, a regular since we'd opened. A human genome researcher currently on sabbatical from Queen City University, John Staufregan had a crush on Maggie and had helped find her daughter, four-year-old Emily, when Maggie's ex forgot to pick her up at preschool. Although Maggie had finally warmed to the Professor, he hadn't exactly captured her heart. But he definitely looked better. He had taken Maggie's throwaway comment about another patron—"I bet you'd look good with a haircut like that"—and exchanged his tired, forty-something comb-over for a buzz cut. It had shaved at least ten years off his appearance.

Maggie brought his breakfast cupcake and coffee, then stood back, arms crossed, and really looked at him. "I like it," she said appraisingly.

He blushed like a pimply boy whose voice had just changed. "Well, it saves time getting ready in the morning, that's for sure," he said, brushing his palm over the top of his head. "I still can't quite get used to it."

"Well, you get our approval," I said, holding both thumbs up.

"You definitely do," agreed Maggie.

The rosy rhubarb-colored T-shirt she wore today made her eyes look even bluer. I could swear they twinkled, but maybe it was an optical illusion. I didn't notice that my eyes looked any greener and I was wearing the same thing.

As the last of the morning rush dissipated, I was behind the counter checking our inventory on cinnamon rolls. We were almost out—good. There was nothing more disheartening to a bakery owner than display cases full of cinnamon rolls by late afternoon. Butter and sugar cookies could hold for several days; cinnamon rolls and Danish pastry could not.

Maggie went over to refill the Professor's coffee.

"Do you ever like to go to the movies or out to dinner or anything?" he muttered into his cup as Maggie's hand on the coffeepot hovered above it.

Look her in the eye. Smile! I tried to telepathically coach from the sidelines.

Maggie's eyes widened. She filled his coffee cup briskly, suddenly all business. "I'm so busy with the bakery and my daughter that I just don't go out much," she said with a shrug that didn't fool me for a second. "Don't really feel like it. Too tired."

"Sure, sure," he said. "Just a thought."

"Can I get you anything else?" Maggie asked, as if she didn't know him at all.

He gave her a defeated smile. "No."

After a minute or so, he left his full mug untouched and walked out, shoulders slumped.

"Why did you do that? What harm would it do to go out with him just once?" I asked Maggie. "You've known him for months now."

"He caught me off guard," she confessed as she cleared away his coffee mug. "I've said no to so many jerks that it just came out that way. It's my standard answer."

"Well, you have to fix this the next time he comes in," I said.

Maggie sighed.

Oh, Lord, I needed to go to my happy place again.

Back in my inner sanctum, the peaceful workroom with the milk chocolate walls and cool marble counters, I had to clear my head and come up with some tarts for the "hillbilly" wedding. I let the chilled pastry dough rest at room temperature and took the various fillings I had made out of the refrigerator. I rummaged through the plastic bins for the pastry cutters I wanted to use. I sprinkled a little flour on the counter and found my vintage tartlet pans. I centered myself, bypassing the knot in my stomach for the calm deep inside me.

I glanced once again at my sketches, then rolled out the pastry. With a few deft turns, the pale dough flecked with tiny shards of butter obeyed my commands. I cut out rounds to line the pans, then spooned in the fillings. I moved the pastry scraps to the side of the marble countertop and rolled out a second batch.

I rimmed the golden custard tartlets with tiny circles of dough for a scalloped effect. The berry tartlets got a lattice design that made them look like patterns on a vintage quilt. The bourbon chocolate tartlet was supposed to feature a pastry cutout of a log

The Memory of Lemon

cabin, but, looking at it again, I decided the design would pop more if I baked the cutout separately, then outlined the "logs" in chocolate, applied after baking. I scribbled a note to myself. I gently brushed the pastry designs with egg white and sprinkled them with sanding sugar so that they would glisten and sparkle.

Quickly, I rolled out the puff pastry sheets and formed small square tartlets, which I would fill after they had baked. I rolled out another sheet, cut it into squares, and spooned in strawberry-rhubarb filling, then folded them into tiny triangles for hand pies with decorative vents on the top. They, too, got a brush of egg white and a dusting of sugar.

When they all came out of the oven, my heart lifted.

I never tired of the thrill I got when my abstract ideas turned out better than I had imagined.

Whatever else happened, at least I had this.

Later that afternoon, I welcomed Lydia Ballou and Cadence Stidham back to my parlor. Ro had a detailed plan that she handed to them both. Gavin showed them his watercolor renderings of the tobacco barn interior, the garden set up for the wedding ceremony, the wedding pie table—everything they couldn't imagine for themselves.

Roshonda explained her proposed menu and a full wedding plan, and the mother and daughter were pleasantly nodding. All good so far.

And then my little tartlets—including the square puff pastry case filled with a dollop of sweetened, flavored mascarpone and an artful scattering of fresh berries—stole the show.

Lydia and her mother sat side by side on my settee, looking at each other.

"This is exactly the wedding I wanted, Mother, but I didn't know how to express it," Lydia said, eyes shining.

"I'm glad you love it, sweetheart. I think your father will approve."

Lydia bit her lip, as if she were thinking, *He's not really my father*, but maybe I was just imagining that. The mention of Gene Stidham seemed to take a little bit of the pleasure away from Lydia for some reason. At least she managed to meet her mother halfway.

Gavin, Roshonda, and I breathed a collective sigh of relief. We all settled back to enjoy our French press coffee or herbal tea and the tartlets.

I had skipped lunch, so I sampled the custard. It was beautiful—it tasted rich and sweet—but it needed something more. I typed a note into my phone.

"I was wondering if you might use this as a flavoring in one of the tarts," Lydia said to me. She handed me a little plastic sandwich bag of what looked like tiny, round allspice. I opened the bag and took a whiff. It smelled like allspice, a combination of nutmeg and clove and a little cinnamon. But it wasn't allspice.

"Spicebush berries," explained Lydia. "My grandmother used to pick them in the woods and dry them. It's an old-time Kentucky flavoring."

"I remember," said Mrs. Stidham. "Vangie used to make custard pie with a little spicebush flavoring. She always got lots of orders for that pie when Deuce and I were little kids, before she went to work in the drugstore. But I vote for something else. I never really liked spicebush."

Lydia scowled. *Here we go again.*

The Memory of Lemon

Spicebush berries. The flavor gave me the feeling of a long-ago time, when a peaceful evening meant watching the river flow by.

I thought again of the twin cabins, joined together by the dogtrot. The Kentucky garden. The tobacco barn. But, again, the flavor vanished before I could get a full story.

"We could do both," said Roshonda, bringing me back to the present as she artfully brokered yet another peace deal between mother and bride. "Right, Claire?"

She only called me Claire when it was important.

"Of course," I said. "Golden custard with spicebush and golden custard with something else."

As if on cue, I finally got a text from Ben.

We have to talk.

11

Neely

"I couldn't think where else to meet," said Ben, sitting with his elbows on the table in our booth at the House of Chili. "I had Sammy let me in the back door."

We both looked around, but didn't see anyone with a cell phone or a camera.

"I thought you'd given up on me," I whispered, grabbing both his hands as I sat down across from him. I had robin's egg blue stains on my fingers from coloring our signature buttercream frosting. I still had on my pastry chef's jacket with a few chocolate squiggles that were not part of the all-white design. I had been able to pull my hair into a more presentable ponytail and swipe on a quick swath of lipstick, but that was it. After not seeing or talking to Ben for all this time, I was in too much of a hurry to go full-out primp.

"Not you, Neely. Never you," he said with a grim smile. "But I hate this."

The ever-present Bluetooth hovered over his ear. I searched his face like I was mapping a new planet. I noted the spot he had missed shaving that morning, the nicks and dents from his football-playing days, the crow's-feet just appearing around his eyes. He was perfect.

"We have to have a plan," I said.

"You mean other than avoiding each other?"

"Roshonda says my attorney is more lapdog than pit bull, but he wants us to wait this out. Maybe he's got a point. He says that high-asset divorces are usually more volatile because there's more at stake. It's only two more weeks until I can file for divorce, and then Luke will have to know it's a lost cause."

"Unless it means big bucks."

"What do you mean?"

"Unless Luke is up for an endorsement deal or a big commercial or something that would require him to have an image as a family man."

"Well, when your wife has left you, moved to another state, and filed for divorce, there is no family." I bristled. "Luke is going to have to give his image a single-guy makeover because I'm not going back or pretending to be his wife. Not for any amount of money."

"I'm just saying that there's something else going on here. Most of the rich divorced guys I've worked with, especially the pro ball players, just go with the settlement terms outlined in the prenup and call it a day. Those agreements tend to favor the breadwinning partner anyway, and I bet yours does, too. So there has to be a reason Luke doesn't want to pay you and move on."

"Yes. Charlie Wheeler."

"He's not such a bad guy, Neely. He was a punter, for God's sake."

I knew that was "football" for not being a guy who stood strong on the battlefield, but Ben didn't know Charlie like I did. Charlie was manipulative. He had paid off Luke's conquests so they never talked to sports writers. He had arranged for at least one woman to keep Luke happy after a Pro Bowl I had to miss because of a big wedding. When I finally had had enough and left Luke, I kept receiving flowers and lavish gifts, as if I could be bought, just like the others. Luke wouldn't have thought of that without Charlie's help.

"Charlie is a snake," I said simply.

"Maybe Luke thinks he can win you back."

"Not happening."

We ordered our food and sat in silence.

Ben's five-way arrived, that quintessentially Queen City concoction of spaghetti, chili, kidney beans, finely chopped raw onion, and shredded cheese served on an oval plate. I eyed my two mini chili dogs; I was suddenly hungry. I passed Ben the packets of oyster crackers I knew he liked to crumble on top.

He sighed. "The door opens for us and then slams shut."

"We need something to prop it open," I said. "We need information. If I can find out why Luke is playing hardball, I can get myself off the hook."

"I can help with that," said Ben. "I know people who know things."

"You can help by staying out of it," I said. "If anyone finds out you're involved, it will rebound on me. I have to be the one to dig."

After we had finished our lunch and rose to go our separate ways, I wanted to walk into his arms and just say the hell with it all. But the thought of Gran living in one of those places that smelled of urine and old food held me back.

"I miss you," I said. "Now we can't even connect through texting or e-mail. I wouldn't put it past Charlie to tap my phone or hack into my computer."

"I'll write you a letter," Ben said half-jokingly, and then we realized that was a pretty good idea.

"The last I checked, it was a federal offense to tamper with the mail," he said.

"Send it to the bakery, just to be safe," I said. "I'll write to you, too."

"Maybe I'll have Dave deliver it, attach it to your porch goose. Who would look there?"

We walked over to the cashier's counter, delaying our separate departures as long as we could. "Lunch is on me," Ben said.

"Big spender."

I finally got him to smile and I felt like the sun had just come out.

That safe and warm feeling must have prompted what I said next. "My dad has been writing to me. He's living in a trailer in a Kansas City scrapyard. He has a black dog. He says he wants to come home."

"Why Kansas City?"

"That's just where he landed, I guess. He had been living in some fleabag motel. The stationery is stained and yellowed and smells like cigarette smoke."

"At least he's in touch," said Ben, gently.

"I'm not getting my hopes up this time."

"Well, look at it this way. Now you have not one, but two new pen pals."

I reached up to kiss him.

When I got back to work, as if on cue, the mail had come. Maggie had left it in a pile on the counter.

"Well?" she asked.

"We're going to send love letters."

"Good plan," she said, rolling her eyes.

The lunch crowd had thinned out and Jett wasn't due in for another half hour, so I took the mail back to the workroom to sort.

The thought of an actual letter from Ben was sort of romantic. I picked up a junk mail envelope and pressed it to my heart, just for practice.

Maybe this wasn't all bad, a take-your-time, old-fashioned kind of romance, even if it wasn't by choice. Ben was that sort of guy, one who stood for honor and steadfastness and intelligence. There was a lot of sexiness in that.

Anybody could promise something he couldn't or wouldn't deliver. Anybody could think of himself first. It took a real somebody to stay with you when there didn't seem to be anything in it for him.

I threw the junk mail in the recycling bin, then sorted through the rest.

Junk. Junk. Bakery business. Junk. Bill. Letter. Letter.

City Vue stationery. But the return address was crossed out and the scrapyard address written in. So he was still there.

I opened the envelope.

Dear Claire,

We had a big storm last night. Ranger the dog hates storms about as much as I do. Especially waiting one out in a tin can trailer. Makes me remember my helicopter pilot days in Vietnam.

The folks at the VA hospital say I have to tell the people I love what is going on with me. I have to tell my story. So I'm going to try to tell you what I think has gotten me hung up—and I mean that literally. One of the things.

That damn dream. The storm made me relive it. But I didn't fight it so much this time.

It always starts with a thudding in my chest. I'm in danger. It feels like I'm falling from the sky. I can't stop myself. I have no control. And I know something really bad is going to happen. I'm scared shitless. (Sorry, honey.)

Next thing I know, everything is black. There is no pain, but I know there is, if that makes any sense. I mean I can't feel anything, but there is the taste of pain, sort of tinny and metallic like I had the blade of a sword in my mouth. You will know what I mean.

My throat constricts. My eyes water.

And then from out of the darkness comes this girl with blue hands. They're stained dark blue, like she stuck her hands in a vat of ink. And the smell of piss. I think I must have pissed my pants for days, it's so strong. And I'm cold. I'm in the back of a shack and people come in to look at me lying there, and they bend down and get up in my face, but the only one who brings me water or rice is the girl with blue hands.

I know my helicopter went down over North Vietnam, but the rest of it is a black hole. My Army records say I turned up as a prisoner of war just outside Hanoi, but I don't know how I got from my helicopter to the camp. They don't, either. According to some of the other guys at the camp, I was brought in on a stretcher, or so they told me. So I must have been in bad shape.

Claire, honey, I think if I could remember what happened, I might be able to put my life back together. I might be able to be the father you deserve.

I sure miss you, sweetie.

You can write me back at the Blue River Scrapyard.

Love,
Dad

That evening, at home in my upstairs office, I Googled *blue hands*. First, I found medical reasons for a person's hands turning blue, such as Raynaud's syndrome or cyanosis, but the photos showed hands just tinged blue, not a dark blue as Dad remembered.

Then I added more terms. *Hands* plus *blue stain. Blue ink. Blue dye.*

What was the name of that blue dye made from plants? *Indigo.* I searched *Indigo* then *Vietnam.*

I got a hit right away. *Cây chàm.* The indigo plant.

From there, I found the villages of Lao Chai and Sa Pa, in northwestern Vietnam where indigo grew. By a lengthy process, villagers made the dark blue dye from the plant, using urine to set the color.

So he wasn't crazy.

I found recent photos on travel blogs. Hills terraced with rice fields. Vats of indigo dye. Women with blue hands dipping textiles into the dark dye.

I printed the photos to mail with the letter I had yet to write. Maybe I would also send some lemon cookies we had left over from a special order. Couldn't hurt.

Lao Chai was twelve hours from Hanoi today, by train and motorbike. Who knew how long it took during the war? Maybe several days. If Dad had been carried into the prisoner-of-war camp on a stretcher, the journey must have been extremely painful.

Then I read first-person accounts of American prisoners of war detained in Vietnam. Some of them had shipped out when the Beatles had their first stateside hit song "I Want to Hold Your Hand" in 1964 and finally came back after the Beatles had broken up nine years later, when the Vietnam War officially ended. The troops left with crew cuts and came back to hippies with long hair.

When I looked up again, it was after midnight.

Jack O'Neil was not alone in feeling that he had lost big chunks of time.

Maybe something in these images, these place-names would prompt his memory.

Maybe he could finally come back from the war.

Maybe he could move on from 1973.

Or maybe not, knowing my dad.

12

Neely

"Who thought Pie Night was a good idea?" complained Maggie.

It was six o'clock, the bakery's normal closing time, and the place was empty, despite the row of signature pies, running the length of the counter, that Jett and I had just set out.

Chocolate. Strawberry-rhubarb. Apple. Blackberry. Bourbon chocolate. Coconut cream. Sour cherry. Lemon meringue.

All with scalloped edges, lattice tops, pastry cutouts artfully arranged, or peaks of Italian meringue scorched with a pastry torch for a toasted marshmallow effect. *All that work.*

Granted, one of the reasons we were doing Pie Night was to test how each of these pie varieties held up before we had to bake and take them to Lydia's wedding reception in June.

Pastry dough was such a touchy thing. So much depended on the coolness of my fingers and the marble countertop where I rolled out the dough. The smooth way the rolling pin glided over the disk of chilled dough. There was a certain feel to pastry that you didn't need with cake. You didn't have to feel a cake batter to judge if it was ready, but you had to touch pastry to know. The tiniest change in the weather—humid versus dry, warm versus chilly—seemed to make the dough come together and then roll out differently.

We had baked the pies earlier in the morning. Now, ten hours later, if the pastry was soggy, tough, or otherwise imperfect, I would have to try again with another pastry recipe or filling combinations that could hold up better. And I only had a little over a month.

I sent up a prayer to the pastry gods: *Please let this be all right.*

But I also wanted to make a little money here. "Did you send out another social media blast? Tweet and Instagram?" I asked Maggie.

"You were looking over my shoulder when I did."

"Let's not freak out here," Jett said, ever the diplomat in venom green nail polish and little skull earrings. "People aren't going to come until after they've had their dinner. Pie is for dessert."

Maggie and I stood behind the counter, arms folded, and stared out the display window.

Jett shook her head. Leave it to her to be remarkably upbeat while the rest of us were uncharacteristically morose. "Maybe we should open up so that this wonderful pie aroma brings them in," she said brightly. She opened the door and used it to fan the pie air out onto the street.

And it worked.

Somebody walked in.

"This is Pie Night, right?" the older lady asked, pointing to the sign in the front window.

Signs, portents, e-mail, or the aroma of a just-baked pie. Something was working.

We introduced ourselves to silver-haired Mrs. Hefron, who looked to be in her seventies. I got her settled with a slice of coconut cream and a decaf coffee. Pie was a friendly kind of dessert, so it was only natural to begin chatting.

"I've been looking forward to this all week. I don't make pie like I used to, but my mother made the flakiest crust," she reminisced. "It used to shatter when your fork cut into it. She always used leaf lard, the best kind. She used to buy it in a metal tub. It was snowy white. I can still see her cutting it into the flour with two knives she used like scissors." She took another bite. "But this is very good, too."

Maggie must have called her mother, because in she came with little Emily in tow.

"Well, Patsy!" Mrs. Hefron exclaimed to Maggie's mother. "Where have you been keeping yourself, neighbor? You and that adorable grandchild come over here and sit with me. I'll treat you two to pie."

A single mom and her three kids came in next, and then the Professor, whom Maggie corralled away from her mother. She sat him down with a slice of blackberry pie, the closest we had to his favorite blueberry and lemon morning muffin—*I mean, breakfast cupcake.*

I was surprised when Mrs. Amici's grandson Bobby stopped in. Mrs. Amici used to be a regular customer until she moved up to Mount Saint Mary's memory care wing with Gran. I don't remember Bobby ever coming into the bakery, but I was glad to see him anyway. I cut him a slice of strawberry-rhubarb. "How is your grandma doing?"

"She has good days and bad," he said. "I take Barney up there when I go. Sometimes she doesn't even recognize him, but that dog is always a big hit."

I smiled at Bobby. Barney, part beagle, part dachshund, with a long and low body and droopy ears, had christened every streetlight, lamppost, and mailbox along Benson Street. I missed seeing Barney and Mrs. Amici walk by the bakery every day.

People I had never seen before flocked in, their faces showing a longing you never saw for cake. People's eyes lit up for a cupcake; cake seemed to signal celebration. But their eyes got filmy, watery, misty when we handed them a slice of pie. Pie was memory. Nostalgia. Pie made people recall simpler, maybe happier times.

"I haven't had pie this good since I was a boy," the Professor told Maggie. I saw her pat his hand. Maybe he would ask her out again, and this time, she would say yes. He looked sad. Wistful. Unsure of himself.

But my attention was drawn back to our pie customers.

"My aunt Fanny used to make a hickory nut pie, but she died before she could write down the recipe for me," another woman told me.

As I refilled coffee cups and moved around the bakery, I drifted in and out of pie conversations.

"We used to go cherry picking when we lived in Michigan, and my mom made pies all week that we froze and would bake all year. You can bake a pie from frozen, you know; you just bake it longer. Sour cherry is still my favorite."

The Memory of Lemon

"My mother-in-law and I used to pick black raspberries at a farm near Wilmington, buckets and buckets of 'em. They make the best pies."

"Have you ever had that Shaker lemon pie, the one with the whole lemons sliced thin? You want to talk lemon, that's lemon. It's real sour."

"When I was on the road, I used to stop in a diner outside of Indianapolis that had fantastic lemon meringue pie."

"I clipped a recipe from the newspaper years ago that had a chocolate pie like this one. I wonder where that recipe went."

"When are you going to have Pie Night again?"

By eight o'clock, every pie pan was empty and we had to shoo people out.

Maggie and I were delighted. It was now Jett's turn to go to the dark side. "I've never seen such a bunch of doom cookies," she said, wiping down the tables.

"What?"

"Doom cookies. You know, people who pretend to be something they're not, like girls in my class who pretend to be bad-ass but go home and read *The Little House on the Prairie* in their Disney princess bedrooms."

"Who were the Pie Night people pretending to be? I don't quite follow."

"They're pretending to be bad-ass pie bakers." Jett trilled in a church-lady falsetto, "*'Oh, leaf lard is the best.' 'No, I swear by a mixture of Crisco and butter.'* When was the last time they actually baked a pie? If they did, they wouldn't be gorging themselves here on Pie Night. They probably don't even own a rolling pin." Jett sniffed. And then she added, diplomatically, "But your pie was good."

By the time I got home, it was after nine. I changed into comfy clothes and made myself a peanut butter and apple jelly sandwich, a taste of my childhood. I first had that combination at Maggie's house. Patsy, Maggie's mother, would make after-school sandwiches for us, then one for herself. Patsy was always snacking on something. "Pleasingly plump," Maggie's father used to say, eyes twinkling as he gave Patsy a little pinch on the behind, even in front of us kids. Maggie found that embarrassing, but I thought it was wonderful—to be loved for yourself by someone who found your quirks charming, quite the opposite of the strained silences between my parents at home.

Patsy also had a baby doll dressed in a dimity gown, which she displayed in her living room. No one, not even little Emily, was ever allowed to touch it. "It was what I wore when I was adopted as an infant," she once told me, matter-of-factly. "My birth mother probably intended for it to be a clue of some kind, but it's a reminder to me that I have a happy life. I don't need to look for more."

Dimity. The word stopped me. What was it I was trying to remember about dimity? Whatever it was, I would think about it again tomorrow. I had something important to do yet tonight.

I sank into the settee in my front parlor. I put my feet up on the ottoman and nibbled my sandwich.

The flavor also took me back to elementary school on Millcreek Valley's hilltop, where Ben and I had been in the same class since second grade. When I looked back at my childhood self from an adult's perspective, I wanted to hug that ponytailed, long-legged, smart girl with the permanent teeth that were as yet too big for her little face and tell her everything was going to work out fine. Not to worry.

The Memory of Lemon

When I looked back at Ben as a child, I wanted to tell that shy, husky boy with the blue eyes and sandy hair that one day, he would grow into his strength and self-assurance. He wouldn't have to take a backseat to anyone. Ever.

I needed to write Ben a letter, since we could no longer text or talk by phone.

I wanted it to be a love letter. But what do you write to someone you've known since you were kids, but don't know yet in an intimate way?

I took my sandwich plate into the kitchen and poured myself a glass of pinot gris.

I took the wineglass—and the rest of the bottle—upstairs to my office.

I hadn't penned a handwritten letter since the night Luke and I finally broke up in March, except for a letter to my dad in April. I had torn up the many versions of my letter to Luke and thrown them away. Writing that letter had only been a way to help me work through the breakup.

But I had also written a second letter that night. To my troubled, homeless dad. And he had answered it. We were now connected for the first time since he'd left when I was fifteen. Who knew if it would continue? He could wander off again, but I had high hopes this time.

I had high hopes for Ben's letter, too.

So, what did I feel?

I took a sheet of paper from the printer feed and started freewriting all the feelings that came up when I conjured Ben.

I felt warmth, the kind that starts in your chest and radiates out. I felt happy and buoyant because I knew that a good, good man loved me. I felt grounded because Ben knew me, really knew me, and loved me anyway. I felt safe because Ben, unlike Luke, had no selfish side that could lead him to betray me. When Ben looked at me, when he held me, I felt cherished.

I wanted to be as close to him as I possibly could. I wanted the two of us to become one.

And at that, the longing, the ache, the physical thrill that was always the first thing I felt with Luke became the ultimate thing I felt for Ben. It was all of Ben that I wanted.

I gulped my wine and fanned my face with the paper.

I placed a sheet of stationery on my desk blotter and caressed it with my fingers.

Ben,

Not seeing you is so hard. We were off to a good start—again—and then the stupid prenup had to ruin everything. If it weren't for Gran, I would tell Luke to keep everything and I would just walk away, happily empty-handed and free. But I can't do that.

I don't know how long this has to last. I hope not long. You have been so patient and understanding. Please know I am doing everything I can to make this ridiculous situation go away. I have an appointment with my attorney to file for divorce. I will let you know how that goes.

I miss you more every day. I miss being in your arms, my head under your chin, listening to the beat of your heart.

Yours,
Neely

I sat back and put my pen down. What good was it to sit by patiently, passively, like the little woman at home that Luke and Charlie Wheeler wanted me to be?

I had to do something.

Against my attorney's strict advice, I called Luke.

I doubted whether he would even hear his phone ring, buzz, bleat, trumpet, or whatever sound it made these days. He was probably out socializing or bedding a barmaid.

But he picked up on the first ring.

"I was hoping you'd call." His voice was like velvet, tender like a caress. And there was no noise in the background. Maybe he was having a quiet evening at home for a change.

"I wasn't sure you'd be home."

"I'm a changed man, Claire. That's what I've been trying to tell you."

"You haven't been trying to tell me. I haven't talked to you in months."

"I have been trying, but you haven't been responding."

He was right. I had blocked his number from my phone and sent his e-mail address to the spam folder.

"So you thought, good guy that you are, that threatening me with that stupid prenup was a good plan?"

"I had to get your attention somehow, Claire," he said, tiredly, as if this were a last resort. "Look, just say the word and I'll drop whatever I'm supposed to be doing and come to you. You can have whatever you want. Your bakery. Your life there. We'll just go back and forth. Other couples have long-distance marriages and they make it work."

"Except you can't be by yourself for fifteen minutes."

"I'm by myself now. It's lonely, I'll admit it. But the only one I want is you."

I took this all in. Luke, alone. Sounding sad, bordering on pathetic. Something was off. "This isn't like you, Luke. What's really going on? Was your strained ACL worse than what the doctors thought? Are you having symptoms from that concussion you had a few years ago?"

"Ha," he said, mirthlessly. "I do feel a little beat up, Claire. Every year, it takes a little longer to recover from the season. But I'll be fine, come time for training camp."

"So what is it, then?"

"I know I totally screwed us up. We had a great thing going. And this might not be something that I can fix."

"You can't fix it, Luke. So let's just part as friends and go on with our lives."

"I'm just not ready to do that yet, Claire." He sighed. "It's ironic, isn't it? And predictable, I guess. And I hate to be predictable. But you don't know what you've got 'til it's gone. I love you," he whispered, and then he ended the call.

13

Neely

After Pie Night and Luke's unexpectedly lovelorn phone conversation, I was ready for an easy day at the bakery. But that didn't mean I was going to get one.

"The phone's been ringing," said Norb as I walked in. "Who calls at six in the morning?"

"People who are desperate for cupcakes," I said, and Norb rolled his eyes.

When I checked the phone messages, I found we had several new pie orders.

"I was wrong, Norb," I shouted to him in the back. "People are desperate for pie."

It seemed that cake and cookie people were happy to order online, but pie aficionados did their ordering the old-fashioned way. I was going to have to teach Jett about pastry. We were going to need the extra help.

I sidled up to the La Marzocco, part Italian coffee machine, part seer. What message would I get in the foam of my latte today?

I ground the dark-roast beans and tamped them down. I streamed the water over the grounds and then poured the ebony brew into my cup. I foamed the milk and used a long-handled spoon to guide the froth over the espresso in what I hoped was a triangular slice of pie.

Voilà! Pie. I couldn't believe it. Was this a sign that I could have what I wanted?

Be careful what you wish for, I reminded myself. A month prior, I'd been worried about business. But according to Maggie's chart, our foot traffic had gone way up since we'd introduced pies, turnovers, and tarts. And that didn't even include everyone at Pie Night. Our sales were up, too. But we were all running ragged. I guess it was a good thing that my social life was stuck in neutral for the moment.

No point in checking my text messages. I was still blocking Luke. There wouldn't be any texts from Ben. Maybe I would get a letter from him later in the day.

I summarized my love letter to Roshonda when she came for her caramel macchiato, and she tut-tutted. "That sounds a bit tepid, don't you think? You sound like his pen pal."

"Well, I am. Sort of."

"Well, don't you want to be a sexy pen pal? Don't you want drool marks on your letters after he reads them?"

"Ben doesn't drool."

"He's a man, Neely. He drools."

Roshonda looked me up and down. "And I hope you don't mind my sayin' so, but you gotta get your sexy back. This isn't cuttin' it."

"I'm at work."

"I mean when you get home. You can't write sexy if you don't feel sexy. Were you wearing your old robe and bunny slippers when you wrote that letter?"

"Yes," I admitted. *What are you supposed to wear late at night, at home, by yourself?*

"My favorite outfit!" Maggie joined in. "Perfect for mindless snacking and TV watching after Mom and Emily go to bed." She sighed. Maggie's domestic situation was not enviable. Patsy was a big help to her, but living with your mother was nobody's idea of the good life.

"Well, you've got a professional man interested in you," Roshonda said, turning to Maggie. "What's the holdup?"

"The Professor is a nice guy, and he's been good to Emily and me, but I just don't want to start anything with him," Maggie said. "It would be awkward if it didn't work out."

"Well, it's lonely and boring if you keep doing what you've been doing. Seems to me that 'awkward' would be an improvement."

Roshonda had a point. Maggie looked suitably chastened.

Roshonda turned to me. "Did you at least spritz some of your Chanel No. 5 on that letter?"

"No, I didn't think of that."

Roshonda let out a big sigh and shrugged her shoulders.

"Girls, you need a refresher course in romance. I'll be in later for lesson number two."

"We're still stuck on lesson one, Getting Our Sexy Back," muttered Maggie.

"Well, work on it. Do some visualization. Imagine yourselves as magnetic, charming, irresistible women," said Roshonda on her way out the door. "That's your homework."

I looked at Maggie. No makeup. Circles under her eyes. Day two hair.

She looked at me. Robin's egg blue buttercream tinting my fingernails yet again. A smear of chocolate pie filling on my pastry chef jacket. Disobedient ponytail.

"Homework," we murmured.

Right on schedule, the Professor came in. He barely nodded to me, but went straight for Maggie. She looked a little flustered, small wonder.

"Do some visualization on him, too, while you're at it," I whispered to her when the Professor was occupied with his breakfast cupcake and coffee. "He's solid, reliable, well educated, and kind, and he adores you. Find the sexy in that. If he asks you for a date again, say yes this time!" Considering that her bad-boy ex-husband was chronically late with child support, barely saw little Emily, and was just an all-around jerk, that should be easy. But the Professor still had some spiffing up to do in the looks department. His new buzz cut was so much better than his tired combover. But there were still those baggy, old-man pants and rumpled shirt.

I vowed to drop a subtle hint later that would encourage the Professor to trade the dad pants for slimmer jeans. Maybe just this one tweak would be the tipping point that would get Maggie to see him in the way he deserved.

I readied the little cakes, buttercream frostings, mousses, and fillings to take next door for my morning wedding cake appointment.

I walked up to my own front door to make sure the entry looked welcoming. I noticed that Gran's old-fashioned plants were flowering. The bridal wreath hedges that lined the sidewalk bloomed white. Her flowering dogwood in the tiny front yard matched the pink tulips I had planted in the black iron urns on either side of the porch. On the shady side of the house, lilies of the valley were releasing their wonderful scent.

My heart lifted, and I wasn't even in the bakery workroom.

My wedding cake baker goose, guarding my porch, held a clutch of pink tulips under his concrete wing. Who put those there? Maybe, I hoped, Ben?

Despite having a wedding cake tasting in just fifteen minutes, I grabbed the bouquet and found the enclosed letter. Yes!

I let myself in the front door and quickly went through the shotgun-style house to the kitchen in the back. I filled a vase with water and plunged in the tulips. I took a quick peek at the letter, but only to make sure it was from Ben. I wanted to take my time to savor every word later.

With a lighter heart, I arranged the buttercreams, mousses, and fillings on the artist's palette I'd had specially made, and I put the little cakes on a tiered stand. While the water heated for French press coffee and tea, I did one last tidy-up in the front parlor.

We wouldn't need the white marble Victorian fireplace on

today, so I lit a small votive candleholder in the hearth instead. A little flame or candlelight seemed to make the French gray plaster walls more elegant, as did the gilded frames around my favorite paintings. I liked to think these tastings were all about the cake, but it was also about the ambience.

Everything was ready, so I checked my Excel spreadsheet again.

Cathy Barnett and Dan Loeffler. She was a retired teacher, and he owned his own insurance business. Second marriage for both.

When I opened my door to them, they were laughing like two naughty children.

"We have to get a goose like that," Cathy said. "We'd be the talk of the old folks' home."

"They already talk about us," Dan teased, and we all laughed.

Cathy, a petite blonde, and Dan, a tall and athletic-looking man, sat close together on the settee. He held her hand and she beamed at him.

I poured them each a coffee as we got started.

"How did you two meet?" I asked them.

"In kindergarten," Dan said. "Cathy was the cutest girl."

"And Dan was the smartest boy," Cathy said.

"We dated in high school, but we lost touch when Dan went away to college. We both married other people," added Cathy. "And had families."

"But there was always something missing," Dan said.

They looked at each other, then at me.

"After both of our spouses died, we saw each other again at our high school reunion," said Dan. "And that was that."

The Memory of Lemon

"I could watch paint dry with Dan and it would be interesting," Cathy said.

He squeezed her hand.

I took a moment to center myself and allow my intuition to kick in.

The flavor that came to me was a luscious Suncrest peach that I once had in California. This heirloom variety needed time to ripen on the tree to achieve its peak flavor. Unlike other peaches that were picked unripe so they would ship more easily, Suncrest peaches had to be eaten right away. But they were worth it—fragrant, luscious, juice-dripping-down-your-chin perfection.

The problem was that I didn't have any peach mousse or filling. But I quickly improvised.

"You're getting married in August, when peaches are in season," I said. "Taste our browned butter yellow cake with a little apricot and some vanilla-almond buttercream, and see what you think."

As they each took a small bite of what I hoped would be their signature cake flavors, I was drawn back into the taste of the peach. It was juicy and sweet, but as I got close to the center of the peach, there was an off flavor of rot. In my mind's eye, I could see a darkened area close to the center that would soon cause the peach to wither. I knew what that meant.

I didn't know whose life would be blighted, but these golden days were few. They wouldn't have much time together.

I wanted to cry. Here these two lovely people had found each other again and were so ready to be happy together. What if Ben and I had waited too long?

Luke had always dodged the issue of children. "We've got all the time in the world for kids, Neely," was his usual response. "Let's have our fun now."

I was in my midthirties. I could feel my biological clock starting to tick, louder and louder. What if this divorce dragged on for years? What if waiting kept Ben and me from having children? He would be a great dad. I could picture a tiny baby nestled in his arms, how tender and protective he would be.

I offered Cathy and Dan more cupcakes, then took one for myself and piled on the sweet buttercream, willing the sugar to do its calming work.

When I got back to the bakery, I simply said to Maggie, "Peach and almond."

Perhaps all that had softened me up for Ben's first letter. I read it in the back workroom. And promptly allowed myself to quietly sob.

Dear Neely,

If you're reading this, then the florist delivery guy did his job. I had to explain what I meant by "Put them in the goose" to the lady who took my order. If the tulips are fresh and this letter isn't soggy, I'll be sort of happy.

I miss you.

It's hard for me to talk about my feelings, but here goes.

We have known each other for a long time, and it always seems that we get to that dividing line between friendship and love, and then something happens and we never step over.

I would be good to you, you know that.

The Memory of Lemon

*I want to make you happy. I want us to be happy together.
I want us to be happy together for a long, long time.
I hope this is the way you feel, too.
But if you don't feel this way, have second thoughts, or
think I'm rushing you, tell me.*

*Take care,
Ben*

14

Neely

Today is the first day of the rest of my life.

I was filing for divorce from Luke.

It was May 15, exactly six months since I had closed on Gran's house and officially established residency in Ohio. My appointment with my attorney was later that morning.

I sprang out of bed, dressed quickly, and tucked Ben's letter, folded into a manageable square, in my bra. Maybe that sounded weird, but I wanted it close to my heart. I looked at myself in the mirror and didn't see any geometric outline through my rhubarb-colored T-shirt, so it was all good.

When I arrived at the bakery at dawn, Norb was baking sugar cookies shaped like spring flower baskets that Jett would decorate for a special order when she came in that afternoon.

"Everything's coming up roses, Norb," I said.

"If you say so." Norb was a man of few words, a person who liked routine. Lining trays with parchment paper, arranging these nonspreading cookies so they were exactly one inch apart, sliding the tray into the oven with the same smooth motion. Over and over and over again. Watching his calm efficiency, it was easy to forget that Norb had enough built-in domestic drama from his wife, Bonnie, for two men. Baking dozens of sugar cookies probably helped keep him sane.

I made myself a Cuban coffee: dark-roast beans and hot milk with just a hint of sweetness. I didn't want to tempt fate with a message in the latte foam. What if it forecast a bad day?

I checked our orders, the spreadsheet, the phone messages. A slow day for a change.

Maggie could deal with all of it when she came in, so I decided to visit Gran. She was most lucid in the morning. At Mount Saint Mary's, relatives could visit at any time if they knew the security code to get in the memory care wing.

"I'll be back in a little bit, Norb. Going to see Gran."

"Without treats?"

Good point. I opened one of our robin's egg blue bakery boxes. I picked up a dozen still-warm, orange-frosted cinnamon rolls with tissuelike bakery paper, nestling them together in the box. Maybe the flavors would nudge Gran's memory to the "orange day" she recalled a few months back, or to any day, for that matter. Anything to light up her face from the frozen mask it had become.

As I pulled into the parking lot, I could see the flickering candlelight in the stained glass windows of Bernadette's grotto, where I had come in the past winter to soothe my weary soul.

I walked toward the nursing facility's entrance.

The male and female concrete geese, guarding the door, had molted April's yellow slickers and umbrellas for May's new look. Their outfits channeled Marie Antoinette Meets Mozart, complete with white wigs made out of cotton batting and pastel brocade clothing. Each goose held a bouquet of silk flowers under one wing.

Fortified with a little humor, I punched in the security code and entered the memory care wing. Gran was in her wheelchair, pulled up to a table. Her name tag proclaimed she was Dorothy M. O'Neil, and I hoped she knew that today. Her hair was brushed and she had on a pale pink blouse and navy pants that were a little too big. I made a note to tell Aunt Helen that Gran needed new clothes in a smaller size. I brought a chair over, opened the box of bakery goodies, and let Gran smell the orange-frosted cinnamon rolls. Her eyes lit up.

"Brand-new day," she said.

"And it's going to be a good one." I tore off a piece of cinnamon roll and fed it to her.

"Jack," she said, opening her eyes wide as she looked at me.

"You mean Dad?"

"Jack. Brand-new day." She sat up a little straighter.

"I remember that, Gran. You made these rolls for him when I was a little girl. He seemed so happy." I gave Gran another piece of cinnamon roll.

"Happy."

"Dad has been writing to me, Gran. He's in Kansas City. He says maybe he can come home soon."

"Home."

"I miss him, Gran, but I'm mad at him, too. He left us. Not just me and Mom, but you, too. And Aunt Helen."

"Us."

"I was fifteen years old. You were still working."

"Emmert's."

"Yes, you worked at Emmert's Insurance." I offered another piece of cinnamon roll. Gran opened her mouth for more roll.

She looked at me blankly and kept chewing.

I gave her a sip of orange juice. "If he did come back, all of us would be on edge, especially Mom. There would be drama. I've got enough drama right now just trying to get divorced."

"I should have," Gran said.

"Should have what?"

"Divorced George. He was a bastard."

"He died before I was born. But Helen, Mom, Dad, you—nobody seems to have a good word to say about him."

"He drank."

"Dad has a drinking problem, too. Did you know that?"

"My daddy drove a taxi," Gran said unexpectedly, her gaze drifting over to slender Sister Agnes in her trademark pale blue velour pantsuit as she eased her walker toward Olive Amici's room.

I first met Sister Agnes when I took her story-writing day camp session at Mount Saint Mary's the summer before sixth grade. During the past few months, I had learned a lot more about her life.

But I was still surprised when I suddenly got the twin flavors of apple jelly and peanut butter.

I closed my eyes. That combination reminded me of Maggie's

The Memory of Lemon

mother, Patsy, but I let that thought go so the story would build on its own.

I could see the front seat of an old-fashioned black taxicab. A little pad of June 1942 calendar cards that read *Mooney's Taxi* was stuck in the sun visor. The taxi was waiting in front of the old brick convent with its mansard roof. In the front seat, with the driver, was Gran, who looked to be a young teenager. She had a lot of papers in her school bag, but a happy, I'm-finished-with-that air to her, so it must have been the last day of convent school.

"I made all A's," the young Gran proudly announced to her father.

"We'll stop at the Friendly Café for lemon meringue pie after we take this poor girl to St. Joseph's," he replied. "Remember, sweetie, we must be kind."

"I know, Dad."

He reached over and took his daughter's hand. They both knew, without saying, that having to be taken to St. Joseph's was the worst thing that could happen to a promising young woman.

But why was I seeing this? As I started to ask, the scene shifted, out of the taxi window, across the brick drive, and up three stories and through an open window into what must have been an infirmary room, judging from the metal hospital bed.

I saw a peanut butter and apple jelly sandwich with several visible bites gone from the soft white bread. The lunch tray must have been sitting on the little table for hours, as the bread was dry.

A tall young woman rose from her sitting position on the narrow bed. She smoothed the creases from her thin cotton dress that was now shorter in front and longer in the back. She gave up trying to fasten the belt. She took it off and put it with the length of dimity fabric and her few other personal items in the carpetbag.

She looked at her reflection in the window of the little room. Her wavy blond hair was parted on the side and swept back from her face with hair combs. Gone were the dark circles under her eyes. Her cheeks were plumper.

Sister Michael Mary, the head of the convent, urged her to sew while she was away. "It's best to keep busy, my child."

Sister also reminded her that if all went well, the young woman would be back to start her novitiate in the fall. Sister assured her that she would be welcomed back. What happened couldn't have been her fault. The terrible incident had made her lose her memory.

The nuns at St. Joseph's would take care of her, just like they took care of all the girls who came to them.

And they would find a good home for the baby.

I looked up again at Sister Agnes and smiled, a little sadly.

Gran's moment of clarity and my vision had come and gone.

But it made me think again of Patsy. *The dimity dress on her doll. Could she possibly be Sister Agnes's child?*

Gran chewed her roll and reached out for another sip of orange juice.

"Blue hands," she said.

I looked at my fingernails. Sure enough, there was a faint trace of robin's egg blue in my cuticles.

"I know. Maybe I should wear gloves when I work with buttercream. But back to Dad. Maybe he still has a drinking problem. And if he came back, he'd make it our problem again."

Gran's eyes glazed over. She slumped to the side of her chair. Maybe I had upset her, the last thing I wanted to do.

"Well, Gran, maybe I shouldn't be mad at him. Maybe he did the best he could. Maybe I should be more understanding."

"Orange."

"Orange you going to feed me more cinnamon roll?" I smiled and offered Gran another bite.

When Gran had eaten all she wanted, I kissed her, left the remaining rolls at the nurses' station, and headed to Rainbow Cake.

There, the morning rush was making Maggie look a little frazzled, so I quickly put on my apron and started helping customers.

When the crowd died down, Roshonda came in, eager for news and her standard macchiato with caramel syrup. "Give it to me," she said, holding out her well-manicured hand. I plunked her coffee mug on the table. She gave me a look. "*The letter.* Let me read it before you send it this time."

"I don't have anything to show you just yet."

"Girl, do you want this man or not?"

"I'm serious, Ro. I'm going to write Ben after I see my attorney this morning."

"What's he going to do?"

"File my divorce petition. It's been six months to the day."

"Well, at least you're getting somewhere." She took a sip of her coffee and did that little shiver she does when she's pleased. "And I know you have Ben's letter in your bra."

"What?" I looked down at my chest.

"I knew it!" she said, laughing. "The women in your family always store their valuables there. Your gran put that little muslin bag with rolled-up cash in her bra when we went to Gatlinburg, and your aunt Helen put her whole checkbook in her bra when we went to look at Notre Dame for college."

"No wonder I didn't get a scholarship," I murmured.

"Well, spill."

"I'm not going to show you the letter, but he says he wants us to finally cross over the line from friendship into love."

"And?"

"He doesn't want anything coming out of the blue to wreck things at the last minute."

"Fool me once, shame on me. Fool me twice—oh, yeah, he was fooled twice," Roshonda said, sipping her coffee. "Two really bad dates with you, when the same man screwed things up. Ben must hate Luke Davis."

"That makes two of us."

"You don't hate Luke. He's too damn sexy to hate. The charm just wore off," Roshonda said. Her smug look was replaced by a frown. "But Ben could hate him. Luke is every decent, trustworthy guy's nightmare. The smooth-talking, good-looking, successful guy who can steal your girlfriend right out from under you. Except there's been no 'under' yet with Ben"—she raised her eyebrows meaningfully—"and technically, you're still Luke's wife."

"Give me back that free coffee."

"You know I'm on your side. But you have really dug yourself a hole here, girl."

I glared at Roshonda and said with a bit of an edge, "Ben says he wants us to be forever."

Roshonda sighed. "Now, that's romantic." She checked a text message on her phone, hurriedly rose from the table, and grabbed my arm. "When you write the letter this time, it has to be good. *Good*." She squeezed my arm for emphasis. "You call me! We'll talk!" And she did that sexy-woman power walk out the door, across the street, and straight to her office. As I watched her from our display window, two cars slowed down, all the better for their drivers to get a look at a sleek, tall, Kerry Washington lookalike in a pale blue sheath and killer heels.

I wondered whom she was seeing. Was the handsome guy she had been dating in March still on the scene?

Roshonda was a love-'em-and-leave-'em type. She was picky. She was immune to charm. A guy couldn't use the same old tired lines on her. He had to work hard. And she never introduced us to a guy, never even told us his name, unless she was serious about him and pretty sure she'd let him stick around.

But the Roshonda of the past few weeks was normal Roshonda times ten. I had never seen her like that before. She practically exuded sexiness and power. Who was the mystery man?

Speaking of mystery men, there was a guy in an SUV with dark tinted windows parked across the street. He had been there at least since I had returned from my visit with Gran two hours before. Who waited for somebody that long in Millcreek Valley? Hmm.

Maybe it was time to find out, or at least rule out the one possibility that concerned me. I suspected this was the start of the Luke Davis Reign of Psychological Terror. *You can't leave me if I don't want you to.* If so, it would end today when I filed for divorce and became officially separated. *Bring it, sleazeball.*

I put on a clean white pastry chef's jacket and did a quick touch-up in the bathroom. At least I would look a little more professional when I saw my attorney.

As I drove west on Benson Street across the little bridge into Lockton that always gave me the shivers, I noticed that the SUV was following me. He kept a few cars back from me on Mill Street, through Lockton, and then continued as Mill Street turned into Fairview Avenue.

What an exciting life I led. I was being tailed. I hoped Luke—or more likely Charlie Wheeler representing Luke—was paying this guy extra for boring duty. *Knock yourself out.*

I thought about going into a shop, then leaving through the back door and finding an alternate route to my attorney's office. But no. I wanted Charlie and Luke to know that I was seeing my own attorney. Why keep that a secret?

I slammed my car door with a little more vehemence than usual. I marched in the door with a little more purpose, startling the receptionist.

When she saw me through to Jonathan Billings's office, I sat down with a flourish, ready to sign a stack of papers and set the legal ball rolling.

"There has been a development, Neely," he said.

I narrowed my eyes. "Yes, I know. I'm being followed this morning."

His eyes widened. Jonathan was a slender, pale man with coal black hair that he surely had to lacquer with hair spray to keep it in such a perfect coif. His firm specialized in divorce. But it was never a confidence-building sight to see your attorney gulp.

"That doesn't surprise me. I just got this letter today." He passed a paper across the desk to me. "It cites your prenup again. It reiterates that Luke could claim all property accumulated during your marriage if he can prove you've been unfaithful. Like your current residence. And the bakery."

I was stunned. How had Luke and Charlie known to send the

letter here? If I didn't quite believe it before, I believed it now. I was being followed—in cyberspace, on my phone, in person. Why was Luke pushing so hard? The night we'd talked on the phone, he had sounded lonely, not angry. Why was he trying to take everything away from me?

"These photos also came today."

Jonathan opened a manila envelope and took out several eight-by-ten black-and-white glossies.

I looked at them, one by one. Ben and me holding hands, walking into Boca for our ill-fated date. Me in my sexy dress. An intimate close-up of Ben's hand pressing the small of my back. The two of us clinking champagne glasses at dinner. Smiling for Charlie's camera.

The evening had started out so magically, it made my heart ache. There was nothing sordid here, just two people falling in love. The problem was that one of them was still married. And Charlie Wheeler was setting her up for a fall. A big fall.

"But I haven't done anything. And I'm filing for divorce."

"Well, maybe not today."

15

SEPTEMBER 1948
MILLCREEK VALLEY

The Wanderer

"It's a lot to take in," the newly bereaved man said.

Two deaths were a lot for anyone to take in, thought Dorothy Mooney.

Small boned with reddish blond hair and clear gray eyes, she sat across the large partner's desk from the beneficiary as he read and signed the stack of papers: the deed to the house, the bank account statements, the life insurance policy, and the inventory of the contents of the safety-deposit box. She also had a ring of keys for the Benson Street house, the car, and the detached garage.

Emmert's Insurance was in the same building as the man's attorney, Joseph Sand. Twenty-year-old Dorothy sometimes worked at the attorney's office when there was an overflow, like that morning, and not as much business for Emmert's. Mr. Sand had explained everything to Mr. O'Neil and witnessed his signature of the will. Dorothy was completing the follow-up.

George O'Neil's curly auburn head bent over the papers, but Dorothy had noticed his frayed cuffs, the short and wide old-fashioned tie, the well-worn leather bomber jacket, his scuffed shoes, and his general air of being down-at-the-heels. Still, he seemed saddened at the sudden loss of both parents in an automobile accident. He looked to be about thirty, maybe a little older. No wedding ring.

Mr. and Mrs. Thomas O'Neil had seemed a courteous couple. He worked on the railroad and she was a homemaker. They never talked about a son. Dorothy had thought they were childless, but here he was.

She leaned back in the wooden swivel desk chair as he read the documents, allowing her mind to wander. It was sort of a game, really. Seeing what flavor came to mind when she focused on him, what story she could make up to go with it. Dorothy imagined she would taste his late mother's pot roast or his father's favorite breath mint. And then would come a cozy family scene of birthday dinners or Sunday drives.

No, that was an unfortunate thought, Dorothy chided herself. A Sunday drive had been the cause of their deaths.

She started over. She relaxed.

George O'Neil.

Something with a bitter edge, sort of an apple-like fruity middle, a burning finish. Bourbon. A twist of lemon.

Of course, he must be drinking at such a loss. But the flavor pulled her into a deeper place. Old resentments. She gazed out

The Memory of Lemon

the window, letting her mind wander, and in a few moments, the stories came.

"Where is the lazy son of a bitch?" *A younger version of Thomas O'Neil in a railroad conductor's uniform walked into the kitchen, slamming the back door behind him.*

"Now, Tom, don't get yourself all worked up again," *his wife, Grace, said as she mashed the potatoes at the stove.* "Dinner's almost ready."

"I told him to put the trash out in the alley this morning, and the trash is still by the back door. Now we'll have rats." *He slung his metal lunchbox across the room, where it hit the low windowsill and then clattered to the linoleum floor.*

"Tom!"

He rammed his coat on a peg. Then barged through the door to the pantry where the medicinal whiskey was kept. He pulled a glass from the junk drawer and poured himself a slug, downed it, then another and another. He leaned in to the counter of the Hoosier cabinet where Grace kept the spices, sugar, and flour. The small stained glass window high up in the pantry wall sparkled colors on the back of the pantry door. But Tom didn't see them.

He heard muffled voices through the door. Tom squeezed the glass, trying to control his rage.

"You were supposed to take the trash to the alley before you went to school, George."

"Sorry, Ma, I forgot. Jimmy was going to show me his Ted Kluszewski baseball card."

"Well, your father is angry."

"He's always mad, Ma."

Tom slammed the whiskey glass down on the counter and stormed back into the kitchen. He grabbed eight-year-old George by the collar and slammed him up against the board and batten wall.

George's green eyes bulged and his face grew red.

Grace pulled Tom off his son, and the boy slid to the floor. Tom elbowed Grace out of the way and struck George, leaving a white handprint on the boy's flushed cheek.

Grace sobbed into her apron.

Dorothy couldn't watch any more of this scene, which played in her mind like the black-and-white film noir she had just seen at the Emory Theater.

Poor George. What a rotten childhood.

When George looked up from signing the papers, she gave him a warm smile.

"When the dust settles, do you want to go out dancing sometime? Maybe the Friendly Cafe? They've got a good jukebox," George asked a little nervously.

It wouldn't hurt to go out with him. It might cheer him up.

"I love to dance," she told him.

16

Neely

"Now my attorney wants a fifty-thousand-dollar retainer!" I shrieked.

"Calm down, girl," Roshonda said. We sat across from each other in the conversation area of her office, four white leather club chairs arranged around a glass-topped hammered metal table. She slid a tall glass of sparkling water with a sprig of mint and a lemon slice across the table to me, along with a lemongrass-colored coaster. "So, the teacup poodle has a mean bite after all. But he bit you instead of Luke. You didn't pay him the extra money, did you?"

"I don't have fifty thousand dollars to throw at this. And my head is spinning from all this legal stuff. Now we have to go through arbitration. And if I file in Ohio, it will take longer because Luke lives in another state."

"Well, did you really think this was going to be easy?"

"Whose side are you on?"

"Yours, of course." Roshonda reached across to me, her elegant, manicured, completely-in-control hand calming my shaking one.

I took a deep breath and a gulp of water.

"And you haven't heard the best part yet. I really could lose a big chunk of the settlement and maybe my house and business. I thought that was just cage rattling."

"Well, you already knew about the prenup and how it left things to Luke's discretion."

"Charlie Wheeler took photos of Ben and me on our date and we looked very cozy together. He just sent them to my attorney as another warning shot. And someone followed me over to Jonathan's office today. I don't know what Luke and Charlie are trying to do."

She nodded, gravely considering the shifting landscape of my life.

"Has Luke seen the photos?"

"I don't know. I don't think he had seen them when I talked to him the other night."

"Do you still have Ben's letter?"

I touched my chest. It was still there.

"Give it to me."

I shrank back.

"I'm not going to read it. I'm going to keep it for you. I'm going to keep all of them. If Luke has someone following you, and someone hacking into your e-mail and phone, he could also have someone sneak into your house every so often. They don't need to be finding letters."

"But why?" My shoulders sagged. I sat forward, my elbows on my knees, and pressed the cool glass of water to my flushed face. "What's really going on here, Neely? Luke never struck me as a cheap, vindictive person. He's got plenty of money without going after what you've worked so hard to establish here. He knows Ben is a good guy. I never pegged Luke as the 'if I can't have her, I'll trash her' type. I don't get it."

"I don't, either." I pressed my lips together.

We sat in silence. Roshonda leaned back in her chair, with arms crossed. She pressed her pointer finger to her upper lip, something she always did when she was pondering something.

My thoughts were going in circles, not finding a viable way out of this mess. But Roshonda suddenly sat up straight.

"It sounds like Luke and Charlie are playing good cop/bad cop. Luke appeals to your heart, Charlie scares you to death."

Roshonda took a sip of her drink and tapped a manicured nail on the glass-topped table. "Here's the plan. Before you pay your attorney another dime, you have to find out what's really going on with Luke. You have to talk to him again. You have to go directly to Luke to get him to stop this."

"How?"

"You call him and talk to him. As many times as it takes. Simple as that."

She tapped a text message into her phone. "And I know people in the entertainment industry that I can discreetly ask for a favor or two. We have to know if Luke is up for some big commercial, a reality show, something where he has to have a certain image. Don't worry, Neely." She raised her glass and toasted mine. "We'll get this fixed."

I relaxed a little bit. I had a plan. It was a good plan. Instead of retreating, I was going forward.

"And what do I do about the fifty thousand dollars?"

"Well, don't look at me." Roshonda chuckled, and then got serious. "Let's try this two-pronged approach first and then see what happens."

When I walked across the street to the bakery, my step was much lighter than when I had trudged over to Roshonda's office an hour earlier.

"We got a few more graduation party orders today," Maggie said as I came in. "Jett's working on the sugar cookie baskets.

"Cuban coffee again?" she asked. She sprinkled a little sugar in the bottom of my Tiffany-blue mug, then added the dark brew and a froth of milk before she handed it over to me. "How did the meeting with your attorney go?"

"Well . . ." I took a sip and let the sugar-calming magic happen. "It's going to be a lot more complicated than I thought."

"Isn't it always? And speaking of complicated, John and I are going out tonight."

"John?"

"The *Professor*," Maggie growled. "I'm amazed that peer pressure still works. You better hope this date isn't a total disaster or we could lose our best customer."

"Where are you going on a Thursday night?"

"A lecture on campus. Something about telomeres."

My raised eyebrow said it all.

"Don't ask because I don't know, either. And then we're going for ice cream afterward."

"You'll need it," I said, patting her on the shoulder. "So how

The Memory of Lemon

bad can it be? First dates are always awkward. At least you'll be able to tell us all about the fascinating world of telomeres tomorrow." I gave her shoulder a squeeze. "Remember, he's a good guy who thinks you're really hot. And Roshonda's homework: You're a magnetic, charming, sexy woman."

She rolled her eyes, handed me the stack of mail, and harrumphed back to the workroom to check on Jett.

There was another letter from my dad. I slipped it into my purse to read later.

If there ever was a night I needed my mom's home cooking, this was it.

I closed up just after six o'clock, grateful for a slow afternoon for once.

I brought a coconut cream pie, Mom's favorite. Coconut's hard, dirty, shaggy exterior didn't promise much. But when you cracked it open and then cleaned it up, it surprised you with the smooth white riches inside. In a coconut shell, this was my mother's mission in life—to tackle the litter, the dust, the stains, the residue of life and tidy them all up. Her sweet reward was that exotic state of everything-in-its-clean-place, always a mirage in the distance while she was living with Helen. Coconut cream pie fed her soul.

At our weekly dinners, I was in charge of dessert. Helen poured cocktails. And Mom, of course, made dinner. We all cleaned up the kitchen afterward. I washed, Helen dried, and Mom put away, even though she had a dishwasher. It was actually quite soothing, another reliable rhythm to my new life here.

As I drove past my old piano teacher's brick bungalow, I checked out her porch goose, dressed as Beethoven, complete with a tiny piano, the same outfit from when I was taking lessons.

Mrs. Elmlinger had recycled a bobbed wig to make Beethoven's unruly hair.

Thank goodness for things that never seem to change.

And I was doubly thankful when Aunt Helen handed me one of her obligatory whiskey sours when I walked in their door. Homemade lemonade and bourbon, our family's signature cocktail.

Helen and Mom, sisters-in-law, had settled into their Odd Couple living arrangement after I went off to college. Mom was a neat freak; Helen was a slob. But somehow it worked. Little rituals like Helen making the cocktails before a dinner of Mom's home cooking were part of the glue that held them together.

Helen looked different, more put together. She had colored her hair. She wore lipstick. A high-necked white blouse replaced her usual Fighting Irish sweatshirt and her jeans were of the skinny, not the mom, variety. The moccasins on her feet were a step up from tennis shoes, but still made allowances for her bunions. Maybe she had had a meeting today.

"You look a little stressed out, honey," Mom said as we sat down to dinner, with maternal radar that was unerringly accurate.

"Busy day," I said, sipping my drink.

"Did you file for divorce yet?" Helen asked, disregarding the kick I felt Mom give her under the table.

"Well, we started the proceedings. But we have to wait to file for a bit more. I just want this to be over with." I sighed.

"Well, meatloaf always makes everything better," Helen said, putting a thick slice on my plate.

Mom added a mound of mashed potatoes and gave me a helping of slow-simmered green beans.

The Memory of Lemon

We chatted about our day. Mom at the parochial elementary school, Helen at the sprinkler company.

I talked about my visit with Gran that morning. "She remembered Emmert's and her father driving a taxi. She even talked about George, the grandfather I never met. Why didn't anybody seem to like him?"

Helen looked at me, then at my mom. *Uh-oh.* "He died when I was six," said Helen. "But from what I gathered, he hit the bars every night and then came home drunk and mean. I remember waking up once, thinking I was having a bad dream, but it was him yelling at our mom."

"How did he die?"

"He was walking home drunk one night. They think he hit his head somehow. They found him in the creek under the bridge to Lockton. After that, Mom got her old job back at Emmert's Insurance and she never really talked about him again. I haven't even thought about him in years."

So, Dad must have been eight, old enough to notice more than his little sister. No wonder he kept his drinking secret in high school.

After the main course, I cleared the plates, rinsed them out in the sink, and cut us each a slice of pie. Helen poured the coffee.

"Well, Claire, I've got some news," Aunt Helen said when we sat back down. "I haven't even told your mother."

Mom and I both looked up from our coconut cream pie.

"I have a date this weekend."

"A what?" Mom sputtered.

"A date. With a man. You know, when two people go out to the movies or have dinner or something like that?" said Helen.

"Well, that's wonderful," I said. "Who is he?"

"I met him at work. He's a plumber we use a lot for commercial installations. He just got divorced."

"Well, he could be on the rebound. He could be trouble, Helen," Mom warned.

"Don't worry, Cindy. I'm not going to bring him home here and make out on the couch or anything."

"Helen!"

"Where are you going on your date?" I asked, taking us back to safer territory.

"There's a fried catfish supper at the VFW this weekend."

"Sounds perfect," I said. *A fried catfish supper and a lecture on telomeres. Be still, my heart.*

When I got home, I took Dad's letter upstairs to my office to read. I settled into the oversized leather club chair with the ottoman, meant as a holiday gift for Luke, which I didn't end up giving him. I hated it, but it would do for now. And I reluctantly had to admit that it was comfortable.

Dad must have cleaned out the City Vue's stationery because this letter was several pages.

Dear Claire,

Thanks for writing back. I can't tell you what that means to me, how I look forward to your letters.

And the lemon cookies!

I don't know if it was the cookies or the print-outs you sent about indigo and blue hands and North Vietnam, but I feel like I'm getting closer to remembering what happened to me.

The Memory of Lemon

But here's what I do remember.

You wanted to know how I became a helicopter pilot.

A week after I graduated from high school—that was June 1968—I went to the Navy recruiting office and told them I wanted to be a pilot. They said I had to have a college degree and then apply. That wasn't gonna happen. So I went to the Army recruiting office. They said I could be a warrant officer, a rank in between enlisted men and commissioned officers. Basically, a fancy name for a helicopter pilot. A warrant officer was in charge of the helicopter and the flight to and from, but not the mission itself. The only hitch was I had to be eighteen to take the warrant officer flight test. I was seventeen.

I remembered Dad's senior photo from high school. The serious young man in a sport coat with a white shirt and tie. So young. So clean-cut. I didn't want to imagine what he looked like now after years of living rough. I went back to reading his letter.

I waited. I spent the summer at a lot of backyard kegger parties with my buddies, listened to a lot of Beatles and Rolling Stones. Drank a lot of beer. I worked at Hinky's, this crummy bar, where I washed glasses and served crappy hamburgers to the drunks. But the main attraction for me was that I could sneak all the drinks I wanted. At the end of the night, when the bartenders were too tired to notice, I'd pour off a little booze into my own bottle and sneak it home. I had a drinking buddy, this girl who was a friend of my sister Helen's. Diane Amici. We used to hole up in a neighbor's garage and pass the bottle.

My dad. Drinking to feel better.

Just for the record, Diane Amici was not my type at all. We just drank. Mom always said that drinking alone is what killed my dad. I told Diane that if we drank with other people, we'd be okay. We were all wrong.

But back to the helicopter pilot stuff.

I had to wait a couple of months for an opening at Hunter Army Airfield in Savannah.

Mom made our turkey dinner early because I started the Monday before Thanksgiving. November 25, 1968.

I loved flight school. There's no better feeling in the world than piloting this big ol' bird—you're making it fly with just a two-blade rotor on top and a smaller two-blade rotor on the tail. Everything below you is so tiny, so inconsequential. All your cares, all your worries, all your fears. None of it mattered.

But it could be scary as shit, too. You had to know how to get out of any situation. You'd be at the controls, up in the air, and your instructor would just turn the engine off. You had to figure it out damn quick. You prayed that you didn't screw up and get someone else hurt or killed.

I left for Vietnam on May 15, 1970. Another red-letter date because the countdown started from there. I didn't know that in Vietnam I would never know what day of the week it was. Friday was like Sunday was like Wednesday. But I always knew the date because everybody was counting down the days until their tour of duty was up. I couldn't wait to go and then, once I got there, I couldn't wait to go back home.

The Memory of Lemon

When we landed at Cam Ranh Bay, the first thing that hit me was the smell. Piss and rot and gunpowder all rolled into one. And then the heat and humidity like someone trying to suffocate you with a pillow over your face.

We had five days of training about Vietnam. It wasn't like World War II—D-day and tanks and take back territory. Our mission in 'Nam was search and destroy—locate the enemy and their supplies and take everything out, but not leave men on the ground to hold the fort. There was no fort.

I dropped troops into battle. I flew the wounded back to the base hospital. I dropped Army Rangers into Laos and Cambodia for reconnaissance missions. I flew Army brass up to Quang Tri and Khe San. After a while, I didn't ask myself if what I was doing was right or wrong. I just kept my head down and did my job so that nobody I knew got killed.

Simple as that.

You're the person I love best in the world, Claire. I don't want to burden you with this. Thank you for helping me understand myself.

Love,
Dad

17

Neely

The next morning, I found another bouquet under the wing of my front porch goose. Fragrant sweet peas and a letter in a sealed plastic bag wrapped around the stems. I quickly brought the bouquet inside and put the ruffled lavender blossoms in water. As my coffee brewed, I took the letter out of the bag and tried to make it lie flat, to no avail. With the letter in one hand and my mug in the other, I went into my parlor and curled up on the settee. As the pale light poured in the windows, I read Ben's letter.

Neely,

In a weird way, I like this old-fashioned courtship. Maybe I am old-fashioned. I'm definitely more of a planner. But that doesn't mean I can't be flexible. I could make adjustments on the football field. I can make adjustments in business. But for some reason, I have a hard time making adjustments when it comes to you. We almost get "there" and something always happens.

Hope everything went well at Billings's, but if it didn't, I will adjust.

There. I really like declaring my intentions. I said I was old-fashioned, didn't I?

So here goes.

I want us to grow old together.

Okay, maybe that's not going to sweep you off your feet, but that's not my style anyway.

I want us to have a home. Argue over whether my ratty old recliner goes in the living room or is banished to the basement. Bicker over who left the dirty dishes in the sink.

I want us to have a family. I want to teach our kids how to play soccer and how to drive. Remember when I taught you how to drive a stick shift? My neck has never quite recovered from the whiplash.

I want us to laugh.

I want to know that your face on the pillow will be the last thing I see at night and the first thing I see the next morning.

I want to hold you again. Sooner, rather than later.
Ben

The letter rolled up on itself again and I just let it go. I let the coffee go cold.

How I wished . . .

The Memory of Lemon

How I wished I didn't have to tell Ben about the exorbitant retainer, about the delay.

I went back to the kitchen and took my cell phone out of my purse. I had to get this settled with Luke.

Luke had two lines on his phone, one for business and the other personal, with Charlie micromanaging both accounts. Both lines had a 212 New York City area code. Charlie monitored sponsorship and media calls on the business line; Charlie also fended off—or paid off—the ladies who tried to make themselves permanent fixtures in Luke's personal life.

But I also knew Luke had another cell phone, one with a 513 Queen City area code, the one his mother always called. The one I had called the other night. That line was our "if anything happens" number, a way to stay connected, but sane, if and when the media camped out on our doorstep. He used to keep this phone permanently charging in an outlet in the corner of our Brooklyn brownstone bedroom; he didn't carry it with him every day. Since he didn't have this phone with him, he'd only hear it ring when he was at home and near the bedroom on the third floor.

I looked at the time. It was just after six a.m. For Luke, in the off-season, the night was still young. He could be out. He could be home but *unavailable*. He could be traveling. But I called him anyway.

No answer. I didn't leave a voice mail message.

Instead, I texted him: I have someone camped out on my doorstep this time. Please call me.

I put the coffee mug in the dishwasher and went upstairs to my bedroom.

At my dressing table, I poufed my hair on top of my head, put on lipstick, and spritzed myself with Chanel. I opened the buttons on my blouse to show a little cleavage. My skinny jeans were all right as they were. It felt a little silly to me, but I was doing my Roshonda homework. At the last minute. Right before school started.

I was imagining myself as a magnetic, charming, sexy woman. I grabbed the bottle of perfume and ignored my robin's egg blue–stained fingernails. I eased my feet into my tallest heels and sashayed across the hall into my office.

I sat down at my desk and spritzed my new stationery, thinking about what I needed to write to Ben. The news from Jonathan Billings the previous day hadn't been good.

Maybe by the time Ben got my letter in the mail, Luke would have called and this trying time would be behind us.

After Ben's latest letter, I couldn't let him down again. I couldn't give him this much bad news.

Maybe I needed to tell Ben that I was going to start dealing directly with Luke, the new plan that Roshonda had suggested. But then I didn't want Ben getting all protective and worried. I decided to save that disclosure for another time.

I settled back in my chair, picked up the pen, and conjured up an image of Ben. His sandy hair, tousled. His chiseled face with all the nicks and dents I loved so much. The scar above his eyebrow. His nose that would never be perfectly straight again. Stubble on his cheeks. His lips, so soft and yet so insistent.

His broad shoulders and muscled chest. His powerful legs. I imagined myself lying next to him in the dark, right before sleep, our faces almost touching. I imagined the kind of pillow talk we might have after making love.

Fond. Funny. Serious. Loving.

Planning our future.
And then I began to write.

Ben,

> *I loved the sweet peas and your letter this morning.*
> *I have to say I like this old-fashioned courtship, too.*
> *You can have your ratty old recliner in whatever room you want, as long as I get to have a claw-foot tub and a scented bath.*
> *Put your nose here xxxxx for a preview. You can wash my back. Or better yet, join me.*
> *For now, let's hold on to that.*
> *Jonathan said there might be another complication if I try to file in Ohio, while Luke lives in New York. So he suggests we wait a while longer. This is so frustrating, I know, but I want to do this right. For Gran, for you, and for me.*
> *Before you know it, we'll be at the Ballou wedding in Augusta, where both of us have every work reason to be. Maybe we'll find a way to sneak off before the bloodhounds follow.*
> *I'm trying to be brave and patient and upbeat, but I miss you so, so much.*

Yours,
Neely

I straggled into the bakery later than I had planned. "Here." Maggie came up behind me, tapped me on the shoulder, and handed me a latte. "I asked for special guidance on this one, and I think you'll like what you see."

I looked down at the milky foam on top of the latte and there it was: a wavy star.

"Is that a telomere, by any chance?"

She guffawed. "I actually fell asleep during the lecture and woke up leaning against John's shoulder. He had his arm around me. I don't know how I feel about that," she said, stiffly.

"I think it's sweet. He didn't have his hand anywhere else, did he?" I teased.

Maggie rolled her eyes. "Torrid romance and a preschooler don't go together."

"Things to look forward to," I muttered, and then pointed to the wavy star in my coffee. "Well, tell me what this sign means before my coffee gets cold."

"It's your lodestar. The thing you know is true. All you have to do is keep it in sight, and it will lead you home."

"You've been reading too much Martha Beck," I said. My smirk was supposed to be ironic, but Maggie wasn't fooled. She patted my arm again.

"Ten minutes to opening."

What was the one thing I knew to be true? I took another sip of my latte. The lodestar disappeared. I quoted Norb: *Damn*.

"Where are you going on your next date?"

"John's taking all of us to the fried catfish dinner at the VFW tonight."

"That was fast." I whistled. "You'll have to check out Aunt Helen's new boyfriend while you're there."

When Roshonda came into the bakery for her ritual caramel macchiato that afternoon, she had news.

"It pays to know people," she said smugly.

My eyes widened. "Luke's up for a pizza commercial," I guessed. She shook her head no. "Insurance?" No. "Luxury car?" No.

"Better than any of that. Much better."

"An ESPN football series shot in preseason? You know, those in-depth looks at one team and how they fight adversity both personal and professional, blah, blah, blah?"

"You're close."

"I give up."

"I put a bug in someone's ear in L.A. She's looking for a new bachelor for network reality TV. You know—the guy who entertains all those hot young women and then chooses one by giving her a rose at the end?"

"I never watch that."

"Well, you'll host a watch party for this one. My contact is very interested in Luke, providing that he is divorced and new on the dating scene by the time they want to film in February, after football season is over. The sooner he wraps up your legal proceedings, the sooner he can sign a TV contract."

18

Neely

On Monday, I stood in the baking area holding a tray with a dozen tartlets, which I had just brushed with an egg wash and sprinkled with sugar so they would bake to a golden, sparkly finish.

I hoped they tasted like Lydia would expect. She had sent me a barely readable copy of an old family recipe—Little Abigail's custard pie—very similar to one in Gran's recipe file. But Gran had crossed out *spicebush berries* and written in *whole allspice*. I thought a thimbleful was about a teaspoon or so.

I don't remember Gran ever making custard pie. It was usually lemon.

I LOATHE spicebush, Mrs. Stidham had texted. I think that custard pie is a bit homemade-y for a wedding of this caliber. I hope you're going to offer tarts like this—she attached a link to a dazzling, free-form tart from a Michelin-starred restaurant in the south of France. Too bad that sprays of fresh red currants, each little red fruit de-seeded with a goose quill, were not yet in season here.

But I was doing my best to dazzle, anyway.

For the authentic spicebush berries, I had had to call a boutique ice cream company in Columbus that I knew made a spicebush-flavored confection. The ice cream company had gotten its dried spicebush berries from Integration Acres in southern Ohio, so I called and ordered some, too.

What had probably taken Little Abigail a short walk in the woods to get had taken me several phone calls and a FedEx package.

These little tarts were like gold. They needed to go in the oven. *Now.*

"You're breaking my concentration," the usually unflappable Norb said, rather bluntly. "I have a system this morning, Neely, like I do every morning. Breakfast pastries as soon as I get here so they're fresh for the morning rush. Cookies and cakes next, then pie, so if the filling runs over, we have the bulk of the baking done before I have to shut everything down and clean out the damn oven."

Damn. He must be bothered. Norb never cussed.

"Sorry, Norb. It's my fault. I forgot to tell you I need these tarts for the final Ballou wedding meeting later this morning."

Norb muttered something thankfully unintelligible as he expertly removed three trays of cookies to the rolling rack to cool and put another three trays in to bake.

"How long will those tarts take?"

"Thirty minutes. Tops."

"Okay," grumbled Norb. "When these cookies come out, I'll put your tarts in. Put them on this rack," he said.

"Thanks, Norb," I said, carefully sliding the tray on the top of the many-tiered rolling rack. In my mind, I did a fake salute, as in, *Aye, aye, Captain*. Norb was my *employee*. I was the boss. But everyone was entitled to a bad day and making Norb's bad day worse was not in my best interest. I was edgy enough as it was.

I walked to the front of the bakery and glared at May's display, arms crossed. After an all-work-and-no-play weekend of cleaning my house and tidying up the yard, with no message from Ben, I was ready for this godawful month to be over. Maggie and the Professor were dating. Even Aunt Helen was seeing someone. Jett seemed to be more attentive than usual to her phone, and in a good mood, which made me wonder if she had a crush on a boy at school.

Why couldn't I have a life, too?

I wanted to rip down the rhubarb-colored curtain, sweep all the carefully arranged goodies to the floor with one dramatic swing of my arm, and throw a full-on tantrum.

I was sick of strawberry and rhubarb.

I was sick of hard-to-please brides and their nouveau riche mothers who had it so good, but didn't seem to know it.

I was sick of being a good girl who followed the rules. I was sick of almost ex-husbands who could turn into reality TV stars. Sick of Ben suddenly dropping out of sight. Sick of my attorney demanding money for a problem I didn't create. Sick of anonymous men in dark SUVs following my every move outside the bakery.

The rest of the morning flew by as customers picked up their graduation and holiday orders for Memorial Day weekend, which was early this year. Every time the door opened, Maggie looked up expectantly until the Professor finally came in for his usual breakfast of blueberry and lemon muffin and a coffee. He beamed when he saw Maggie.

By ten o'clock, the morning rush had ended.

I sent another text to Luke: Let's part ways as friends. Fresh start for us both.

I was hoping that Charlie Wheeler, as Luke's attorney and agent, had heard from Roshonda's L.A. talent scout. Maybe Charlie would nudge Luke to end his marriage if it meant more money in their pockets. As Luke's legal wife, I was hoping to move from the asset to the liability category—fast.

With a lighter step, I went back to the baking area and grabbed the tray of tartlets, golden and flaky and sparkly with sugar. At least there was one thing that had gone right that morning.

I carefully packed them up in bakery boxes to take next door.

As I walked past my front porch goose, there was no bouquet of flowers, no letter. There hadn't been since last week.

I couldn't let myself feel deflated before Rainbow Cake's most influential wedding clients arrived, so I busied myself with brewing coffee and herbal tea. I arranged the tartlets on a tiered stand and set a stack of dessert plates and silver forks on the table.

Roshonda and Gavin arrived with their laptops. Lydia and Mrs. Stidham still seemed testy. We all sat in the parlor to go over last-minute details.

"We'll have the tent company ready to set up for the ceremony in the garden, but we won't actually put up the tent unless the weather forces us to," Roshonda said. "This way, we can be ready for anything. I've already hired a landscape service to tidy up the garden so it will be in pristine condition. We'll set up the rows of white chairs in front of the tobacco barn. You'll say your vows, Lydia—"

Lydia interrupted. "We won't be *saying* our vows," she said, earnestly. "We'll be *playing and singing* our vows. We've written our own song."

Mrs. Stidham looked blank. "I don't understand," she said. "How is that going to work? You'll have on a wedding dress and a veil. You'll be holding a bouquet."

"We'll have the instruments up there by the minister. I'll give the bouquet to Melissa to hold, and we'll play and sing our song," Lydia replied, her blue eyes taking on a steely cast that I was now translating as *determined*. Much better than *obstinate*. "It's going to be all right, Mom." She patted her mom's knee. "It will be wonderful. Even if I don't have a veil. I'm having flowers in my hair instead."

Mrs. Stidham fanned herself with the menu card.

"Will you need microphones or speakers or anything like that?" asked Roshonda, making notes on the spreadsheet.

"Yes, I guess we will," said Lydia. "We want everyone to be able to hear. We've been working on this song for a year."

Mrs. Stidham cleared her throat. "Can you tell us just a little more about the song, sweetheart?"

"It's sort of bluegrassy. A ballad. About love that stands the test of time."

What could we do but nod as if playing and singing your own vows was something we encountered every day?

But there was more.

"A few hours before the wedding, Christopher and his groomsmen are going to canoe across the river in a flotilla. Dave Pearce is going to organize it. To bring awareness to the Ohio River ecosystem. You know him, right, Neely?" asked Lydia, turning to me.

If Dave Pearce mucks this up for all of us, I will personally drown him in the treated effluent of the Mill Creek.

"Maybe they could paddle in special T-shirts, then get freshened up afterward," I volunteered. I couldn't imagine anyone canoeing in a tuxedo, but, again, better not to assume.

"So, the groom's party will need their tuxes and dress shirts and shoes and Dopp kits ready in the hotel rooms," Roshonda said as she made more notes.

"As long as they're dressed and ready to go on time, I don't have a problem," Mrs. Stidham said. She looked as if she was going to say something else, but then thought better of it. She pressed her lips together.

"So here are the latest sketches of what the tobacco barn will look like inside." Gavin bravely entered the breach. "We can't have open flames, for obvious reasons, so we'll use LED candles like this one."

"And I think you saw the menu card," added Roshonda. "We'll have that signature bourbon cocktail. The catering company is setting up the grills in back of the barn. We'll put up another tent back there for plating the food and cleaning up, so it will all go smoothly."

"And the pie table?" I asked.

"We'll have tiered stands on long tables so people can come up and get whichever kind of tartlet they want for dessert," said Gavin. "Lydia will cut the wedding pie at a round center table

The Memory of Lemon

in the middle of the barn, just like you would do for wedding cake. We'll have the pie on an elevated stand." Lydia smiled. Her mother looked long-suffering.

"There's something else," said Mrs. Stidham. "I know we talked about using the abiding cabin for an extra restroom, but it's so tiny and very basic, I'd hate to ruin the effect of the tobacco barn with a substandard restroom. Gene and I have been to a magical outdoor wedding and reception at a ranch in Sonoma and no one blinked an eye at porta-potties. We really can't have all the guests trooping in and out all night. I thought we might be able to get our hair and makeup done in my mother's abiding cabin, but there aren't enough electrical outlets. When we've finished getting ready at the hotel suite, we'll drive to the site and just wait in the cabin, ready to go, so no one sees Lydia before the wedding."

"We'll hire porta-potties to go on the other side of the tobacco barn, so they're convenient." Roshonda made another note. "Do you want an ice bucket of champagne and glasses in the hotel suite or in the cabin?"

"Both," said Mrs. Stidham, clutching the menu card tighter. "We might need a little Dutch courage, or I guess that would be French courage if it's champagne." She took a sip and placed her coffee cup back in its saucer. "Back to the cabins. You all feel free to use the abiding cabin, the one that has furniture. Stay there overnight if you need to. Sometimes bourbon cocktails are a little stronger than you think," she said, eyeing us meaningfully. "I don't want you driving back late at night if you've had one too many. So if you end up staying, just close the door when you leave. Nobody in Augusta worries about locking up. I'll have my local cleaning lady take care of everything on Monday."

"Is there anything else we haven't talked about?" Roshonda asked. "If not, it's time for pie!"

When Mrs. Stidham saw how pretty the tartlets looked, she eagerly picked up a plate. "I think this pie thing might work out just fine," she said, bypassing the spicebush custard tarts for the free-form one that most closely resembled its Michelin-starred inspiration, with tiny strawberries on their stems and orange mint leaves. The problem with this little tart was that it looked fabulous, but you had to fussily pick it apart to eat it. But Mrs. Stidham didn't seem to mind.

Hey, at this point, whatever.

Lydia chose the custard tart from Little Abigail's recipe. "It tastes just like the ones Grandma Vangie used to make," Lydia said after one forkful. High praise indeed.

"Let's try the lemon," said Mrs. Stidham. It was another heirloom recipe with a simple filling of thin lemon slices, sugar, and eggs. She took a forkful—"Mm-mm"—and then passed the rest of it to Lydia.

"Another winner," Lydia said.

"My grandmother made this pie," I said. "It was my father's favorite."

"And I'm all about the blackberry," said Roshonda, "as long as I don't have blackberry seeds in my teeth when I leave here. But I like those little turnovers, too."

"I suggest we narrow this down to five," I recommended, "each a different color and pastry design and flavor."

"As long as we have Grandma's custard, I can leave the rest up to you," Lydia quickly chimed in. "If you want the fancy tartlet, we can have that, Mom."

"Your father will go for the bourbon and chocolate, no question about that."

Lydia gave her mother a level look that seemed to say a lot to her mother, even as it gave away nothing to the rest of us.

"We owe your father," her mother sniffed.

"I was there, Mom. I know."

"We found ourselves in a rather difficult position once," Cadence said, twisting her napkin. "I don't know why I'm thinking about all of that now."

Again, I got a flavor that started out as citrus, which I was coming to recognize as the flavor that signified a wanderer for this family. And then it morphed into an unpleasant lime flavor, citrus that was fake. Maybe a wanderer who pretended otherwise. A wanderer who was manipulated, backed into a corner. And then something in Cadence Stidham shifted. She dropped her guard. And I saw what had prompted it.

A blue haze of cigarette smoke hung in the dim, noisy tavern like fog over a river of spilled beer.

"I have to go upstairs and check on my daughter."

Behind the bar, a bleached-blond, frazzled, younger version of Cadence Stidham tried to work her way around the man who blocked her path. Her eyes had that wary yet fed-up look of a trapped woman.

"It's gonna cost you." *He was skinny, older, with slicked-back hair that had gone out of style with Elvis.*

"Les, let me get by."

He made a point of reaching over her for the dusty, fluorescent yellow-green bottle of lime cordial from the shelf at the back of the bar, rubbing his front against her. He unscrewed the top and poured a glug into his beer, over her head.

The cloying smell of lime almost choked her.

"That's a nasty habit," said Cadence, coughing.

"You're my nasty habit," he said.

She looked up at him. At the nicotine-stained teeth, at those pale blue eyes that could seem so kind, then the next minute look at her so cruelly. Les had offered Cadence the apartment and a job with flexible hours after her boyfriend, Lydia's father, had died in a motorcycle accident. Cadence had once been grateful. She could raise her child, be independent, not go back to that sleepy backwater where nothing much ever happened.

Then, Les wanted more.

First, her pride. Then, her body. And now, whatever shred of human dignity she had left.

"Ooh, baby, that's good," he crooned, cigarette dangling from his mouth. "You're my nasty."

Something in her snapped. She untied her waitress apron and stuffed it behind the bar.

"Not anymore. I quit."

"You quit and you leave, darlin'." He pointed upstairs. "You and the kiddo. That was the deal."

"Well, I quit."

"Then get out. Now."

"Now? It's almost two o'clock in the morning! The bar's almost ready to close."

"I don't give a shit. You want out, you get out. Now."

Lydia was still awake. Cady could hear her daughter coughing.

Les was drunk. And when he was drunk, he was mean.

This was her moment. The door had opened. A few clothes thrown into a suitcase. The wad of bills hidden under the mattress. She and Lydia didn't need anything else.

Somehow, they'd get back to Vangie. She'd take them in, no question.

A small man with thinning hair and clear glasses stepped up to the bar. Cady had seen him the past few nights. He wasn't a regular, wasn't a drunk, just a quiet guy who sipped his beer all night. And observed.

Rumor was he had invented some card game, made a fortune, and was now trying to buy the entire, run-down city block. He was welcome to it.

Les was the holdout.

"You and your child need a safe place to stay tonight, miss?" the would-be real estate investor asked. *"My sister lives in Hyde Park. She's a night owl and is probably still up. I could give her a call."*

I shivered. Cadence and Lydia had wandered into a dangerous place, leaving the safe haven of Vangie and the Augusta cabin.

No wonder Cadence clung to the new life she had made with Gene. No wonder lime cordial signaled the bad old days.

No wonder Lydia rejected her mother's ideas.

The scene snapped shut and I was back with mother and daughter, in my parlor.

"Let's not think about those days, Mom. I know my getting married has dredged up a lot of stuff for both of us," Lydia was saying. "But I don't have any issue with Gene. Never did."

Mrs. Stidham dabbed her eyes with her napkin.

"We're very different people," Lydia continued, "and we will never vote for the same candidate, but I know Gene's heart is in the right place. Of course he should have what he likes."

Mrs. Stidham visibly relaxed.

And the rest of us did, too.

"Lemon is usually ranked as the second-favorite dessert flavor in food magazine polls," added Gavin, as if nothing had happened. "It gets my vote."

After everyone left and before I headed back to the bakery, I took another moment to send a text to Luke: Let me go.

19

SEPTEMBER 1948
MILLCREEK VALLEY

The Healer

Eighteen-year-old Vangie Ballou, in side-buttoned, wide-legged pants and a striped blouse, hung her sister-in-law's wash out to dry on the clothesline.

With wooden clothespins clamped in her mouth, she arranged the crib sheet on the line, then pegged it on each end. She reached down in the wash basket for one of the many cloth diapers that would flutter down the line like surrender flags.

"You should be wearing a housedress, Vangie," Stella Mae called out the back door. "You'll ruin your good clothes. And don't get your sandals muddy."

But Vangie wouldn't be caught dead in a housedress or a pinafore apron like Stella Mae wore. She had big dreams. They didn't include being stuck at home. She kept her movie star magazines under her pillow, and her lipstick and compact at the ready in her purse. A Hollywood scout could discover her. Maybe she would be known by her full first name, Evangeline.

She could see her name roll on the big-screen credits. Evangeline Scott. Evangeline Adams. Evangeline Taylor. *Evangeline Something.*

Here she was just Vangie, the hillbilly sister.

When she'd lived in Kentucky, she never thought of herself that way. She was just herself and she sounded like everyone else. But this tiny backyard bordered by a weeping willow and the Mill Creek was a far cry from the old home place in more ways than one.

Here it was noisy, crowded, and hot. With the windows open at night, Vangie could hear cars and trains and trucks into the wee hours of the morning. The neighbors were only a stone's throw away on each side and referred to her brother's family as "briar hoppers." This muddy, smelly creek was nothing like the wide Ohio River, which changed colors with the passing of sun and clouds. And the brick house held in the heat of the day unlike their cabin, which was snug in winter and cool in summer.

But Vangie knew there was no turning back. Her future was here. At least for a while.

All the able-bodied farmers had left Augusta to fight the war or find factory jobs in the Queen City area after gas was rationed. It had become too expensive to farm with machinery instead of mules and horses. The few tobacco farmers who had big wagons and horses that could haul tobacco all the way to Maysville did all right, but the Ballous weren't among them.

Vangie was to start her own factory job in the office of the Simms and Taylor mattress factory on Monday. She had taken a correspondence course in stenography and had learned to type in high school. Plus, she was young, tall, and good-looking. She wore her dark, pin-curled hair parted in the middle and swept back from her face with hair combs, just like Bess Myerson, who had been Miss America right after Japan surrendered and the war ended. Bess was the daughter of a Jewish house painter, so why couldn't the daughter of a Baptist tobacco farmer make it big? Anything could happen. This was America.

The washtub sat on an oilcloth-covered table outside. Vangie used the cloudy rinse to water the pots of gladiolas and the morning glories climbing up the porch trellis. Then she dumped the rest of the water and turned the washtub on its side to dry on the tiny back porch.

"Vangie, can you watch Cadence?" Stella Mae called out to her in the yard. "I'm going upstairs to lie down for a while."

Vangie opened the screen door and hoisted her baby niece, who always had a runny nose, up on her hip. Cadence was teething on a carrot and there were carrot shreds all over the floor. The pots and pans that Deuce had taken off the low shelf were littered all over the kitchen and into the middle room, where the family listened to the big Crosley radio. Three-year-old Deuce was filling a battered saucepan with cigarette butts from the ashtray. The front parlor had no furniture.

To be fair, Stella Mae had tried her best to make this a home. But this rented place still had the feeling of "just for now." Vangie's brother, Harold, hoped he could save enough money to move back home to the family farm. But Harold and Stella Mae had already been in this little house for four years. Harold spent his days making mattress covers on the assembly line. You'd think, thought Vangie, that he'd at least put in a garden out back to keep his hand in, but when he got home, he just sat in his chair by the radio, smoked, and yelled at the kids.

Cadence started to fuss. Vangie got her bottle out of the icebox and put her down in the middle room's playpen. Cadence was happy to lie back and feed herself. Deuce was taking the cigarette butts out of the saucepan and putting them back in the ashtray. His fingers were sooty. He would soon take a nap, too.

Now would have been the perfect time for Vangie to escape. Maybe walk down to the drugstore on Millcreek Valley Road.

A movie producer motoring from Queen City to Chicago could be nursing a hangover and stop in at the drugstore for a Bromo-Seltzer at the soda fountain. He'd gulp it down, start to feel better, and turn around on his counter stool to discover Vangie trying on a new shade of lipstick. She would end up playing the ingenue in his new movie and be on the cover of Photoplay *and...*

That wasn't going to happen today.

Vangie's second tried-and-true escape was more domestic. Making pie. She scooped flour into a large bowl, cut off a chunk of leaf lard from the icebox, sprinkled in a little salt, and used two table knives in a scissor fashion to cut the fat into the flour. She added ice water, a little at a time, to make the dough. The familiar motions took her back to the double cabin on top of the hill where she could hear the birds singing and the river running.

If she were back home, she could go out and pick Indian summer blackberries and have enough for a pie. Or take out a jar of home-canned fruit. But here?

Vangie had to make do with milk, flour, sugar, and eggs from Amici's around the corner. But she had her mama's favorite pie recipe.

In the middle room, Cadence was asleep and Deuce was curled up in his daddy's chair with his thumb in his mouth, just dozing off.

Vangie quietly crept upstairs and pulled her suitcase out from under her bed in the children's room. From the quilted pocket, she pulled out a small handful of dried spicebush berries, crushed them in her palm, and inhaled the nutmeg fragrance with the citrus and spice notes.

For a second, she was back on top of the hill, sitting on her mama's rocker in the dogtrot and watching the river flow by, always the same yet ever changing.

Back in the kitchen, Vangie took out the brown school notebook that her mother had filled with recipes in her sprawling, penciled script. Vangie didn't know who Little Abigail was, perhaps some long-distant relative who was probably bossy. But Vangie loved the pie.

Little Abigail's Custard Pie

Take a thimbleful of crushed spicebush berries and put them in a pot. Add a quart of sweet milk and put over a low fire. The milk should feel hot to your fingers. Take the pot off the fire and cover it. Don't rush. The longer it sits, the better the flavor.

Go about making your pie pastry. Line a pie pan with your dough. Lift the spicebush berries with your fingers from the milk and rinse them off. Leave the berries to dry so you can use them again. Beat 8 eggs and 2 teacups of white sugar together in the yellow bowl. Pour this into the pie shell. Sprinkle the top of each pie with a little more sugar.

Bake in a hot oven for 15 minutes, then turn down the heat and bake until you can stick the tip of a silver knife in the middle of the pie and it comes out clean.

Back in the kitchen, Vangie put the spicebush berries in the saucepan, poured the milk over them, and put the saucepan over a low flame on the stove.

While the kids slept, she let the milk and spicy berries steep. *Mama would approve.*

She rolled out the chilled dough for the crust with a deftness that came from much practice. She lined her mother's old pie tin.

With her fingers, as Little Abigail had once instructed, Vangie removed the spicebush berries and rinsed them at the sink. Vangie washed her hands, getting out all of the milk residue. She dried her hands and inspected them. Her red-lacquered nails had held up just fine. But there was more to do.

She made the filling and spooned it into the pie. With the pastry trimmings, she cut out little leaves and glued them with a little beaten egg yolk to make a decorative border around each pie. She carefully brushed the leaves on the outer rim of the pastry with the rest of the beaten egg and dusted the border and the filling with sugar.

So pretty.

While the pie was baking and everybody was still sleeping, Vangie wrote out the recipe for Dorothy Mooney, that nice girl at Emmert's Insurance. Vangie had brought her a slice of pie last week when Harold was late with his insurance payment and Dorothy had told old Mr. Emmert that she had simply forgotten to record it on the correct day. Dorothy had gone on and on about how good that pie was, so Vangie felt beholden. Vangie would drop the recipe off when Stella Mae woke up.

Dorothy had given Vangie a recipe for Shaker lemon pie that

you made with thin sliced whole lemons. But lemons were a luxury right now. That would have to wait.

Later that Tuesday evening, when they had finished their dinner, the family went into the middle room to sit around the radio. Vangie cleaned up the dishes. Stella Mae looked beat, so Vangie offered to bathe the kids and put them to bed.

When Vangie came downstairs an hour later, Harold sat in his favorite chair and Stella Mae was stretched out on the divan. Into the room on the WLW airwaves came Fibber McGee and Molly, a tall-tale teller and his commonsense wife who lived in a place called Wistful Vista. Fibber's get-rich-quick schemes never panned out except for laughs, and even Harold chuckled.

When Harold and Stella Mae went up to bed, Vangie indulged in her third form of escape—her fiddle. It was an old one, as old as the abiding cabin. The red velvet lining in the bottom of the fiddle case had faded to pink. A paper pasted to the inside lid held the signatures of all the women who had played and loved this instrument: Abigail Newcomb, Sarah O'Neil, Little Abigail, Lizzie, and, lastly, Vangie's mother, Daisy Ballou. One day, Vangie would sign her name to the list, but not yet. Who knew what lay ahead of her? Maybe she'd meet a movie star and get married.

Vangie picked up the fiddle and tucked it between her chin and shoulder, just like her mama had taught her. Lightly, she drew the bow over the strings and felt the familiar tingling that went through her arm and into the instrument.

She played the first few notes of "Wildwood Flower," her mother's favorite song.

I will twine, I will mingle my raven black hair
With the roses so red and the lilies so fair . . .

In the corner of the room, Vangie conjured the image of her mother, lit only by the pale light of the cabin's kerosene lamp, and it brought tears to her eyes.

He taught me to love him and promised to love
And to cherish me over all others above
My poor heart is wondering no misery can tell
He left me in silence, no word of farewell.

That song, as beautiful as it was, left Vangie feeling unsettled rather than comforted. Her mother used to say that such a feeling was a portent. But who was leaving? Who was staying?

MAY 1949
AUGUSTA, KENTUCKY

Vangie's heart was heavy.
 She had to grow up. And grow up fast. All those stupid dreams about Hollywood.
 Real life had a way of smacking you in the face.
 Vangie rocked on the steps of the dogtrot, soothed by the evening breeze off the river below. She smoked a cigarette, taking a long draw and puffing out the smoke into rings that floated off into the night air. She would have to make a new life right here where her old one had been.

Deuce and Cadence were tucked in under the rafters upstairs.

Oh, if her mother were only here now. Vangie brushed away a tear. It was not good to cry. That wouldn't help anything.

When Stella Mae lost the baby, it started a downward spiral. Stella Mae was never right in the head after that. Vangie had to quit her job and stay home to take care of the little ones.

And then Stella Mae started wandering. She'd get up in the night, take off all her clothes, and roam the streets, talking to imaginary people and telling stories that would make your hair curl. Stella Mae, the quiet one, as noisy and showy as a guinea hen. The police would bring her back, muttering, "Damn hillbillies," under their breath.

Harold was mortified. And scared. And helpless as a man usually was in a domestic crisis.

Eventually, Harold had to put Stella Mae in a mental hospital in Queen City. It was all very hush-hush; it had to be if Harold was to keep his job. If they knew you had a wife in a mental institution, they looked at you funny, too, Harold had said. So Harold and Vangie just told everyone that they were taking Stella Mae and the kids back to Kentucky.

Good riddance, their neighbors seemed to indicate. No one had offered to help them pack up the truck that Harold had borrowed.

After Vangie and the kids were back in Augusta, Harold moved to a boardinghouse. He promised to send money to Vangie every month.

Step by step.

The first week, Vangie had cleaned out the abiding cabin, washing the windows, airing out the mattresses, reacquainting herself with fireplace cooking. There wasn't anything she couldn't make in a big iron pot or a skillet with a lid.

The next week, Vangie had planted a big garden. She kept the herbs that had been there forever. Horehound, comfrey, sage. She could maybe make the tinctures her mother had taught her, sell them to people who still valued home remedies.

Vangie leafed through her mother's recipe book, one of Vangie's little brown composition books that she had used for writing practice in school. She brushed her fingers over her mother's sprawling writing.

When it got too dark to see, Vangie stubbed out her cigarette and went back in the abiding cabin.

A kerosene lamp lit the way.

Vangie took down the fiddle case from the mantel over the fireplace. She had forgotten to put it up the night before and in the morning Deuce had opened it and ripped that old pastel drawing of a mother and baby by that artist whose name she could barely read. Was it J. J. Anderson? J. J. Andubon? That wasn't a name. Oh, well. It was so faded, though, it wasn't worth keeping. Why her mother and her mother's mother had kept it all these years, Vangie didn't know. She used it to help light the fire.

She picked up the fiddle and tucked it between her chin and shoulder, feeling the calming presence of her mother and her grandmother—and all the women before them—called to life again in the dark corner of the room. Lightly, she drew the bow over the strings and felt the tingle that told her the song and her loved ones were there, waiting.

The Memory of Lemon

JULY 1970
AUGUSTA, KENTUCKY

In a pale blue sleeveless blouse and denim short-shorts, Cady Ballou watched her old life recede as the ferry plied its way across the Ohio River from Kentucky to Ohio. She had her ash brown hair in a ponytail but tied a scarf on all the same. From where the ferry docked on the Ohio side, it was a fifty-mile ride to Queen City on the back of Deuce's motorcycle, and her brother tended to go really fast.

Roped to the back of the motorcycle was her turquoise and cream Samsonite suitcase, which held the clothes she'd need for her new city life. Minidresses that Vangie had sewn, a pair of white go-go boots, baby-doll pajamas, a few A-line skirts and sweaters. She'd had to leave her hair dryer with the hood at the cabin; there was no room on Deuce's motorcycle for anything else. But once she started her job, she'd buy another one.

At twenty-two, Cady's only regret was leaving Vangie, who had been a mother to them both.

"I know you gotta go," Vangie had told Cady the night before as they sat on the dogtrot, the breeze blowing up from the river. "I was like that myself when I was your age. Just promise me that you'll take care of yourself and go see your mother every now and again."

"You are my mother, Vangie," Cady had told her. And it was true. Vangie had raised them, practically all by herself. After

Stella Mae had been in the mental institution for a few years, Harold had divorced her and married a secretary at the mattress factory. They started another family. After that, Cady and Deuce hardly ever saw their father.

When Vangie took them to see Stella Mae, it was hard. It wasn't that Stella Mae got emotional and clung to Cady and Deuce, it was more like she wasn't *there* anymore. Stella Mae could remember events from her distant past, but not the little house in Millcreek Valley, not her babies. *Electric shock therapy,* a nurse had stage-whispered once to Vangie when Cady was still little, as if that explained anything.

Until Cady and her brother started school, Vangie had raised a big garden, made her old-time remedies, sold her famous pies, and took in a little money from the lease of their land and barn to a tobacco farmer. As soon as Cady started first grade, Vangie got a job at the drugstore in town. Now she was the manager.

And Vangie had done well for them all. The abiding cabin had electricity, a little kitchen, a color television, and a bathroom with a claw-foot tub. The working cabin had a lean-to addition for the washer and dryer.

Still, Vangie liked to keep things simple. "Old-timey," was how Deuce always described it. The beds, dressed in homemade quilts, were still tucked away in the loft. Blue-green glass Mason jars filled with flowers from the garden or whatever Vangie could gather on her walk to and from town. Simple white curtains at the windows, the cabin snug and quiet. Old rocking chairs in the shade of the dogtrot and in front of the fireplace.

Cady would miss the sound of Vangie playing the old songs on her fiddle, always peering into the dark corners of the cabin as if she expected someone to walk right into the room from there.

But Cady's taste was more Rolling Stones than "Barbry Allen." And she couldn't just fossilize here, waiting for her boyfriend to come home from his tour of duty in Vietnam. She had to do *something*.

When the ferry docked on the Ohio side, Deuce revved up the 'cycle. Cady threw one leg over behind Deuce, put her arms around her brother's midsection, and braced herself for what she hoped would be a thrilling ride.

20

Neely

After everyone left, I tidied up the parlor, put the dishes in the dishwasher, and had a strawberry-rhubarb turnover at the ready.

Like clockwork, I heard my mailman's familiar tread on the front porch.

I opened the door and handed him the turnover, wrapped in a paper napkin. "We have to stop meeting like this," I deadpanned.

"Except it's my job," he replied, handing me my home mail. He was always going to be a literal, connect-the-dots kind of person, the type who never skipped a step in following directions.

I hoped the telescopic lens on the camera being aimed at me from across the street was catching this exciting moment in my life.

A short letter from my dad. He was applying for a free cell

phone, some disadvantaged veterans' benefit that required a lot of paperwork. He had to live at the scrapyard for three months and have someone certify that residence in order to get the phone with 250 prepaid minutes.

The luxury of that struck me. I knew where he was. I knew he loved me. I knew I loved him, in spite of everything. He was taking steps toward a normal life.

I read on:

> You wanted to know what it was like to fly a helicopter.
>
> It was an adrenaline rush, for sure. It was the worst place you could be and it was the best place you could be.
>
> The Huey lifts off, slow, struggling, shaking, whipping up dust or whatever shit is on the ground, fanning the smell of diesel fumes and rotting fish and cordite. I can still smell that. You think to yourself, "This could be my last moment on Earth." And then you're up. The white sands of the South China Sea or the jungle canopy and the hell that hides in it recede like they never existed at all. The air is cooler. It smells fresh. You're in this tin can up in the sky, but you're far safer than you would be on the ground.
>
> I always dreaded landing in the jungle. Anytime I had to drop off or pick up troops in the LZ—that's the landing zone—it was always life or death. You're under fire from rockets, rifles, tracers, you name it.
>
> When I got back to base, I just wanted to zone out. Somebody always had beer or booze or dope. And then sometimes there was a package from home. A letter. A book. Mom and Helen were good about sending stuff. This one time

they sent bar cookies—lemon—that were still moist and intact when I got them, a rare feat, even packed well in a tin. I took a bite and I was back at home, in my old room. I promised myself that if I got back home, I would never drink another drop. I would never work at Hinky's again. I would never cause my mother or anyone I loved another moment of anguish. I would be good.

I'm still trying to keep that promise, Claire.

Love,
Dad

On impulse, I packed up the rest of the lemon tartlets, a taste of home, to send some to him in Kansas City. I was pretty sure that the Blue River Scrapyard was not on the FedEx or UPS route, so I stopped at the post office to mail the package, trailed by the black SUV.

I waved to the man in dark glasses and a baseball cap.

Knock yourself out.

I took another box of the lemon tartlets up to Mount Saint Mary's. Maybe something in the tart would spark Gran's recognition, just for a moment, and I would have her back with me again. This was her recipe, one she made for every family occasion, even Thanksgiving.

But when I got to the memory care wing, she was sleeping. I didn't want to wake her. I left the tartlets with the duty nurse. I'd make extra tarts for Lydia's wedding and try this again.

When I got back to Rainbow Cake, I sorted through the bakery mail. There was a letter from Ozarks Treehouse Cabins.

The handwriting was familiar, so I went back to the baking area, quiet with Norb gone for the day, to read it.

Neely,

I hope you got my message through Dave Pearce about my fishing trip. He helped me find a pair of waders and a new fishing reel. He said he'd let you know.

No, that idiot Dave Pearce had not told me. No surprise there.

I sent this to you at the bakery so it wouldn't be lying around for Somebody to find on your porch.

Every year in May we go to the White River in the Ozarks and fish for trout. We drink a lot of beer, paddle around in canoes, stay in treehouse cabins, and eat a lot of country fried steak. Fun, huh?

And we unplug. No cell phone service. No Internet. Kinda perfect for our situation, right?

But to get back to your letter.

Definitely a claw-foot tub. And I did like the perfume.

It's a good thing I'm far away or I'd be tempted to carry you off, Luke be damned.

We will be together.
Ben

Later that night, loud cricket chirps woke me out of a sound sleep. What was that? My phone.

"Hello?" I answered, groggily.

"What's going on, Claire? What's with all these 'let me go' texts you've been sending?" The deep, velvety voice was one I immediately recognized, a voice like a he-knows-what-he's-doing caress. Once again, it stirred something deep within me and I almost let myself get swept away. With half-closed eyes, I looked at the display: 513 area code. The safe phone.

I could just see him as clearly as if he were beside me. Tall, athletic build. His sun-streaked hair, green eyes, the intensity he could turn on like a high-voltage current.

Gone was the "poor me" Luke. Here was the Luke I knew so well. He would be great on TV.

I threw off the covers and sat on the side of the bed, alert. I had to be alert. I had to get this done.

Breathlessly, I launched in. "Did you know that Charlie Wheeler is having me followed? That you're paying for around-the-clock private detectives who take photos of me opening my mail?"

"What are you talking about?"

"I tried to file for divorce last week, Luke. But I couldn't. Charlie says that I have violated the terms of our prenup. The clause that says that if I were unfaithful, you could revoke the settlement. Charlie has photos of Ben and me having dinner—with *him*, by the way, although Charlie conveniently left himself out. And we both know who was unfaithful during our marriage."

There was silence on the other end.

"Charlie says you could take everything and leave me with nothing. Is this what you want to do, Luke? Is this how you want things to end?"

I heard him sigh. "Claire . . ."

"Do you know how much it costs to have Gran in the memory care wing each month? Her money is going to run out soon. And I can't pay that out of my own pocket yet. The bakery is exceeding projections, but it won't really turn a profit until maybe late this year, if we're lucky and I work my ass off."

"Claire..."

"And on top of that, my attorney now wants a fifty-thousand-dollar retainer because he thinks our divorce is going to be really, really difficult. I don't have fifty thousand dollars."

"Claire..."

"This isn't like you, Luke." I took a deep breath and tried not to sob. "This isn't like you."

"Can I say something here? Okay, I'll admit it. I didn't want this divorce. I still think we can work this out."

"Work out what? How many more times we'll go through this same thing? I don't have it in me anymore. I just don't."

"I can change."

"No, you can't. We could be having this same conversation thirty years from now. I want to be with someone I can trust. I want kids."

"We can have kids, Claire. Someday."

"It's always 'someday.'"

Neither one of us said anything for a long moment.

"Okay. I probably wouldn't want to live with me, either." I could imagine Luke's trademark grin.

Then he got serious. "Okay, I had you followed. I wanted to know what was going on in your life because you wouldn't talk to me. You're my wife, Claire."

"How could you think that was a good idea? I felt threatened, especially financially. I got angry with that moron in the black SUV who photographed my every exciting move. It has made me think a lot less of you, Luke, not more. Spying on me did not make my heart grow fonder. Quite the opposite."

"That's not what I meant to happen. I would never harm you. I was just trying to buy some time. I wanted to know if there was somebody else. Like Ben."

"I like Ben. I've always liked Ben. You know that."

"When Charlie sent me the photos he took of your dinner at Boca, you and Ben—"

"And Charlie," I reminded him.

"Okay, but Charlie was an add-on. You two were already there." Luke paused, cleared his throat. "I get it, now, how you must have felt when I stepped out of line. The bottom dropped out of my world the second I saw those photos. And then I could have punched the next guy I saw. I began to question everything. Maybe I didn't really know you at all. Maybe there had been other guys that I didn't know about. And then I had to do anything I could to get you back. Over and over again."

"It's not fun, is it? And multiply that by how many times?"

"I get it now." He sounded contrite again.

I didn't say anything. I had said it all before.

"Ben is a great guy," Luke said, sounding reasonable. Then he got angry. "But you're still my wife. *My* wife."

"I'm only your wife in the legal sense. Please, let's end this. So we can both get on with our lives." *Hint, hint.*

"What about Tranter?"

"What about him?"

"Don't do this, Claire."

"If you want to know something, just ask me."

"Okay." His voice was softer, almost contrite.

But I knew he wouldn't ask. He might have been brave and daring on the football field, but that didn't translate to emotional courage. And if he didn't ask, I wouldn't tell.

"I'll tell the PI to stop."

I waited. I needed more from Luke.

I heard him sigh again. "Send me the damn papers, Claire. I'll sign whatever you want. Better yet, I'll be in Queen City next weekend. I'll sign them in person. But we both know we're not really over. I still love you."

An hour later, just as I was falling back to sleep, my phone buzzed with a text message from Roshonda: Two people we know are flying to L.A. tomorrow.

21

Neely

For the next few days at Rainbow Cake, I worked with renewed purpose.

As I sipped my Cuban coffee, before we opened, I sighed with relief once again. No black SUV. No guy with a telescopic camera lens. No one to make me feel trapped, hemmed in, constrained.

I felt freer than I had in weeks.

I would meet with Luke. He'd sign the divorce papers. Our divorce would move along.

I had had a wonderful letter from Ben. I would see him soon and we would see where things would go.

Now I could focus again on work.

In the back, while Norb was baking, I assembled our signature rainbow cakes for a special order—those coral, butter yellow, pale green, rose, and lavender layers all frosted with a robin's egg blue buttercream. As much as I loved this cake—and our customers did, too—that teal blue coloring always found its way to outline my fingernails, sort of a litmus test of how busy we were.

When we opened our doors, Maggie wore that expectant look again that quickly faded to resignation. We hadn't seen the Professor since his last date with Maggie at the VFW. Mornings just weren't the same without him.

Maggie wasn't the same without him. She had pale, shadowy circles under her eyes. Even the rhubarb-colored T-shirt she wore couldn't make her blue eyes pop. She looked faded.

"Maybe he went on vacation," I said, as I put an order of our vegan cinnamon rolls in a box for a customer.

"Yes. A vacation from me."

"Don't say that. We don't know why he hasn't been here. Maybe it has nothing to do with you."

"I think it has everything to do with me. Maybe I introduced him to my mother too soon."

"Everybody likes Patsy, and I'm sure the Professor did, too."

She sighed. "He hasn't even kissed me yet, Neely."

"We all know he's the shy type. Just give him some time. And some encouragement."

"If I ever see him again."

I squeezed Maggie's arm, tagged the order for pickup, and went to the next order on the list.

The morning went by, smoothly and uneventfully, and I found myself with time on my hands.

I scooped up a half dozen more of our lemon tartlets and

made another attempt to see Gran in the memory care wing of Mount Saint Mary's.

She was awake and sitting up in a wheelchair.

"I think Dorothy knew somebody was coming today," said a staff nurse. "She's been a little more animated. Kept looking at the door."

I sat down beside Gran and opened the box of tartlets. "Gran, I brought you a treat. Your famous lemon pie. Can you smell it?"

I held a tartlet up to her nose and she inhaled the sharp, buttery fragrance. And smiled.

"Jack," she said and put her hand up to my face.

Close enough.

"Jack is getting better," I said. "I've been writing to Dad. He's been writing back. He's been telling me about his time in Vietnam."

"Blue hands," Gran said. Slowly and shakily, she took one of my hands—stained from making rainbow cakes—and kissed it.

"Occupational hazard," I said and kissed her back.

"Do you want to try a bit of tartlet?" I asked. "Your famous recipe."

I put the tartlet on the paper plate I had brought and gave her a forkful.

"I'm making these for a big wedding in Augusta, Kentucky."

Gran looked at me.

"Vangie," she said.

How many people had I ever heard of who were named Vangie? Only one. "Did you know Vangie Ballou, Gran?" And then the other shoe fell. The pie recipe with spicebush berries. Little Abigail's custard pie. Did Vangie ever live here? I would have to ask Lydia or her mother. How strange that our families might have known each other.

Gran took a third bite and sank back into her chair. She turned her head and closed her eyes.

I knew it was time to go back to Rainbow Cake.

While I had been gone, another thick letter came from my dad. How much of that City Vue stationery had he taken with him? Maybe I should send him paper, envelopes, and stamps in my next care package.

But this was a good sign.

I had a breakthrough, Claire, in my group therapy session. Maybe it was all those lemon goodies you keep sending. I don't know. But something that was knotted up in me got smoothed out. Some things that were fuzzy all of a sudden became clear.

I'm not going to ramble on like some crazy person. That is me, being ironic.

But I want to write this down while it is fresh from my newfound memory. It hurts like hell to even think about it, sort of like physical therapy. But this is emotional therapy, the guys say. And it's supposed to hurt.

I remembered the girl with blue hands. I know this isn't all of it, but it's a start.

My last mission was to fly a major and his party up to Quang Tri near the North Vietnam border.

It was October 25, 1970, almost two years after I left home for the Army.

Clear day. But Typhoon Kate had hit the Philippines to the south a few days earlier and was coming up the coast.

The Memory of Lemon

The typhoon meant my layover in Quang Tri was a lot shorter. The Army brass moved up my next mission to take a team of four men for a drop into northern Laos for a long-range reconnaissance mission. We weren't at war with Laos, so it had to be secret.

We took off, no problem. The sky to the south and east was turning blue-black with that weird green like a tornado sky, so I churned up the Huey to its full capacity.

The drop into Laos went fine. Quick down, quick up. The men made for cover just as the rain started falling. In just that time—five minutes, maybe—the wind formed a massive wall.

Jimbo, my gunner, and I were in midair when I felt the pedals go soft. I couldn't turn the chopper. I was scared shitless.

The Huey made big loops at first.

And then the loops got tighter and tighter.

We started to spin. When your tail rotor fails, it's like you're driving a car on an icy road and doing doughnuts at high speed. It's happening fast, but it feels like slow motion.

I knew I had to drop us down as close to the ground as possible.

I white-knuckled us down into a valley, trying to aim for the small space between where the jungle stopped and the terraced hillside started before I cut the rotors and the Huey fell. But we blew in too close. We rammed into this stone tower that cropped up out of the bush. I thought my neck would snap off.

But we stopped. Jimbo opened his door and fell out, sideways.

I struggled to get out of my door and my parachute deployed. I was lost in this silky white cloud. But I jumped anyway. And then I felt the tug of my harness. I didn't clear the chopper. I dangled like a marionette.

Then the rain came, sheets of rain straight into my face, into my nose and lungs.

I hung there in midair pounded by rain for what seemed like hours. But maybe it was only minutes. I don't know. But in a split second, I fell.

When I came to, one side of my face was stuck in the mud. The rain had stopped temporarily. A skinny little boy leading a baby goat by a piece of rope prodded me with a stick. I hobbled over to the other side of the chopper. I saw that Jimbo was dead. I wanted to bury him, but I had to get out before the Viet Cong came.

I took Jimbo's rifle to use as a cane.

I followed the boy back to a wooden hut at the end of a cluster of huts. Inside it was dark and smoky. There was a big vat over a fire in the center and a smoke hole in the ceiling above it. Everything smelled like piss. A scared young woman offered me a cup of water and a bowl of rice. She had dark blue hands. She said something to the young boy and he took the goat and left.

I don't know what this means, but I remembered it, like the cobwebs had been dusted off or something.

There's more. I know there's more. And when it comes, I'll be ready for it. This is the only way to get better, honey.

I've blathered on enough.

Thank you, thank you for the lemon tarts. I think that's what did it, sweetie.

Love,
Dad

22

NOVEMBER 1950
MILLCREEK VALLEY

The Healer

The cellar still had the warm smell of coal dust and they hadn't even burned any coal yet.

Dorothy O'Neil knew it was silly to wash the white net curtains again. They would only get increasingly dingy every week once the coal furnace got going when the weather turned. By spring, the curtains would be grayish yellow. That was the price a modern homemaker in an old house had to pay for staying warm in winter.

Still, it was a fine house. Shotgun style. Parlor in the front, dining room in the center, kitchen at the back. A long hallway leading from the front door to the bathroom.

It had been the home of former clients at Emmert's Insurance, Mr. and Mrs. Tom O'Neil. Their deaths had led her to their son,

George, whom Dorothy had married, and from there to baby Jack, just weeks old.

She should be tired from childbirth and caring for a newborn.

But Dorothy was filled with a restless energy. She needed something to do.

Baby Jack was asleep in his little blue bunting on top of the folded laundry in the willow basket. He had another hour to go before his next feed. Dorothy had the bottles of formula already made up in the icebox, where the lemon Jell-O salad with the grated carrots was chilling in individual metal molds.

The peeled potatoes were in the saucepan, covered with cold water, ready to boil. The pot roast was in the oven. No one could say that she drove her husband to drink at Hinky's because she didn't have dinner on the table when he came home from work.

Dorothy leaned down and patted her son in the basket. He was so perfect, so innocent. His whole life before him. Once again, a fierce love overtook her and she trembled. Once again, she vowed to herself that no matter what, her son would have a good life.

Dorothy stood up and turned her attention back to the laundry. She had soaked the curtains in borax, drained out the dirty water, and filled the tub of the wringer washer with clear water. Dorothy always added bluing to the rinse when she was doing the whites. She put a few drops of bluing into a jug of water until the water turned a dark blue. As she poured the bluing into the rinse tub, Dorothy saw the shack again, out of the corner of her eye. And the little boy with a goat. The boy looked Chinese. *Were they . . . ?* She turned sharply to look and splashed the bluing over her left hand.

There was nothing there in the corner of the cellar. But as the bluing stained her hand, an inky dark taste filled her mouth, the deep empty blue of an abyss, a bitter flavor of hopelessness.

She dropped the jug into the rinse tub and looked at her left hand in horror. Now she was marked. She plunged her hand into the rinse water, grabbed the scrub brush, and furiously went at her hand until it was raw.

But she could still see the bluing around her fingernails.

And still she could taste the bitterness. She could also feel the knot in her stomach, the sensation that something was terribly wrong. Usually, when she sensed a flavor, it emanated from someone close to her, someone she let in to her mind, and she understood that the person's story that unfolded had taken place in the past. The only two people in this cellar were Dorothy and Jack.

Jack, sleeping peacefully. Jack was too little to have stories just yet. Dorothy had never gotten tastes, then glimpses, of her own stories. Why would she? She already knew them.

This must be what they call the "baby blues," when you aren't quite yourself.

Dorothy had just read an article in *McCall's* magazine about the baby blues, about how young mothers didn't realize what was happening to them. How their husbands and best friends might not know, either. In the end, the article said, the young mother just had to find a way to snap out of it. *Stay busy. Think cheerful thoughts. Get enough rest. Eat right. Have something to look forward to.*

Dorothy dried her hand on her apron, picked up each net curtain from the rinse tub with her laundry stick, and guided each curtain through the mangle as she turned the wringer. She took each flattened curtain between both hands and shook it out to full form, then pegged the curtains to the clothesline she had strung up in the cellar. When all the curtains were hanging on the clothesline, she picked up the basket with the sleeping baby and went back upstairs.

Dorothy put the basket down on the kitchen floor and went through the swinging door into the tiny pantry. She took a spoon out of the drawer of the Hoosier cabinet and plunged it into the sugar canister, then into her mouth.

The sugar melted on her tongue, softening the bitter edges of the terrible taste, making the hallucination go away. The shack. The boy with the goat. The feeling that a towering black storm cloud was coming. The feeling of being trapped.

When she had this disaster dream at night, Dorothy always had to save the baby. George never seemed to be in the dream. It was always just Dorothy and Jack.

If she and Jack were in the car, she had to drive away from the cloud. If they were shipwrecked, she had to grab a floating spar—and the baby—and paddle away. If the tornado was approaching, she had to run into the cellar as the storm broke in its black fury.

The little stained glass window high up in the pantry wall sparkled colored lights on the linoleum floor as the sun shone through.

Dorothy sighed.

She took a glass custard cup, a mixing bowl, the rotary beater, vanilla, and the sugar canister out into the kitchen. She cracked and separated three eggs: yolks in the custard cup, whites in the mixing bowl. She whipped the egg whites with sugar and vanilla until they were white and billowy. White clouds. She spooned the meringues onto a baking sheet. She took the pot roast out of the oven and checked it with a fork; it was tender. It could stay on top of the stove for a while. She put the egg yolks in the refrigerator. She'd use them to enrich a cream sauce for tomorrow's fricassee. She turned off the oven and put in the meringues to slowly bake and get crisp.

By the time she went to bed this evening, the meringues would be ready.

She would eat this sweet nothing in her nightgown and keep another by the bed. When the dream came this time, she would be ready.

NOVEMBER 1968
MILLCREEK VALLEY

They celebrated their turkey dinner on the Friday before Thanksgiving.

Jack was leaving for helicopter pilot training on Saturday. He had to be in Savannah to report for duty on Monday morning. Dorothy was thankful just to have him there. Ever since he had enlisted in the Army, she had dreaded this day.

But Dorothy was not going to send him off with tears and bad feeling. She wanted to send him off with confidence, with strength, with the safety net of family.

The night before, Dorothy had made a lemon pie and a pumpkin pie, noticing how the moonlight shone through the stained glass window up high in the pantry as she brought the sugar and flour and spice through to the workspace on her kitchen table.

Friday morning, before she left for work, she set the table in the small dining room with her ceramic turkey and Pilgrim boy and girl candleholders as the centerpiece. Helen and Jack always made fun of the holiday figurines, but that was the point. Family memories. Even a running joke.

When she went home for lunch from Emmert's Insurance, she put the turkey in the oven, the lid of the roaster on tight to keep the bird moist. When she got home, she'd remove the lid so the turkey would brown and warm up the sweet potatoes and the spinach casserole, Jack's favorites.

She had asked Helen to open the can of jelled cranberry sauce and put it on a serving plate when she got home from school. And then peel potatoes and put them in a saucepan of cold water. Helen was no cook—she just didn't have a feel for it—but those were two dishes it would have been hard to ruin.

After Dorothy picked up her bakery order at Oster's on the way home from work, she put the cloverleaf rolls in the kitchen, then went upstairs to put the meringues on her bedside table.

That old dream had come back. The one she had had since Jack was a baby and her husband George was still alive. And with it the taste of bitterness, like blue-black ink that spilled and spread and ruined everything in its path.

This particular bitterness did not signal danger. Dorothy wasn't afraid for her son's life. Yes, he was going to war. But she had the feeling he would come back to them.

If she had tasted spice, that would have been different. Spice was for loss, for remembrance, for the past.

This bitter, ink-dark flavor brought on more a feeling of hopelessness. Of blackest night, the absence of light.

The Memory of Lemon

And then flashes of story. A girl with blue hands. A little Asian boy. A baby goat. There they were in suspended animation, surrounding Dorothy, looking as if something was just about to happen. By now, Dorothy had figured out it had something to do with Jack. She was tasting a flavor, seeing a story that was yet to be. His story.

Like any mother, she had prayed that whatever it was, it should happen to her, not her child. She was strong. She could take it.

Jack was young. He was just starting his life.

As they sat down to dinner and said grace, Dorothy looked at her son, Jack, and her daughter, Helen. Her children. And she felt a fierce maternal love surge through her.

Let this terrible thing be taken from him, whatever it is. Give it to me. Let it be me.

But the next morning, at the bus station, she could only hold him tight for one last time and send him off with a taste of home. Turkey sandwiches with cranberry sauce. And the lemon pie he loved so much.

23

JUNE

Apricot and Lavender

Neely

I hoped the message in the latte foam, like the oracle at Delphi, would have an interesting message for me that morning. From what I knew about oracles, they always spoke in cryptic symbols that at first led you to a wrong conclusion. If you were lucky—or good at symbols—you eventually figured it out.

"Why do you have your eyes closed?" asked our Saturday barista, as he made my latte.

"I want to be surprised by the design you make in the froth," I said, eyes clamped shut.

"Well, see what you think of this."

I opened my eyes. He held up my favorite mug, then slowly and dramatically pulled it down to eye level.

I took it from him, careful not to jiggle the coffee and change the pattern. I peered into the foam. A wagon wheel.

"Is there something wrong, Neely? A bug in your coffee?" Maggie asked, coming back behind the counter with used cups, plates, and silverware from a now-empty table. She bent to put them in the gray plastic bin, now almost overflowing. Justin was busy with the coffees. I'd have to ask Jett to come up to the front and deal with the dishes.

June marked the end of high thinking-about-a-wedding season, and we were busy with mothers and daughters making the rounds of bridal gown shops, honeymoon travel agents, wedding paper goods stores, and florists. From what my fellow bridal business owners told me, the "season" was characterized by a flurry in January that built to a peak in June. The summer months were slower. And then things picked up again in September, tapering off during the holidays.

Happily, during the peak season mothers and daughters stopped to refuel at Rainbow Cake, but crumbs and coffee residue wouldn't give them the Parisian tearoom feel I wanted the bakery to project. I'd have to get Jett out here right away.

"Neely?"

"Oh, sorry, Maggie. I was just figuring out our dirty dish problem. And now this." I slowly passed my coffee mug toward her so as not to disturb the design in the froth. "Look. I have a wagon wheel in my latte this morning. I don't know what to make of that."

"It means you're going to be hauling a lot of pie down to Kentucky today," Maggie said. "Bet you didn't realize that I was psychic."

I rolled my eyes, took a sip to make the design go away, and walked back to the workroom to get Jett.

Wagon wheel. Wagon wheel. Maybe if I chanted it enough, like a mantra, a lightning bolt from the blue would hit me and reveal the answer.

"What's with the wagon wheel?" Jett asked, looking up from her work. She was brushing the last of the tartlet shells with egg wash and sprinkling them with sparkle sugar before they were baked.

"Oh, it's the design in my latte foam this morning. What do you think it means?"

"Easy. *Heart Like a Wheel*. My mom's favorite movie. It's about a woman drag racer going against society's expectations."

Having met Jett's mother, I wasn't surprised. She looked like an aging biker babe, one who had lived through a lot of disappointment and heartbreak. I wanted a better life for Jett, and I'm sure her mother did, too. But this morning, the mother/daughter penchant for going against society's expectations was colorfully evident.

Jett looked like she was auditioning for the sequel to *Edward Scissorhands*. Spiky hair dyed a delectable "Deadly Nightshade" color that dripped brownish purple if she got caught in the rain. Venom green fingernail polish, leather jacket, a nose ring, multiple piercings in each ear, and ripped jeans. Pale face, purple lips. From the earbud of her iPod escaped a dark tune I wasn't sure I recognized. Maybe that was just as well.

Maybe I should also rethink having her come out to the front, even to get the dirty dishes. Chic Parisian tearooms didn't usually feature servers with raccoon eye makeup.

I stood for a moment and watched her.

Jett went to such lengths to appear tough on the outside, but

Judith Fertig

I knew better than anyone how fragile she could be. At least she got to channel that delicate side in her work here at Rainbow Cake. The fern fronds, lavender flowers, and rosebuds she had hand-painted on each of the iced lavender and lemon sugar cookies were little works of botanical art. We had boxes and boxes of these wedding favors, in cellophane bags tied with ribbon, to take to Kentucky later that day as well. She had also piped out tiny chocolate lines on the cutout pastry log cabins that would go in the middle of rich Derby tartlets. Every week she took on a new skill and excelled at it.

"Jett," I said, waving my hand in front of her face so she would notice me over the gloom and doom music. Her eyes widened in alarm. She used to jump if she was startled, back in the days when she was stalked by an abusive ex-boyfriend. I judged how well she was recovering by how calmly she took interruptions. This was a small improvement. "Could you help with the dishwashing today? We're slammed."

She took both earbuds out and I could hear guitars that sounded like sirens accompanying the dark, halting beat of a zombie walk. "My heart is stone," Jett sang in her best mournful vibrato.

"I'll take that as a yes." I smiled. "And we need you sooner rather than later."

"One minute," she said to me, finishing the last row of tartlets as she sang another lyric, "'In the refuse of the city, I stalk the night bird's lair . . .'"

I walked back to the front of the bakery to see a knot of people stalking our display for June. Apricot and lavender might seem like an unusual pairing, but it made perfect sense to me.

Luscious, sweet apricots taste best when they're baked and the flavor is concentrated. On the other hand, lavender likes it cool; the buds have a floral, almost astringent flavor. Lavender was a line drawing that I filled in with brushstrokes of lush apricot.

The apricot-colored curtain showed off our little upside-down apricot cakes with a hint of almond garnished with little lavender sprigs, Jett's hand-painted lavender cookies, and our polka-dot meringues in apricot and lavender. We would put out apricot tartlets with an almond frangipane filling the following week.

At the moment, with the Ballou wedding front and center, we had nary a tart pan to spare.

It was a little after nine a.m. Just three hours until I needed to leave for Augusta, my van loaded with the ceremonial wedding pie, trays of tartlets, boxes of bagged cookies, my pastry chef's tool kit, and my wedding uniform—the navy lace sheath dress and heels I wore to "present" the cake to the bridal couple. It was my custom, and built into my price, to stand guard at the cake—or in this case, the wedding pie—until the bride or groom took over. Mrs. Stidham was paying me to stay until Lydia and Christopher cut the pie.

Gavin and Roshonda were staying until the end; they had reserved rooms in Augusta. Gavin and his team, who would drive back in from Queen City, had to take down all the decor. Roshonda had to make sure the caterers had cleaned up and the rental companies picked up the tent, tables, chairs, linens, china, silver, and glassware on Sunday.

I planned on waiting until Ben was finished with his security duties, probably well after ten p.m. There were always a few guests, usually the younger ones, who wanted to take full advantage of the open bar as long as possible. Mrs. Stidham had said we could hang out in the cabins if we wanted. She and her husband would be staying at the inn. The newlyweds would drive on to Covington to stay nearer the airport. Their honeymoon flight to an ecolodge in Panama left on Sunday.

As I waited on customers, I started to worry about all the things that could go wrong. What if my van stalled or ran out of gas and I was somewhere in the hinterlands?

As each worry came up, I found a solution. Car trouble? Call AAA. What if the ferry wasn't running? Keep going down 52 until I could go over the Ohio River on the Maysville Bridge. That would take an extra hour, but I had an hour to spare built in to my timetable.

What if Ben decided that uncomplicated guy time on his fishing trip was preferable to the trouble of a relationship with me? I had no answer for that one.

At least I didn't have to worry about being tailed and photographed by the not-so-mystery guy in the black SUV.

True to his promise, Luke had called off the hounds. And just the previous day, my attorney had messengered the divorce papers to the bakery—no invoice for a fifty-thousand-dollar retainer—for me to sign, along with quitclaim deeds for my house and my bakery for Luke to sign.

I took a photo of the documents with my phone and texted them to Ben. Good, had been his reply. Can't wait to see you. Tonight after the reception.

What had happened to Mr. Romantic Letter Writer?

Maggie, too, had her own worries.

The Professor still hadn't reappeared. John Staufregan had

been a regular since we'd opened in January. But we hadn't seen him since his last date with Maggie over two weeks ago.

"I miss the Professor," I confided to Maggie when the morning rush died down. "I want one of his mini lectures about mitochondria or amoebae or whatever they are traveling up the nasal passages to register in the brain as flavor."

"I do, too," said Maggie. "I take back every snarky thing I ever said. I'd even be happy to go to another telomere lecture. He's kind of grown on me," she confessed. "Roshonda was right. Here was this really good guy who seemed to like me and I let him drift away."

"Maybe it's not too late," I said, trying to be optimistic.

"I hate, hate, hate being back in that old high school rut, waiting for the boy to call you."

"What boy?" Jett asked, as she picked up yet another bin full of dirty dishes. Thank goodness our industrial-strength dishwasher only took minutes to cycle through.

"The Professor," Maggie and I said in unison.

Jett furrowed her brow. "You know, the phone works both ways. Why don't you call him?"

Maggie looked startled, as if the thought had not occurred to her.

"And you think I'm weird," Jett muttered. "Here, give the phone to me."

Maggie obliged.

"What's his real name?" Jett asked, and she found John Staufregan in Maggie's contacts. "You text something neutral but interesting to pique his attention, something like this . . ." Could your telomeres use a muffin and a cup of coffee? Hope so.

We all looked at the message.

"Now send it," I said.

Maggie took a big breath and pushed the button. She looked not once but twice that her text had gone through. Then she put her phone in her apron pocket.

The rest of the morning flew by in a blur of orders, appointments, and lattes—all with the wagon wheel. I started loading up around eleven o'clock.

When I was carrying the last tray of tartlet boxes to the van, I saw a shadow to my right and felt the presence of a man. A tall man. Millcreek Valley was not a high-crime area, but a woman could never be too careful. Suddenly, I realized I was vulnerable. I hadn't been paying attention to my surroundings.

I set the tray on top of the other boxes in the back of the van and quickly rummaged in my pastry kit for a weapon. A smooth-sided palette knife was better than nothing. I turned around to confront the man.

"What do you . . . ?" I whirled and took a swipe at him with my palette knife.

The tall man quickly wrapped his big hand around my little wrist and I dropped the knife. I barely growled before my shoulders sagged in relief. "Luke!"

"Is that some new pastry chef martial arts move?" he asked. "What the hell is going on here? I would have texted you, but you're still blocking my number. Unless I use the supersecret phone, which is still at home."

I tried to quiet my heart, beating fast in "fight" mode.

Still holding on to my wrist, he lowered my arm, tucked it

behind my back, and pulled me to him. "Look at me," he said. And I peered up at the face I used to love.

"Luke, let me go," I said, lowering my gaze.

"That's what you keep saying." Luke relaxed his hold, and I stepped back.

"I'm here because you asked me. I told you I'd sign those papers," he said. "Until then, you're still my wife. And I want to see your bakery. All your hard work. I never got to see it the last time I was here. Give me the grand tour."

I sighed. I still had a little time before departing for Augusta and I really did want Luke to sign the papers and get this over with. I was also proud of Rainbow Cake and wanted to show him how well I had done without him.

"Come on," I said.

He put his arm companionably around my shoulders and walked with me through the parking lot.

"I'm signing football cards at a collectors' show tonight," he said, his voice like molten chocolate. "But I don't have any plans after that." He turned his famous laser-beam eyes on me, but I wouldn't look at him.

"I've got an out-of-town wedding," I said. "And we're getting divorced."

Luke caused quite a flutter as soon as we went in the front door of Rainbow Cake. Both the brides-to-be and their mothers seemed to know who he was, if not from football, then from those car commercials he did. Luke was his charming self, signing autographs while I packed up a box of mocha cupcakes for him to take, his favorite and so *Luke*.

I couldn't help it. Part of me still believed that if he had nurtured the best parts of himself—like the affable white chocolate that gets along so well with other flavors, the take-charge coffee, and the strong-shoulder-to-lean-on dark chocolate in the frosting instead of the risk-taking devil's food cake—we might have made our marriage work. But Luke had to be the constellation of flavors that he was, and things happened as they did. I couldn't—and now wouldn't—change a thing.

When the fuss died down, I took Luke back to my inner sanctum and had him sign the papers.

Jett was still listening to her music, making tiny marzipan apricots for a special order we'd received. I waved my hands in front of her face, her eyes widened as she looked up, and then she smiled. She took out her earbuds, wiped off her hand on her apron, and extended it to Luke when I introduced him. "Pleased to meet you. I decorate everything here."

Luke shook her hand, grinning. "I can see that," he said, holding her hand so he could admire the poisonous color of her manicure.

Before the infamous Luke Davis charm could bedazzle even my nonconformist pastry artist, I said, "Gotta go," pushing him to the front of the bakery.

"Don't forget your cupcakes," Maggie said when we got to the door. She handed him the box.

"Great place you have here," Luke said to me and Maggie. "I'll definitely be back." He whistled as he walked to the parking lot.

"Your latte foam never mentioned anything about Luke turning up," said Maggie. "Unless he arrived in a station wagon or a Jeep Wagoneer."

We both ran out the door, just in time to see Luke drive off in his rental car, a silver Lexus.

"Stupid oracles," I said.

Inside, we went to our stations—Maggie to wait on customers, me to check my list for the umpteenth time before I finished packing the van for Lydia's wedding.

I walked back to the workroom to get the container of extra baked pastry decorations, just in case some of the tartlets didn't make the journey intact. A little edible glue and a pastry cutout to match, and they'd look like new. Hopefully, I wouldn't need them, but I had to be ready for anything.

But maybe not this. Jett was smiling dreamily at a tall, pale, nerdy-looking guy I hadn't seen come in. He didn't have one ounce of goth in him, but he looked pretty taken with Jett.

"Boss, this is Nick, my lab partner in biology."

"Nice to meet you, Mrs. . . ." And he stumbled.

"Just call me Neely. And it's great to meet you. As you can see, our Jett is very creative," I said, indicating the tiny marzipan apricots she was crafting.

"Nick is all about science," explained Jett. "He has this cool telescope. We're going to look at the stars tonight."

"Maybe you'll get some new ideas for designs," I said.

"If you pay me overtime."

I gave Jett my best lopsided grin. It was good to see her getting back to her old, sassy self.

I was on the road a little before noon.

The day was turning warm and I feared for the pastries, so I turned on the air conditioner. I popped in my *Foreverly* CD to get in the mood. I loved to sing along with Billie Joe Armstrong and Norah Jones, always the harmony, never the melody.

My mind wandered. What did that wagon wheel mean?

My phone buzzed. The bakery. "You'll never guess who just came in," whispered Maggie.

"The Professor?"

"He's wearing blue jeans and a fitted shirt with the cuffs rolled up. I can't believe it. He looks a little like Sting, I think."

Sting? That was maybe taking it a bit too far, but I was glad I had put that bug in his ear. Maybe he decided he needed a makeover before pursuing Maggie seriously. If so, it had worked.

"Well, his grande latte, skinny, and his lemon and blueberry breakfast cupcake are on the house. Even if it's lunchtime. Tell him we're glad he's back. And don't let him get away this time."

"Don't you worry about that," Maggie said. "And you meant to say *muffin*, right?"

I smiled and snapped my phone shut.

The Professor had come back, as had Maggie's sense of humor. The wedding tartlets and cookies looked luscious. Luke had signed the papers. My van hadn't broken down. The ferry was running and I was on it. I would soon see Ben.

As the ferry plied its way over to Augusta, I stepped out of my vehicle and felt the power of the river beneath my feet.

I texted Ben: Luke signed the papers.

Everything was going to be all right.

Soon, I was driving off the Augusta ferry, passing the historic brick town houses on Riverside Drive, then turning off Bracken Street and up the winding lane. I parked my van near the cabins, the garden, and the tobacco barn at the crest of the hill. I was lucky to find a spot not already taken by the other vendors putting this wedding together.

I checked my display again. No text from Ben. *He's busy, too,* I told myself.

As soon as I opened the door of the van, I breathed in the aromatic scent. I could taste it, too, even more vibrant than when I had been there a few months before.

My gift was being able to glimpse a key scene in someone's past when I focused and then let my intuition kick in. The signature wedding dessert usually evolved from that revelation.

Without one key story this time, the trial and error process had taken much longer. But we finally got there. I had to be thankful for that. Lydia Ballou and Cadence Stidham loved the wedding pie and the little tartlets.

They'd love this "hillbilly" wedding, too.

I breathed in the fresh scent, felt it refract into two bands of flavor that I tasted one by one. Citrus. Spice.

Now that the pressure was off and I was more relaxed, I could finally see these flavors like two broad brushstrokes capturing a simple scene: sunlight over a cabin on a hillside near a river.

The scent wafted closer as a guy in a dirty baseball cap, a torn T-shirt, and jeans took a bundle of green branches out of the back of his pickup truck.

I ran over to him.

"What is that you're carrying?"

"Spicebush, ma'am. Grows wild in these parts by the river. Mr. Nichols is using this and the rest of the stuff I foraged." He indicated the tangles of wild grapevines and the buckets of water holding pink wild roses and branches of late-blooming dogwood. "I also found white-flowering viburnum"—he indicated another set of buckets—"florists love the shape of that one." And then he looked at me, his eyes widening in alarm. "These are all legal to pick."

"Oh, no," I assured him. "If Gavin hired you, you must be good at what you do. I'd just like to smell fresh spicebush for a moment. I've only tried it dried."

"Whatever floats your boat."

I breathed in the fragrance and tasted the flavor, all at once. After all the previous misfirings, the first flashes of story took me by surprise. In quick progression, I saw a young man in buckskin pants bearing a striking resemblance to my father. Who was he? I saw a woman hanging herbs to dry in a cabin, drowning in a winter flood. Who was she? I saw the woman who must be Vangie with Cadence and her brother when they were little. And I saw Lydia as I first encountered her in my front parlor, frowning and insisting on wedding pie.

Spicebush was the "tell," the flavor that tried to explain an inner state. But whose inner state? And why had it taken me so long to get a first glimpse of story?

With a prickling sense of awareness, I thought of Gran and Vangie.

Suddenly, it came to me. There were two flavors in spicebush, two families whose stories intertwined. Lydia's and mine.

This place was the touch point. The cabin, the garden, the river, the barn. This was where the two stories had come together at some time in the past. And then went their separate ways.

"Neely!"

Roshonda power walked up to me. She was in full wedding planner mode with her iPhone in one hand, her iPad in the other.

"What are you doing sniffing twigs, girl? Gavin's waiting for those. And we've got work to do." She snapped her fingers in front of my face. "Wedding. Three hours. Wedding pie. Big clients. Remember?"

I hugged Roshonda, thanked the forager, then went around to the back of the van and opened the double doors. Roshonda followed me.

"Luke stopped by, just as I was getting ready to leave. But he signed the papers."

"Now you don't have to keep letters in your bra anymore, but you do have to invite us all over when Luke is on TV. Have you told Ben the coast is clear?"

"I texted him. When is he supposed to get here?" I pulled out the handcart and started stacking boxes of tartlets.

Roshonda pressed her tablet and the security schedule came up. "Let's see. Dave's here already. He's got a guy at the ferry, one stationed at the riverside parking lot where the shuttle will pick up and drop off, and more up here at the barn, all starting at four p.m. I'm surprised Ben isn't here yet. Maybe he had last-minute stuff to do." Roshonda looked up from her tablet. "Promise you two won't get all lovey-dovey until the place is empty?"

I grinned. "I can't promise anything."

I was glad I had work to do. The hours would pass quickly.

I couldn't wait to see what Gavin had created in the barn; his line drawings, with the barest wash of watercolor, had looked wonderful when he presented them at the final planning meeting. My little works of pastry art were part of the scene.

When I wheeled the handcart through the wide-open double barn doors, I stopped in my tracks.

Gavin had used Audubon's description of a nineteenth-century Kentucky frolic as an inspiration. Burlap with crystal. Simple with sophisticated. Country with city.

In the soaring, weathered wood heights of the barn, crystal chandeliers sparkled from long burlap-wrapped cords hung from the rafters. Along the perimeter of the barn, Gavin had placed large ficus trees in tubs, the branches strung with tiny white lights. At night, they would look magical. Between the trees hung large framed Audubon prints festooned with garlands of greenery—I recognized the glittering green Carolina parroquets, passenger pigeons with speckled plumage, and red-winged blackbirds from the Ohio River Valley.

Roshonda put her arm around me and we took in the scene together. "Isn't this the best! For all the trouble this 'hillbilly' wedding has caused, I think it was worth it."

"When I think of all the fancy weddings I've been to at the most expensive hotels," I said, "this barn puts them all to shame. I hope the Stidhams like this as much as we do."

"Oh, they'll like it," said Roshonda with a sly smile. "I've got every wedding magazine editor on speed dial and free pick of all the wedding photos afterward to help a big story happen. I've got a writer here who freelances for *Garden and Gun*. Just make those pies look good. She might ask you later for the recipes."

I wheeled the handcart over to long tables in the back, draped with burlap. Gavin had found long, rectangular tiered stands in weathered tin, so all the tartlets of one flavor could be displayed together on each tier.

"Neely!" he exclaimed, coming down off a ladder, another Audubon print hung. He gave me a sweaty hug, a first from fastidious Gavin. He must be *really* into this. "I've got more greenery for you to place around those tarts if you want."

He put his arm around me and steered me over to a round table in the center with a weathered tin cake pedestal. "I thought this might be good for the wedding pie." An antique, wood-handled pie server lay next to the pedestal. I could just imagine the pie-cutting photo—all of this texture contrasted with Lydia's simple white gown.

"Perfect!" I said.

I unpacked the wedding pie first, carefully placing it on the tin pedestal, then arranged the greenery around it. When I tucked in a slender twig, my fingers brushed the leaves.

"Spicebush," I said, raising the branch to inhale its fragrance again.

"Don't you love the way it smells?" said Gavin, coming down off the ladder. "We wanted this to look like the best version of 'my old Kentucky home.'"

I unloaded and arranged the tartlets, the yellow lemon with a pressed fork-tine design around the rim, lattice-topped blackberry, bourbon chocolate with a center pastry cutout of a tiny log cabin, golden spicebush custard tartlets with tiny circles of dough for a scalloped effect, and strawberry-rhubarb with a pastry leaf design. My old Kentucky home.

I arranged the individual bags of cookies in rustic, handwoven baskets.

I stepped back to survey my work, then snapped photos with my phone.

Almost done.

I took the handcart back to the van, slipped off my chef's jacket, and grabbed my dress on its hanger and my overnight bag. I tucked a box of tartlets and cookies under my arm.

The wedding would start at four thirty and I wanted to change before the wedding party arrived and needed to use the cabins for last-minute touch-ups.

I climbed the few steps to the dogtrot porch that connected the two small cabins. The door to what Lydia called the "abiding cabin" was unlocked. I walked into one room with a fireplace to the right, a small bathroom, and stairs going up to the loft on the left. An old quilt covered the back of the small sofa. An antique rocking chair in old blue paint looked like the perfect place to comfort a child or play a fiddle. Blue-green jelly jars held bouquets of flowers and herbs that looked like they had been picked from the garden. I put the tarts and cookies on the old pine table in the little kitchen.

There was a reason people described cabins as cozy and snug. The thick, solid walls created by the hand-hewn logs seemed to keep the outer world at bay. You could feel safe in a cabin. In the tiny bathroom, I changed out of my jeans and shrugged into my new navy lace sheath dress, sleeveless for warmer weather. I touched up my makeup, pulled my hair up into what I hoped was an artlessly sexy topknot, and spritzed on my perfume.

I put my overnight bag into the space under the open stairway, then climbed to the loft. Why not have a look upstairs before everyone came?

Ohhhh, I thought. So romantic. Sunlight streamed through a tiny window onto a four-poster bed tucked under the eaves, pillows dressed in creamy linens ruffled like an eighteenth-century gentleman's shirt. A summer quilt in bridal white.

I heard voices approaching the cabin, so I backed down the steep steps and slipped into my low heels.

The first guests were arriving from the shuttle, which would take people back and forth all evening.

My heart fluttered. Ben would be here soon.

But he wasn't there when the groomsmen paddled across the water in their Save the River T-shirts pinned with boutonnieres—nice touch, Roshonda—to cheers from onlookers.

Ben wasn't there when the ceremony began.

Lydia, in a simple white embroidered muslin gown with flowers in her hair, stood in the center of the garden. She handed her bouquet to her attendant. She picked up her beautiful old violin and tucked it under her chin. She seemed to wave the bow like a wand, casting a spell as she lowered it, then passed it over the fiddle strings. The music that came forth was as modern as Kentucky bluegrass, as ancient as old Ireland.

She and Christopher sang their vows in the lyrics of the song.

Oh, take my hand, and walk this garden
And pledge to me you'll be my own
Beyond the hills, beyond the river,
Wherever we will call our home.

As their music drifted through the garden, up through the green hills and down to the river, it carried the flavor of spice. If I closed my eyes, I could envision a succession of shadowy women hovering around Lydia and her mother, drawn by the music, by the familiar flavor of spicebush, their taste of home. It was as if they had come back to wish her well.

The ghostly women stayed until the vows were sung, rings slipped on youthful fingers, and the happy couple announced to family and friends. Lydia tucked her violin and bow under her arm and held her bouquet in her hand. She linked her arm with Christopher's and started back down the garden aisle. And then she stopped.

As I had suggested in a whisper to her before the ceremony started, Lydia presented her bouquet to her mother, who dabbed her eyes with a handkerchief as she clutched the flowers to her heart. They, too, were bound together in love.

A murmur of happy surprise rose up to roost in the trees.

I was so caught up in the moment that I didn't notice that the wraithlike figures had faded, once again, into the past. I had been hoping that maybe they would hover around me, too.

I needed their support.

Roshonda, Gavin, and I had helped Lydia's family come together in the place they had called home. The best weddings can celebrate new beginnings, but still honor those that had gone before.

My family, however, was still mired in the past. The people I loved the most were out there, somewhere. Still wandering. My dad hundreds of miles away in a scrapyard trailer. Gran lost in the fog of dementia.

And Ben? Where was he?

Ben was still missing when Lydia and Christopher cut the wedding pie and guests made a champagne toast.

My official dessert duties over, I stepped back into the night and texted Ben: Where are you? Please come soon.

"He said he's on his way, Neely," Dave reassured me for the umpteenth time.

But Ben wasn't there when the guests threw confetti flower petals at the newlyweds as they left the old barn to start their honeymoon.

He wasn't there when the last guest left and the grateful, happy Stidhams took the shuttle to the River Landing Inn in downtown Augusta, where Roshonda and Gavin were also staying. He wasn't there when Gavin turned out the lights and the barn went dark.

"Why don't you come back with us, Neely?" Roshonda said, as she and Gavin were getting in his car. "My room has two beds."

"I'll just wait in the cabin a little longer," I told her. "But thanks for the offer." I smiled. Roshonda squeezed my arm.

The lights were on in the abiding cabin.

I looked at my phone's display again. It was working. But still nothing from Ben.

Why had he texted Dave and not me?

I stood out from the shadows of the dogtrot so I could see down the lane and to the river through a clearing. I could hear the water, coursing past me, always the same, yet ever changing.

I had chosen the wrong man the first time. I thought I had chosen the right man the second time. The man who wasn't coming to me.

All the men in my life ended up leaving. First my father, who'd abandoned my mother and me. Then Luke with his roving eye. And now Ben.

This was a new twist on my old pattern. At least I had had

some time with my father and Luke. Ben was leaving me before we even really got started.

The wind picked up. In the moonlight, gray clouds scudded across the night sky until the stars flickered out. I hoped Jett and Nick had already found the stars they were looking for.

A storm was rising.

I could smell the rain before I heard it. Trees bent in the wind. Thunder boomed and lightning flashed over the river in hieroglyphics that someone, somewhere, might take as a sign.

But not me. I was done with signs. *Slice of pie. Lodestar. Wagon wheel.* I was a fool.

I should have gone inside, but still I stood there.

My dress would be ruined, but I didn't care. I turned my face up to the pelting rain. *Bring it on.* I let it wash away my assumptions and superstitions and that crazy idea that all would be well.

My hair was plastered to my face and neck. I shivered. But I stood there and took it.

And then I saw the headlights. Two headlights. Coming up the lane.

I tasted citrus and spice. I saw ghostly faces whirl before me in a squall. The women were still there, waiting.

With a loud crack, lightning cleaved through the dark night and the lights in the cabin went out.

"Ben!" I called.

He opened his car door and ran through the downpour to the shelter of the dogtrot. I stepped back out of the rain.

"You're soaking wet," he said.

"So are you."

"Why were you standing in the rain?"

"Because I wanted to."

We could barely look at each other. What was holding us back? Why were we so hesitant?

"Roshonda said I could find you here," Ben said. "I've been down at the ferry all night. The Stidhams didn't want to pay two dollars for any car that didn't belong to a wedding guest," he said with a wry tone.

"Couldn't you have had someone else be in charge of that?" I asked.

"I could have."

"So why didn't you?"

"I needed time to think, Neely."

I shivered. "That's never good."

I could hear Ben's smile in his tone. "And you don't have the sense to come in from the rain."

"Give me a minute," I said, opening the abiding cabin door.

A gust of rainy wind blew me forward and I felt the ghostly women push me through the door.

In the darkness, I felt my way to the small bathroom and the towels hanging on the rack. I felt my way back to the entryway and handed Ben one. I bent sideways to towel off the worst of my dripping curls. "There," I said, standing up straight. "You were thinking what?"

"We've been caught between two worlds," he began. "We're friends. We've looked out for each other since we were kids. We will always have that. But I want more now, Neely. I want you. I want us."

He paused, then cleared his throat. "When you texted me that Luke had signed the papers, I really got my hopes up. We get this close. *This close.* And then something happens. I asked myself, *What could possibly happen this time?* The only answer was you. Maybe you would change your mind at the last minute again. I couldn't face it."

"Then why are you here now?"

"I thought this might be my last chance. Maybe you stayed because you were waiting for me. Maybe you stayed for some other reason. There was only one way to find out."

If I hadn't known it before, I knew now the depths of the hurt I had caused him. I was the one who had to take the next step.

"My zipper is stuck," I said, turning my back to Ben, my heart beating fast. I closed my eyes.

Slowly, with hands oh-so-gentle, he unzipped my dress.

I turned around to face him, looked deep into his eyes, slipped my dress off my shoulders, and shimmied it all the way down. I kicked my dress aside, then my shoes.

I held the lapels of Ben's sport coat and helped him ease it off his shoulders. He unknotted his tie while I unbuttoned his shirt. He slipped off his shoes and socks.

I led him upstairs to the bed under the eaves, with the rain beating on the tin roof.

My body quickly warmed as we lay together. I caressed his face, and then we began to kiss, gentle at first, then hungrily. I loved the touch of his hand on my breasts, down the contour of my belly until it reached the place that wanted all of him, and wanted him now. I felt silken and molten and shivery.

When I touched him, he groaned, and I guided him to me. We had no more time to waste.

We moved with each other in a new rhythm that we had the rest of our lives to perfect. Faster, faster, and more forceful, until we broke through every barrier that had ever come between us.

Afterward, we lay in each other's arms.

I rolled over and laid my head on Ben's chest, as if it were the most natural thing in the world.

He stroked my damp hair. "You smell like frosting," he said.

"I do?" I held up my hand, but couldn't see my fingernails in the dark. "That damned buttercream. You think you get it all out . . ."

"No, no, Neely. Frosting is a good thing. A very good thing. But a guy's gotta have cake," he said, stroking my hip again. "Lots of cake."

"Hmm," I murmured. "Cake."

Sometime in the night, I woke up with Ben snoring softly beside me. I should have felt perfectly content and fallen back to sleep. But I had that unerring feeling that there was more for the night to reveal.

I eased out of bed, covering Ben with the sheet, and wrapped myself in the quilt that had fallen to the floor.

Carefully doubling the quilt around me, I backed down the steps from the loft.

The storm had passed. The night sky had cleared. The moon and stars were out again.

I noticed details of the cabin that I had missed in daylight. In clear moonlight and dark shadow, I could clearly see the marks of a long-ago ax that had hewn each beam and made this place a refuge. I ran my finger over clay chinking that still held little pebbles, worn down from bigger rocks over time. I sat in the rocking chair that perhaps this same craftsman had made, in front of the fireplace.

I rocked, the gentle motion loosening more of the knot that my tangled thoughts had made.

After this magical night, I knew, without question, that Ben loved me and I loved him. After all this time, after thinking I knew everything about him, I had discovered that being with Ben was thrilling. Loving Ben hadn't taken me out of myself, but more deeply within. Being with Ben had brought a delicious, long-awaited climax of the body, yes, yes, but more surprisingly, of the heart. I felt illuminated in some way, as if light was beaming from my chest.

I sighed, eased back into the chair, and slowly began the motion that was like a lullaby, holding my tender, new feelings like a baby. As I rocked, the flavor came to me once again.

Spicebush.

Citrus, spice.

A series of scenes flashed through my mind. An herb woman had once sat in this chair, picking up her fiddle to call her loved ones back and to call others who needed refuge with a song. That same woman rowed a frightened slave and her baby across the wide, icy river.

And I thought of Lydia, who had that same gift as the herb woman, binding her new husband to her with a wedding song.

Who would I call to me if I could?

The spice receded as the citrus came forward. I tasted lemon again. I remembered I had left extra tartlets in the kitchen in

The Memory of Lemon

case the wedding party needed a pick-me-up when they were waiting for the ceremony to begin. Suddenly, I was hungry.

I rose from the rocking chair, pulling the quilt around me, and walked the few steps to the kitchen.

There was only one tartlet left in the center of the table. Moonlight, flooding through the window, outlined the yellow tartlet in indigo. I had a startled feeling of something sharpening into clearer focus.

I looked closer at the tart, at the mystery that could be revealed in the everyday, as if I had never really noticed the pattern of the sugared lemon slices. The sections of the lemon slice radiated like the spokes of a wheel.

A wagon wheel.

And if I focused only on the pattern of those spokes, they formed a lodestar shimmering in the moonlight.

The oracle of the La Marzocco, just like the oracle at Delphi, had given me the message in symbols. And the symbols were in a simple slice of lemon.

My stomach rumbled. I wasn't just hungry, I was ravenous. Who could decipher symbols on an empty stomach?

I picked up the tartlet and took a bite, all crisp, sugary pastry and puckery lemon filling.

As I stood there in the moonlight, lemon on my tongue, other flashes of story came to me. Of a gray-eyed woman putting the young man she loved like a son on a boat for America. The young man who grew to manhood in a river town, tramping the woods with a long-haired artist and loving the daughter of the herb woman who had lived in this cabin. Living with his family on the old canal. The family parting when Little Abigail left for Kentucky and childless Lizzie gave the cabin to the Ballous.

And then the dark years for the O'Neil family. The little boy who died of cholera on the canal.

Generations of men easing their pain with whiskey. My brutish great-grandfather Thomas who beat his son, George, who then grew up to be a mean drunk who died young.

The damage went deep.

I drew the quilt around me and shivered. I had never met my grandfather and now I was glad I hadn't.

Gran and her terrible premonition about the girl with blue hands. The taste of bitterness, the hopelessness. The same dream that haunted my father now. What did it mean?

I had started the day with a homeless father whose reasons for leaving our family had been a mystery and a grandmother so lost in the fog of dementia that she couldn't tell me more. Now I had seen.

As I let the stories wash through me, I began to understand.

All the difficulties with this "hillbilly" wedding had been necessary to get me to this place, so I could connect with a past I didn't realize I had.

It was up to me to find a way forward.

The memory of lemon had given me clarity.

Such sadness. Such loss. But such love. That was what endured. Love was the current that ran through every story. I wanted to reach through time and space and tell my father that. It was all about love.

I sat back down in the rocker, feeling my body pulse with

energy. Unlike the women who had lived in this cabin, I had no violin. I had no song to call my loved one to me.

But I had the memory of lemon, the flavor that would send the signal for me, a beacon of hope and comfort for my father.

I held it on my tongue, in my mind, the flavor he would recognize as love. I closed my eyes and opened my heart. I sent my dad a silent message.

He was loved.

It was safe to remember.

The typhoon. The helicopter crash. The girl with blue hands. The little boy with a goat. The dark hut. The smell of urine. What happened in the deep and inky night that had swallowed him whole.

It was time to bring that story out of the darkness. Hold it up to the light.

And come home.

24

AUGUSTA, KENTUCKY

"You two look cozy!" Roshonda beamed as she walked up to our table the next morning. "If a little worse for wear."

Ben and I were sitting across from each other in the breakfast room at the River Landing Inn the morning after the Ballou wedding. Since my dress had still been damp, I had put on my rumpled pastry chef jacket and jeans.

Ben's stubbly cheeks and wrinkled shirt told the same story. We had had better things to do.

But now we were starving. Ben's plate was heaped with eggs, sausage, bacon, cheese grits casserole, and biscuits from the buffet. Mine was a smaller version.

"Don't let that scrumptious food get cold," Roshonda said. "I've already had breakfast." Roshonda gave me the once-over.

"What happened to the magnetic, charming, sexy woman we were going for?"

"She got a little waterlogged in the storm last night," Ben said.

She turned to Ben. "So you didn't drive on to that boutique hotel after all," Roshonda said. "The one where I had to pull strings to get you the room with the skyline view."

"What boutique hotel?" I asked between bites of egg.

"The one we didn't stay at," said Ben, buttering a biscuit. He smiled at me across the table. "Plan A. And thank you again, Ro. But believe me, I'm more than happy with how plan B turned out."

"Oh," I said softly and reached across the table to take his hand.

"Don't let me keep you," said Roshonda tartly. "Some people have to work. I've got a wedding to dismantle."

"That's why they pay you the big bucks, Ro," Ben said.

We said good-bye to Roshonda and finished our breakfast.

Ben leaned back in his chair and sighed contentedly. "Now what?"

"Hey, your letter said that you're a planner."

"Okay." He sat forward, his forearms on the table. "Here's the plan. Let's get rid of that nice leather chair in your office and replace it with my ratty old recliner."

I leaned forward, too. "Sounds good. But let's lounge around in that leather chair a little bit before we give it the boot."

"I'm starting to love plan B."

A week later, on a Monday morning, I arrived at the bakery later than usual, all Ben's fault.

Dad's letter was waiting for me.

The Memory of Lemon

Dear Claire,

I remembered. I feel terrible.

I know that's how this works. You have to feel worse before you get better. The guys in my group said I have to feel the feeling. That I did everything I could to land a disabled helicopter in violent weather. That I already had two strikes against me. That I brought that thing down, and Jimbo and I were both alive when the flight ended. What happened after that was not on me.

But that doesn't make it okay. It doesn't make any of it okay.

Here's the start of the really bad part. The girl with blue hands. The boy was her son. He had the same heart-shaped face, the same nose. He was probably around four. That age when kids start to make up their own funny little songs. I can still hear the tune, although I didn't understand the words. The little goat followed him everywhere, like a dog. He didn't need the rope.

I got to the hut and couldn't go any farther. The boy and I were drenched when we came in. When the girl with the blue hands saw me, she cried out and then covered her mouth. She hugged the boy, then put him behind her. I put up my hand to indicate that I wasn't going to hurt anyone, but then I blacked out.

It must have rained for a while. A few days? A week? Monsoon rains. But it gave me a little time. Somebody had put a splint on my leg and tied it with dark blue rags; it still hurt like hell. I had a bad cough. I must have had a fever, too, because I kept blacking out. My skin felt clammy. The girl brought me rice and this bitter, smoky tea, as dark as ink. I could barely sit up. She'd have to hold my head up to feed me. The little boy and the goat would come over to the raised pallet I was lying on, cock their heads the same way, and look at me like I was someone from another planet.

I watched her dip lengths of cloth into a big vat of dye that was always simmering over a wood fire in the center of the hut. She'd wring out the dyed cloth and hang it up to dry from the rafters. It reminded me of my mother hanging laundry in our old cellar. Dipping the pillowcases and sheets in blue rinse water so they'd stay white, wringing them out, hanging them up to dry.

The last day, I was able to sit up a little bit and smile at the little boy. He smiled back. I gave him a candy bar that had seen better days. But it was all I had.

Then the rains stopped. The girl with blue hands became very agitated and shooed her son and his little goat out of the hut. She seemed to be telling them to go far away. But they didn't go far enough.

I must have passed out again. When I came to, it was all a blur. I thought it was raining again, it was so loud. But it wasn't the monsoon. Shouting and screaming and Viet Cong tearing everything apart in the hut. When I tried to sit up, one of the gooks slammed me with the butt of Jimbo's rifle that I was still using as a crutch. I thought my jaw was broken. I didn't have ammunition or they would have shot me.

I was too weak to even stand up, but I had to do something. I put my hands up to surrender.

The Memory of Lemon

Two guys pulled me off the pallet and started kicking me in the ribs. I could hear the girl with blue hands screaming and her little boy crying. Hell, even the goat was bleating.

It was madness. And then suddenly, it was silent. I heard a sizzling, hissing sound. I looked up slowly. I could see a river of dark liquid trickling down to the embers of the fire and evaporating in a terrible plume of smoke. Two of those damn gooks were wiping their bloody machetes on the banners of dyed cloth hanging from the rafters. They had slit the girl's throat. They all but decapitated the boy and the goat; I can still see their dead eyes. So much blood. So much blood.

I brought this on them. And I've had to live with that.

When you were little, Claire, I would rock you to sleep and sing songs. You didn't know I was lying the whole time. Those lullabies are all about "Go to sleep, I'll watch over you, you're safe." But who was I kidding? I couldn't keep you safe. I couldn't keep anyone safe.

At first, I drank to get away from the bad dream and the bad feelings. But after a while, that didn't work. And then I drank because I was ashamed. You and your mother deserved better.

You still deserve better.

I'm so sorry, Claire.

I love you.
Dad

I sipped my Cuban coffee and felt a wave of sadness move through me.

Oh, Dad. Oh, Dad.

I could picture the girl with blue hands, the little boy, the baby goat. They were real to me.

How would I have handled that? I, who had been thinking my dad was the problem. What if I had had to carry that terrible pain for all that time? What if I had tried to forget, to put it past me, to live a normal life again, but couldn't? What if the only way I could figure out to protect my family was to leave them?

There was a reason for my dad's defection, and it wasn't me. It wasn't Mom. It wasn't Gran. It was the girl with blue hands and all that happened on that terrible day.

I was glad I felt strong enough right then, buoyed by love, to learn Dad's story. If he had shared this even a few weeks back, I might not have been ready to absorb it.

I realized how lucky I was.

I knew I was loved and cherished.

I knew where I belonged, where my family had put down roots so long ago.

I had seen flashes of story—how the strong women in Lydia's family, in my family, had dealt with heartache and fear. How they had risen to the challenge in every generation, finding their way, doing what they felt was right, loving and nurturing the people in their care.

Now it was my turn to be strong.

I had helped my father come this far. But there was more to do.

It wouldn't be easy. I had no illusions about that.

We all had images of each other, frozen in the past. We would probably be shocked to see him. Dad would be shocked to see me, all grown up. And Gran so frail.

The irony didn't escape me. Dad was recovering his memory and sense of self just as Gran was losing hers.

We were running out of time.

Today, I would buy him a cell phone with prepaid minutes and a charger. I would send it with my letter.

I would send him lemon bars, lemon tartlets, lemon pound cake. The memory of lemon that brought him clarity would also help him see his way forward.

And he would come closer and closer.

Soon, I would hear the sound of his voice. We could have a conversation.

And then, one day, I would see him again.

After years of wandering, my father would come back to us.

There would be more pain, more sadness for all that we had lost, but also joy.

Over time, we would find our own meandering, imperfect way across a river that is always changing but always the same.

That's what families do.

Epilogue

JULY
MILLCREEK VALLEY

Black Raspberry and Lemon Balm

My phone *burred* in the pocket of my jeans. When I looked at the number, I ran back to the baking area. With Norb gone after finishing the morning's baking and Jett still cleaning up after the midday crush, it was the only place where I'd have a little privacy.

This is really happening.

"Claire, my girl."

"Hi, Dad," I said quietly. To hear his voice, after all this time, felt like a miracle.

"You sound so grown up."

"Well, I am, you know."

I was laughing and crying at the same time. I hadn't actually talked to him since I was a coltish teenager.

"I know, sweetie," he said, a tinge of sadness in his voice. "Thanks for sending the phone."

"I can't believe we're actually talking."

He sounded like I remembered, a little raspier, probably from years of hard living. His was the voice of long-ago lullabies, when I sat on his lap as a little girl as he sang and I felt that all was well.

"I got the lemon bars you sent, like Mom used to make. One taste and I wanted to leave the trailer and hitch a ride all the way out there, I missed you all so much. This 'tasty/feely' thing is coming back. But I'm not sure I like it all that much." He chuckled, and I could hear the irony in his voice.

You could practically pave a yellow brick road with all the lemon desserts I had sent my dad over the past few weeks so he could taste and feel his way home again. Lemon tarts, cookies, bars, and little cakes were the I-love-yous that our family had savored for generations.

"Maybe we can trade selfies next," I said.

"Whoa, I've got to get to a barber before you actually see your old man again," he said jokingly.

I tried to imagine what he looked like now. Thinner? Weathered? Gray haired? I certainly looked different than I had at fifteen.

"You might actually see me sooner rather than later," he said, nervously.

My heart started beating even faster. I wanted him to come home, but now?

"Still lots of red tape," he said. "It probably won't be right away." I could sense that he was giving me an out if I wasn't ready.

"They have to find a halfway house for me, a place that can handle veterans who were homeless. And I have to have someone who will sponsor me."

"What does that mean, Dad?"

"Someone who will be my emergency contact person. Somebody to look out for me. I don't want to ask you. You're so busy and you're still my little girl. I don't want to burden you with this. I know your mother has every right not to have anything to do with me ever again. But maybe Helen would."

This would all be news to her.

When Dad and I had started sending postcards and then letters earlier in the year, I hadn't told Helen or my mom. They had enough going on with me.

Mom did not take well to change. She still hadn't divorced my dad after he'd deserted her all those years ago. But that didn't mean she wanted anything to do with him now.

When I sent Dad the phone, I thought I had plenty of time to take it slowly.

Now, that was out the window. I'd have to tell Mom and Helen soon.

"I'll ask her, Dad. And I'll ask about halfway houses around here. I'll work on it. Sorry, Dad, but I've got to go now." I could see Roshonda looking for me. "Let me call you back in a little bit." I snapped my phone shut as Roshonda rounded the corner.

"What are you going to do with them today?" she asked, sipping her caramel macchiato and pointing her French-manicured finger at the pints of fresh-picked black raspberries and bouquets of lemon balm.

We stood side by side in Rainbow Cake's baking area, leaning against the stainless steel worktable.

"I'll have to think of something," I said.

Black raspberries had a short season—only three weeks—but they were an intense three weeks.

I was bowing under the strain of abundance, wondering how I was going to use all these berries.

I had folded the dark little gems into our breakfast cupcakes. I'd put the tiny fruits in coffee cakes, turnovers, pies, and cake fillings. I'd whipped up black raspberry buttercream frosting. And still they came.

I'd simmered them with lemon balm to make a fabulous jam. I'd made black raspberry syrup to brush over pound cake. I'd frozen some berries, to fill in for the one week that month when they'd be gone, but certainly not forgotten.

I sipped my latte.

"How's Ben?" Roshonda asked.

My smile was my answer. I took another creamy sip. *Ben.*

"And your mystery man?" I asked Roshonda.

She raised her eyebrows and sighed contentedly.

"Maybe not mysterious for too much longer. We should probably go out, the four of us. It's time."

What Roshonda and I weren't saying, but what we both understood, was that we were both venturing into new relationship territory.

Soon, Luke would take his wandering eye back to training camp where there were, no doubt, plenty of football groupies to console him. Our divorce would be final by the fall and he could go on to more fame and fortune as TV's most eligible bachelor.

I still hadn't met the guy Roshonda was currently seeing. But I had never seen Roshonda look so good. She glowed.

"He's available," Roshonda marveled. "He shows up. He's a grown-up."

"And Ben does what he says he's going to do. I don't have to second-guess him or wonder what he's doing when I'm not around."

"It's weird."

"Well, let me know when you want to schedule the big reveal." Roshonda frowned.

"I'm teasing," I said, swaying to give her a hip bump.

"House of Chili tonight?" she asked, drinking the last of her coffee. "It's Ben, you, me, and Gavin again."

"You bet." I knew I couldn't face cooking, even for Ben, after yet another day of black raspberries. Besides, he loved a good five-way chili.

I walked with her to the front of the bakery and we said our good-byes. For a brief moment, I had Rainbow Cake to myself. Jett was in the workroom, Maggie had gone to pick up Emily from vacation Bible preschool. No customers.

I breathed it all in. The Tiffany blue walls. The mottled chocolate marble counters. The ambience of a Parisian tea salon.

On our feature wall, I had hung the chartreuse green curtain meant to suggest lemon balm. I loved how the pale and dark purples of the black raspberry desserts showed up against it. The showstopper of that month's display was the ombré cake, its five layers going, in varying shades, from deep purple on the bottom to pale lavender on top. It was a "naked" cake, one that had only the lemon balm buttercream frosting piped in between the layers and on top so that the sides showed the colors.

Jett, too, had embraced the black raspberry and lemon balm theme in her own way. Freed from high school dress code constraints for the summer, she had dyed her hair a black raspberry tone (suspiciously similar to her favorite Deadly Nightshade), arranged it in several asymmetrical pigtails, and sprayed the ends bright lime green. I kind of liked it.

"Which customer do I put on the do-not-take-their-order list this time?" she asked, rolling her eyes. She set down a tray on the counter with two more ombré cakes ready for Maggie to box. "If they had any idea how much goes into these . . ." Getting to "naked" on the cake meant Jett had to tediously scrape the browned edges from each colorful layer.

"I know, I know." I patted Jett on the back.

She actually smiled. "Two more to go," she said as she made her way to the workroom in back.

Jett in a happy mood? Everything good for me in the relationship world? Effortless abundance? My father returning?

Moment by moment, I was discovering the sweet flavor of gratitude.

And my heart was full.

Readers Guide

THE MEMORY OF LEMON

DISCUSSION QUESTIONS

1. A recent study from the Emory University School of Medicine shows that memories can be passed on to subsequent generations through DNA. What memories, abilities, or tendencies pass through the families in *The Memory of Lemon*?

2. Neely's gift allows her to sense a flavor that is a hyperlink to someone's hidden issue. The flavor leads to an emotion and then she sees a scene from someone's past. When she tries to resolve a difficult and classic standoff—Bride versus Mother—no flavor comes to her for a long time. Why do you think that is?

3. Do you agree with Neely's customers? Is pie more emotional, more nostalgic than cake? Which dessert is more attached to a certain memory for you—pie or cake?

4. In flashback scenes, we see characters who are Wanderers and Healers. Which one do you think best characterizes Neely? Are there any characters who started out as Wanderers and became Healers?

Readers Guide

5. Neely's father, the homeless Jack O'Neil, knows he has to face a terrible Vietnam War experience in order to begin his journey toward normal life. How can reliving a horrifying experience eventually bring healing?

6. How do characters' perceptions of the river change over time? How does Abigail Newcomb feel about the river, contrasted with her granddaughter Little Abigail in later years? What does the river mean to Lydia? To Lydia's mother Cadence? To Neely and Ben?

7. The artist John James Audubon wandered through the American wilderness and also wandered through this novel. How do the responses of Lydia and her mother to Audubon influences in the wedding underscore their differences?

8. We sense, through one of Neely's surprise flashbacks, that Sister Agnes might have had to give up a baby before she entered the novitiate. And that the child grew into someone Neely knows well. Were you surprised?

9. Some memories come back through flavor, some through song in this novel. What prompts memories for you? A certain aroma? A song on the radio?

10. Do dessert flavors run in families? If so, what flavor is the favorite in your family? Lemon? Spice? Chocolate?

11. In a world of instant communication, Neely is forced by circumstances to send snail mail letters to her father and to Ben. What is special about a letter? How do letters deepen the relationships between Neely and her father? Neely and Ben?

12. Gran, Jack O'Neil, and Neely all share the same gift of sensing a flavor that will lead to a story that reveals something that is hidden. But each of them has experienced the gift differently. Why do you think the young Gran tasted the bitter, inky flavor of a story that *had yet to happen*? Why can't Jack O'Neil "taste" things like Neely can anymore? Why does Neely have trouble deciphering the twin flavors of citrus and spice?

13. Why did Jack O'Neil feel he was helping his family by leaving them?

14. The Wanderers in this novel want to find a home. But when life changes might prompt us to move and lose touch with familiar places, where exactly is home? *What* is home? And how do we know when we're there?